My Wicked Gladiators

MY WICKED GLADIATORS

LAUREN HAWKEYE

An Imprint of HarperCollinsPublishers

This is a work of fiction. Names, characters, places, and incidents are products of the author's imagination or are used fictitiously and are not to be construed as real. Any resemblance to actual events, locales, organizations, or persons, living or dead, is entirely coincidental.

MY WICKED GLADIATORS. Copyright © 2012 by Lauren Hawkeye. All rights reserved under International and Pan-American Copyright Conventions. By payment of the required fees, you have been granted the nonexclusive, nontransferable right to access and read the text of this e-book on screen. No part of this text may be reproduced, transmitted, downloaded, decompiled, reverse-engineered, or stored in or introduced into any information storage and retrieval system, in any form or by any means, whether electronic or mechanical, now known or hereinafter invented, without the express written permission of HarperCollins e-books.

EPub Edition MAY 2012 ISBN: 9780062196897

Print Edition ISBN: 9780062196958

10 9 8 7 6 5 4 3

For Suzanne Rock, the best critique partner a girl could ask for. This book wouldn't exist without you.

Chapter One

I did not want to want him.

Yet as I stood on the balcony that overlooked the training area of my family's *ludus*—the most prestigious of gladiator training schools—my husband by my side, want is what I did. I could see nothing of the mock battle beneath me but him. His sweat, his blood, falling down to the dry dust that ground beneath the worn leather that covered his feet.

Never mind that I could never have him. Dreams of what his touch could bring me only increased the need that thrummed through my veins like flocking birds.

"You're quite flushed, Alba." Lucius, my husband, touched a hand to my elbow and peered into my face with concern. "We should retire inside. Drusilla will draw a bath for you."

A bath . . . clear cool water, the thick silk of oils that smelled like herbs. The slither of limbs through water, and the sheen of dampness on muscles taut from incessant training.

"Come." I could hear the alarm in Lucius' voice, though it

was my slave girl, Drusilla, who moved to support me, not my husband. "Your skin is quite red. Inside. Now."

I alone knew the reason for my flush, but I certainly could not tell it to my husband. And actually, I was not the only one—there was one more who knew in what direction my thoughts lay.

I caught the eyes belonging to that one, and their dense black seemed to swallow the golden gleams given off by the sun. My heart fluttered in my chest, like a young girl with her first feelings of lust, but his expression revealed nothing that was not there when he thrust his battered wooden training sword through the air.

I knew that he felt it, too.

And what kind of *domina* was I, imagining myself seducing a slave?

Uneasy shame brought clamminess to my skin, and I stopped refusing Drusilla's ministrations, allowing myself to be helped inside. Lucius followed closely behind, barking orders at the other slaves, though I could tell that his mind had already moved on, something to do with the ludus, no doubt.

I could not complain, at least not out loud, at his lack of focus on me, his wife. Since my father had given me from his control to that of Lucius, Lucius was my *pater familias*, the head of this house.

Much as our slaves had no choice but to obey us, I had no right to argue with my husband.

And what would I have been complaining about, really? My belly was full, my body draped in silk and gold. The pool that Drusilla led me to was carved from bright white stone, and I could already smell the expensive oils that I could have rubbed into my skin, if I so desired.

I stood still at the bath's edge and waited for Drusilla to remove my garments. Lucius paced, raking a hand through his dark ribbons of hair before crouching to splash a handful of pristine water against the salty sheen on his face.

When he again rose, I was naked. He let his sapphire gaze roam my bare curves, and the thin cloth at his groin tented.

Still warm from the fierce stare of the other, the attention of my husband caused my nipples to peak and a shiver to roll over my skin.

I so very rarely caught my husband's attention. He preferred to take his pleasures quickly with one of the slave girls, women who did not require flattery or coddling. And since he had long ago decided that I was barren, there was no need for him to spill his seed inside of me unless he felt the desire to do so. To be fair, I also could have satisfied my cravings with any of the slaves that I desired.

Any but the gladiators. And it was a gladiator, one particular gladiator, whom I wanted.

But to have caught the attention of my husband, a man whom I did care for after a fashion, after so long a respite made me hopeful, and added to the heat that had begun to pool in my cunt.

Added to the heat was a hope, one that I tried to keep hidden, that I could still, possibly, carry a child.

I shook my head, a move fraught with impatience. It would not do any good for me to go down that route again, to think too long on the one thing I wanted more than anything and couldn't have.

"Lucius?" I held out a hand to him, beckoning him forward. "Join me for my bath." Drusilla, anticipating what was to come, slid her hands from where they had rested at my shoulders, forward and down to cup my breasts.

I had not had her touch me for a long time, though we had once been lovers, experimental young girls. But my husband liked to watch us touch, liked to watch us play.

It excited him.

Lucius' stare grew more avid, and he absently rubbed a hand over his clothed cock as he watched my slave caress my nipples. Relaxing into my girl's familiar touch, I allowed a sigh of pleasure to fall from my lips, and beckoned him forward again.

The movement broke the spell. With a start, he shook his head and stilled his hand.

"I do not have time for this, Alba." Crouching again, he poured handfuls of cool water over his head, seeming not to care when they made large wet splotches on his crisp tunic. "I will be late for my meeting if I do not leave now." And with that as his explanation, he took his leave, leaving me alone with nothing but the attentions of a girl who, though I knew found them pleasant, still had no choice but to give them.

I watched him walk away, watched the beaded ornaments tied to the backs of his red sandals glinting in the undulating beams of light.

A meeting. Of course. I knew better than to ask him with whom or where. I also knew better than to argue, which could result in his foul mood for days. His dealings here in Rome were what supported us, and I knew it. I should have been thankful for the popularity of the gladiators, and for our standing as the top school for them.

We would not stay at the top if Lucius did not do as he did. And I knew that he felt tremendous pressure to live up to the reputation of his ancestors, those great men who had trained giants and champions.

But I was envious of the wives who were doted on by their husbands, who were prized for their beauty and their grace. I missed the ministrations of my husband, the one who had once stroked my skin and whispered in my ear sweet words of wooing. I had not received one of those whispers in a long while, and had been deprived of his touch for even longer.

Shaking Drusilla off, knowing that she knew my feelings well and would not take offense, I stepped into the sparkling pool unaided. The cool water clung rather than refreshed, sucking at me, pulling at my skin.

Though I tried to stop them, thoughts flooded my mind.

They were all thoughts of Marcus.

Sometime later, the slight shuffle of worn leather on stone alerted me to a new presence. Assuming that it was simply Lucius, I took my time opening my eyes, hoping, as always, to lure him into the bath with me, if for nothing else but entertainment's sake.

I was incredibly bored. I had nothing to complain about, since my every need was cared for and my every desire granted, but I had no purpose. Nothing with which to fill my day but leisure.

Leisure was tedious, the feeling of uselessness unpleasant. I was also suffering the inattention of my husband, and was beginning to wonder if perhaps I'd become dull, or unattractive. And here was something new, something bright.

Something burning into my skin with its embarrassed yet entranced stare.

"I beg pardon, Domina." It took me but the blink of an eye to place him.

How was he here, in front of me, as if the gods had suddenly willed it so?

With a noise of distress, Drusilla moved to cover me. I should have let her, but the gorgeous beast of a man who stood before me threw my thoughts and wishes into turmoil. And so instead I cast a look at Drusilla, communicating without words to leave me be. Though she pursed her lips in disapproval—something I would not have tolerated from anyone else—she removed the towel and stepped away.

"What are you doing here?" I made sure my voice was sharp, though in truth I was not at all upset by the appearance of this magnificent-looking man. Clad in nothing but his *subligaculum*, leather briefs worn to preserve modesty, and cheap leather sandals, his muscles were sculpted and raw from what I knew was incessant training, and his gleaming honeyed hair was a delicious contrast to the shadowy depths of the eyes that stared.

My husband had summoned him upstairs, eager to show off his newest prize to the visiting noble with whom Lucius was meeting. But his visitor had fallen ill in the dreadful heat of the day, and Lucius had chosen to escort him home, through the streets of Rome, with the help of Justinus.

My Wicked Gladiators

It would not do for anything amiss to happen to the man, not when it had been known that he was in our home.

In the confusion, no one had thought to show Marcus back down below, to secure him behind the iron gate that separated the quarters of the gladiators from our upstairs lives.

He had wandered, or so he told me, admiring the beautiful things that were displayed in our home: the artisan vases; the rich, finely woven hangings of silk; the gladiatorial galley, where the stone busts—and cocks—of our former champions stood.

This has brought him here, coming upon me in the bath, looking curiously through the arched doorway, while Drusilla rubbed scents into the long coils of my ebony hair.

I was inclined to believe him, since it was a rare thing for a gladiator to wander, unaccompanied, through the halls of our home. I knew that I should have Drusilla escort him back downstairs immediately, back behind the iron gate—knew that that was what Lucius would have me do. Knew from watching Drusilla shift anxiously from foot to foot that that was what she would have me do, too.

I also knew that Lucius would have him punished for coming upon his wife in the bath. I was also more than a little upset that a gladiator would know the contents of my husband's meeting while I, his wife, did not.

Though I did not want the man punished, still I could not say where the boldness that overtook me came from.

I had never been bold, not even as a curious child. I had always been shy, acquiescent—qualities that my husband had praised at our marriage.

I also knew that, despite my own feelings, he had not

come to me. He had been summoned by my husband and had happened upon me accidentally. I had not premeditated our encounter, but I was still the one who had initiated it.

He would not be able to refuse. A slave could not refuse his mistress, and though their lives were different from those of many who served, gladiators were still slaves.

And still I proceeded.

Remaining silent, I motioned Drusilla back and dipped my head under the water to remove the residue of the scented oils. When I surfaced, I refrained from looking across the room to where he stood, instead turning and rising from the water.

I knew what I looked like, naked, with droplets of irresistibly chilled water running down my curves. My mirror, an ornately edged sheet of polished metal that had been a wedding gift from my husband, told me that my skin was fashionably pale, nearly as translucent as the wet, and a stark contrast to the shadows of my hip-length hair. My eyes were bright, my features even, and my body free from disfigurations brought about by disease.

I knew that I was pleasing to most eyes, and I exploited that now. After a long moment in which I simply stood, the bath lapping at my ankles, the excess water running down my limbs I turned. My nipples had peaked under what I knew was intense scrutiny, and I was not disappointed when the gladiator again came into view.

His cock had risen, hardened, and pressed against the leather that covered him there. If it had not, if he had remained unaffected, I might have been able to stop then, to send him away.

My Wicked Gladiators 9

But he wanted me, too, obviously so, and so I shoved the nagging guilt away, buried it deep in my gut, and beckoned him forward.

"Remove your subligaculum and your sandals." His eyes widened, just a fraction, but he moved to comply. The leather ties around his ankles were loosened first, and then the ones at his waist. But instead of the gratifying sight of his skin, the leather stubbornly remained in place, a barrier between me and what I wanted.

In my life it seemed that there was always such a barrier.

"Remove your subligaculum." Though I tried to school my voice into sternness, I could hear the tremor that sounded through it. I was certain that both Drusilla and the man could, as well.

What would I do if he did not comply?

When the clothing fell with a wet-sounding slap on the ground, I drew in a breath, one filled with both relief and desire.

I had not seen a cock besides my husband's for years, even though I was permitted to do so . . . so long as that cock did not belong to a gladiator.

Though I was permitted to fuck a male slave, any slave but one of our warriors, the only one that we had was Justinus, my husband's boy, and I did not care for the man at all.

As such, it had been so very long since I had allowed arousal to whip through me. The thrill of the forbidden, added to the chance that my husband might happen upon us, collided with desire and drugged me. Swallowing thickly, I reached out a hand.

"Come here."

"Domina?" He hesitated, but just for a moment. I was, after all, just as much his mistress as my husband was his master. Still, I could see the war between morals and desire swirling in his stare. Guilt washed over my skin, and with it came anger.

Why should I feel guilt over taking something that I desired, *finally* taking something that I desired? Did my husband not do the same every day of his life?

Slowly, as if unsure that I could really mean as I said, he stepped out of the pool of clothing at his feet, moving toward me. His flesh gleamed in the dim, flickering light of the room, shining with a faint sheen of sweat, one that I could all but smell—the heady aroma of a man who used his body, and used it well.

Though a small voice in my head told me that this was not the wisest idea, I hushed it. I had been deprived of a male touch for far too long, and I wanted this man's hands on me.

He stopped an arm's-length away from me. Seeing this big beast of a man, one who was so sure in the arena, with uncertainty painted over his features caused my stomach to clench with something that I could not quite identify.

I needed the endless cycle of thoughts to cease. I had always thought too much.

"Kiss me." My words caused him to start, then to hesitate again. "Kiss me!"

My every muscle clenched as I waited. I knew that he would do it—he had no choice but to, after I had commanded him to. I knew that he felt, as I did, that these actions were not proper. But even more than that, what if he did not want to? What if this man, this man who had surely not had a woman in a very long time, could not find me attractive enough to even feign enjoyment?

I kept my eyes open wide as he leaned forward. No part of him touched me except his lips, and they were dry, firm, and salty.

I groaned and rocked myself closer to him, until there was but a whisper of space between our naked flesh. I expected him to draw me close, to lift me up and shove his cock into me, as Lucius would have done once.

Instead, as the kiss ended, he straightened and again stood still, his eyes deep and dark and revealing nothing.

I felt tears prickle at the backs of my eyes. What was going on? Was I that undesirable? My beautiful mirror told me that that wasn't so—again, my hair was thick and long, my features even, my skin smooth and unblemished. I had ample hips and breasts, and a small waist with the curve of belly that was pleasing to the eye.

And his cock still quivered under my gaze. So why would he not take me in arms and do as he would?

"Kiss me." I demanded this time in a voice more guttural than it had been, for his first kiss had aroused me, and the arousal combined with my confusion to create a deep morass of . . . I was not sure there was a word for it. "Kiss me again. Now."

And again he leaned forward and pressed his lips to mine. Just a press, nothing more. Angry now, I opened my mouth, licked at the curve of his mouth, slid my tongue in to trace his teeth.

He echoed my movement, kissing me back with lips, with teeth, and with tongue.

Again, he seemed to enjoy it, but would move no further.

Well, the kiss was more than I had had in a long while. I would enjoy it while it lasted. Breathing deeply, I slanted my mouth against his own, rising up on tiptoes to gain purchase. My fingers sought his shoulders, then his neck and the thick glory of that flaxen hair.

After a hesitant moment, his movements echoed mine. His hands slid up my arms, over my shoulders, and then twined into my long, scented hair. There was still space between us, but I could feel the hard ridge of his cock pressing against my belly.

Ah. I was beginning to see just how obedient a slave he was.

I arched my hips against him. After pausing a moment again, as if to make sure that I had really meant it, he rocked against me in return, and the friction of his coarse cock hair against my labia made me gasp.

I now saw. He would not do anything unless I told him to, or indicated that it was what I wanted. He truly was a man bound by the oath of honor undertaken by the gladiators.

For reasons that I could not quite explain, this excited me terribly. Drawing him to me, my arms struggling for purchase against the solidity of his flesh, I let myself kiss him as I had wanted to be kissed for years, hot, wet, and open.

His breathing was as ragged as mine when I drew back, shuddering through his great frame, and his skin flushed. He wanted me as much as I wanted him, this I knew.

So I would take it, and I would enjoy it—*we* would enjoy it—this opportunity that the blessed gods had thrust in front of us. It seemed that Venus was in a fine humor that day. I would have to pray to her later, would have to offer up wine and bread in thanks.

"Drusilla, you may go." I was taking a risk, allowing my slave to leave—being alone with a gladiator, a man whose only purpose in life was to fight, was not a smart or safe thing to do. I knew that she would be irritated beyond belief with me, and that I would endure the sharp side of her tongue later on.

But I did not desire an audience. I wanted to drown in the feeling of man and woman fucking, and nothing more.

My slave girl exited silently, shaking her head but not daring to speak in front of a fellow slave, for fear that he would see our closeness. The friendship was not something that we hid, but nor did we flaunt it, for fear of upsetting the balance of the household.

Had we been alone, Drusilla would have had much to say. But we were not, and she did not. She left, and I was alone with the gladiator. My gladiator, the one who waited silently for orders.

I shivered with anticipation.

"Enter the pool." I gestured toward the stone steps that were swallowed by the wet, and heard the soft slice of his body through it as he descended and the silky water lapped at his hips. I seated myself on the side of the pool, ass against the chilly marble, legs dipped into the liquid from the knee down.

I saw his eyes move from the breasts that were half hidden by the long coils of my hair to the area between my legs that he would not get a clear glimpse of until I parted them.

He kneeled in the shallow water, facing me. Slowly, bit by bit, I opened my legs and let him see what he wanted to see.

I saw the smallest of flickers in his eyes when I finally was spread open wide, and a slight tremor in those tremendous muscles.

He wanted to do this, but would not until I gave him permission.

It was intoxicating.

"Place your mouth between my legs." Before he could reach me, I took up the goblet of wine that sat at my side and poured it over my belly. The bittersweet liquid ran down my pale flesh in rivulets, streaming here and dripping there, the excess falling in fat drops into the water, where it dispersed quickly, a kiss of ruby in the deep blue.

"As you wish, Domina." Bending at the waist, he moved into the space between my legs, pushing them further apart to accommodate his large frame.

I gasped at the first touch of his hard fingers on the soft flesh of my inner thighs. He looked up and smiled for the first time, just the faintest kiss of a smile that held a tinge of wickedness. Then he pushed me back, flat, the ridges of my shoulder blades pressing against the damp, chilled stone until I could no longer see him. His touch was gentle, far softer than I had ever felt the touch of my husband's hands upon my skin. Startled by this, I immediately rose back up to my elbows and stared at him, brow furrowed.

"You need not be gentle." My voice was guttural, raw with wanting.

His stare never wavered from my face as he nodded in acknowledgment, though the press of his hands on my flesh did not deepen in their pressure. "I would not hurt you. I would never hurt you."

My mouth opened to reply, but my words were lost as he

moved his face roughly until it brushed the hot outer folds of my cunt. I understood that though he would wait for permission, and though he may not be gentle, I was safe with the warrior.

He bit first, and a strangled scream escaped my throat. I tried to swallow it, for though I doubted that Lucius was home yet, he could be, very soon. It was a risk that I would take. But it was so very hard to swallow the sounds that kept exploding from my throat when Marcus buried his face between my thighs, the rasp of the stiff hairs on his jaw scratching and inflaming skin that was growing more tender by the minute.

He soothed the sting left by his teeth with his tongue, though there was no softness in his movements. He swiped the rasp of his flesh through my slit firmly and forcefully, occasionally connecting with the inflamed area hidden a little deeper, and I couldn't hold still.

Raising my hips from the hardness of the floor, I begged him soundlessly for more. Replacing the hand that branded one of my thighs with an elbow, he used his newly free fingers to separate the folds of my labia, baring my clitoris. I hissed when the cool air hit it, but the air stopped when his mouth closed over the engorged nub, hot and wet, because the sensation shocked the breath out of me.

I tried my hardest not to scream, and at the same time to close my legs, because the sensation was nearly too much to bear. But I had told him that this was what I wanted, and he was following through. His strength kept my legs apart, and his mouth stayed busy, stroking with his tongue, long, firm strokes, and I could feel myself careening out of control. My fingers scrabbled for purchase on the slick marble but found nothing to grab hold of, so I clenched them in my own hair and tugged as the whirling pleasure built.

It had been so long that the orgasm nearly drowned me. I didn't know if my screams had echoed off the corners of the room or merely off the walls of my mind when the shaking had subsided, but I shook my head from side to side regardless, knowing that I wanted still more and also knowing that time was coming to a close—Lucius would be home soon.

I groaned and arched my hips again, raising myself onto my elbows and willing my quivering muscles to allow me to sit. When Marcus again came into view, I saw him swipe a hand over the excess moisture on his mouth, and I wanted to give him back some of the pleasure that he had given me.

I moved my ass closer to the edge of the pool and let the water lap at my screaming clitoris. I huffed impatiently when he did not immediately move between my wide-spread legs, then remembered through a sex-fogged brain that he would not do so until I bid him to.

"Fuck me." I could not bring to mind any more detail than that . . . and indeed, I did not care how it happened. I just knew that if I did not feel the girth of the cock that was bobbing in the water inside my cunt, and soon, I would surely die.

It happened so quickly that I was not entirely sure of how, precisely, it came to be. I only knew that one moment I was empty, and the next full, a cock of a surely impossible size impaling my most tender cunt. My legs were wrapped around his waist, my arms his shoulders, my bottom still braced against the edge of the pool as he rocked me back and forth. Though he was still on his knees in the shallow bath, he did not lose purchase, though I could feel his thigh muscles, hard as the rocks that covered the mountains outside, bunching beneath the globes of my rear with the effort to stay upright.

I no longer cared if my husband was home and heard me, no longer cared about the fact that this was a forbidden gladiator and I his mistress. I let him ride me, hard and then harder still, until he grunted and the thick smell of salty come tickled my nostrils.

The feel of the viscous liquid as it dripped down my thighs was so immensely satisfying, after so very long, that I again spasmed. Though not nearly as intense, the orgasm still brought a wave of pleasure, and I sighed with amazement at the feeling that I had been so long denied.

Breathless, I lay back on the cold stone, sighing my complaint when he began to ease his thick cock from my body. Every nerve in my body was spent with pleasure, and I felt the ridiculous urge to pull him back down toward me, to wrap his arms around me and enjoy the feeling of skin on skin. But though I wished it, he must have understood as well as I did that he needed to take his leave, and soon. The consequences for Marcus of Lucius finding him wandering the upstairs, let alone what he had just done with the wife of his master, his domina, would be severe. Never mind that Marcus' temporary freedom was because of my husband's carelessness. No, it would be expected that Marcus would have known his place enough to make his way back downstairs.

The reminder of where he lived, where his life was, caused the reality of what I had just done to begin dribbling down upon my head, the chill mixing with the remnants of warm pleasure until the two were indistinguishable. I heard him splash water against his skin in an attempt to clean up, and felt shame.

I had made a slave have relations with me. Never mind that he had enjoyed it—I had not given him a choice, and that was something that I had never entirely agreed with. Biting my lip, I shifted restlessly on the stone floor, closed my legs tight and also shuttered my eyes as I heard him leave the silky wet of the pool. He paused for a moment by me, searing my all-too-naked skin with his stare before padding away to again don his sandals and his subligaculum.

When I again opened my eyes, he was gone.

Chapter Two

I could not sleep.

Seeing Marcus earlier that day—having him connect gazes with me and reveal nothing, no feelings at all over our encounter, had shaken me to the core, though I could not have said why I cared so much. He was a slave, one of my husband's prized slaves, to be sure, but a slave nonetheless. As far as most of my peers were concerned, he did not have feelings at all, or at least none that mattered.

There were Romans who did not agree, however, and I counted myself among them, though Lucius did not want to hear it. And I could not condemn him for his way of thinking, not when so many others did the same.

But I saw our slaves as people, and sought to treat them as such. Perhaps my way of thinking was different because of my own girl, Drusilla. We had been children together, and she had been the closest thing to a friend and playmate that I had ever had. We had even learned lessons together. I had never seen her simply as my slave. This, perhaps, was why I could not condone my commands, the situation that I had put Marcus in. Nor could I seek him out and apologize to him without throwing the dynamics of the entire household off kilter.

If I could just forget about it, I would be fine. But all I could think about as I lay on top of my soft silk sheets was how much I wanted his hard hands on my soft flesh again. He had pleased my flesh in a way that it had never been pleased before, but more than that, his tender assurance that he would never hurt me still whispered in my ears.

I had heard Lucius come in not that long before and retire to his own bed, in the room next to mine. He had not been alone. This was not a surprise to me—he made no secret of the fact that he preferred to take his pleasure quickly and effortlessly by letting one of our many slave girls ride him into oblivion, whether they wanted to or not. It was his due, as pater familias. His favorite was Marina, a beauty who had been purchased from a pleasure house and knew things that many of the others did not. What had surprised me this time was that the grunts coming from the next room that I could not identify as belonging to my husband sounded distinctly male, low and dark.

No matter, I supposed. Lucius had had sex with men before, as I had with women—Romans were fluid in their sexuality, though we were allowed to marry only the opposite sex. But I had never known him to seek a man out, alone, for fucking. And as I had lain there in the dark, the chasm between my thighs aching and my cunt dripping, I pictured Marcus with the husband who had once made love to me in every way imaginable. One dark head and one light, silken strands of hair splayed out across the sheets. Two masculine bodies straining together.

I imagined that Lucius would try to dominate. He would pull Marcus close for a kiss, hard and unyielding, before pushing him down on all fours. My gladiator, my stern warrior, would not acquiesce, would fight his way from underneath. He would lay Lucius out flat on his front on the bed, would smack a large palm across one of the globes of his ass before spitting into his hand and rubbing the stickiness through the crease. Then he would grab his cock by the base, and, ranging his body atop that of my husband, would push into Lucius from behind with the brute strength of a warrior.

The vision made me shake with wanting.

But of course it was not Marcus with my husband in the next room, and I did not really want it to be, though the pictures that it made in my mind's eye aroused me beyond measure. It could not have been Marcus. Lucius would not permit himself sex with a gladiator any more than he would me. Sex sapped the strength that a champion needed in the arena, and though of course the men dallied with each other occasionally, and had visits from whores, visits that Lucius turned a blind eye to—a man could go for only so long without a release, after all—the rule absolutely applied to us.

Though we were of the *plebeian* class, we were firmly entrenched in its upper echelons—we were upstanding Roman citizens. There was a moral code that a true Roman adhered to, and fucking one's gladiators was not a part of it.

When the sounds of ecstasy faded through the plaster wall at my feet, I grew yet more restless still. Pulling my sheer sleep tunic over my head—I preferred to sleep nude in this kind of heat—I poured a cup of wine, a rich ruby stream from the pottery jug on my table, and pushed through the curtain that divided my sleep room from the rest of the house.

It was silent, and the lack of sound was like a sound itself. It rang in my ears, and I was tempted to shuffle the bare soles of my feet loudly on stone still warm from the heat of day to temper the noise. I rarely strayed from my room after I had retired for the night, simply because I usually enjoyed that time to myself, in my own space.

And also, if I could admit it to myself, because I knew that I could happen upon my husband with one of his slave girls, and though I knew that those couplings happened, I was not sure that I wanted to witness one with my own eyes.

It should not have mattered to me in whom my husband dipped his cock. He was a good husband, a good provider. I was well taken care of, and though I might long for his attention, I knew that he did not withhold it to be cruel.

It felt oddly freeing to be out of my room in the night, like I had escaped from a prison cell not all that different from the quarters that housed the gladiators below my feet. Though they each had separate sleep quarters, none was enclosed, and they were free to roam about their area—the sleeping rooms, the baths, the training area—as they would.

Much like myself in the upstairs. With this thought in mind, I decided to visit a place that I saw entirely too often for my liking during the day, but had never seen at night.

The balcony to the ludus was covered with drapes of thick velvet, meant to muffle the noises of the daily training should we tire of them. I pushed through them, and when I emerged on the other side it felt like rising into the air from underwater.

The night air outside was as still as the air in the house but far less stifling. It refreshed me, washed away the weariness and sense of irritability that had plagued me since the afternoon.

The stars were small drops of gold, illuminated against velvet heavier and richer than what hung at my back. The training area below was cast in shadows, empty, and I savored the feeling of solitude. As I lifted my cup to my mouth and let the rich taste of the wine spread over my tongue, I caught sight of a moving shadow in the periphery of the mock arena. Swallowing hard, I knew it was him before I could squint and lock my sight upon the figure thrusting his sword about in the dark corner.

His movements were fluid and beautiful in an otherworldly kind of way. He was fierce and brutish in his actions, and I pitied the next man that he met in the arena, even as I ached to have his body cover mine with the same kind of fierceness.

As I watched, I wondered if Marcus had once been a soldier. His bearing was so rigid, so unyielding—much as his manner had been in the bedroom. He seemed to me to be someone who would have a clearly defined idea of what was right and what was wrong.

Though I supposed that those ideas must have some gray areas as well, for in submitting to my commands, he had dishonored my husband, his *dominus*.

My guilt thickened.

Scared of dropping it and having to explain how the cup

had gotten there when it was brought back upstairs in the morning, I set my goblet down upon the polished wooden railing as carefully as I was able. Still, noise reverberated into the still night air when the pottery met the exposed grain, and Marcus whirled with unimaginable grace in the direction of the noise.

When his eyes sought the sky and found me, standing at the railing of the balcony, watching him, he stilled. Though his face was cast in shadow, I knew that he studied me as intently as I did him.

I did not move. Could not move. I was still ashamed that I had given him no choice in our encounter, though I knew that he had found pleasure in it. I still had not allowed him a say, and that made me no better than those who abused their slaves horribly.

I wanted him with a need that rose up in my throat and choked me, and yet I knew that it could never happen again. Not only because it was not right, because it did not fit with my Roman code of ethics, but because Lucius would raise hell if he found that one of his prized gladiators, one predicted to become the new champion, was fucking his wife.

As I watched, Marcus slowly unfurled his fingers and let his sword drop to the ground. The sand that it fell into puffed up a smoky cloud of dust that swirled away into the night as I watched, mesmerized.

I brought my level of vision up from his feet, roamed over those sharply muscled calves and thighs, skimmed the worn leather of his subligaculum that blocked my view.

Stopped on the fingers that rested on the fastenings of

that leather. Jumped up to his face, which was serious and contained no questions.

My nipples peaked painfully under his stare, and I could not move. I knew that all I had to do to stop this was simply shake my head, but I found that I could not.

More, that I did not want to.

I watched as he pulled on the strings that tied the sides of his leathers together. One tug, then another, and then the garment had loosened, held up only by his fingers. He pulled it out, away from his body, and I caught a glimpse of hipbone, standing out in sharp relief from the taut skin of his flat belly.

Slowly, slowly, he relaxed those fingers, one at a time. The leather fell to the ground beside his blemished wooden sword, and his body—the tough, scarred body of a gladiator—was open for me to feast my eyes upon.

I had not had much of a chance to look at him when we had fucked in the bath, or maybe I just plain had not paid attention. But what I saw now was no less than a work of art, and it took my breath away.

Every muscle in his body was as hard as the rock that made up the walls of our home. I knew that the gladiators trained incessantly, all day, every day, but the reality of that extreme way of life was slapped into my face when I looked at this body, covered with skin tanned a deep brown from the unrelenting Roman sun. Scars crossed every which way over that skin, fine transparent lines over the nutty color, and I knew that each was, to him, a badge of honor.

A time that he had lived, and triumphed over death.

His cock was pale in comparison with the rest of this skin,

an ivory that never saw the sun. It was veined through with blue and purple, and pulsed at full attention under my watchful eyes.

I wanted to touch it. I wanted it in my mouth, under my fingers. I wanted it inside of me, pounding in and out.

I could not have it.

As I watched, he grasped the length of that cock in one of his hands. I bit my lip and fisted my hands in the amber lace of my tunic, pressing my thighs together to stop the ache.

His fist clenched, then loosened, then clenched again. He twisted it around his cock, then began the slow ascent to the top. Just the head was visible above his fist, a dusky plum in the dark shadows, and it glistened in the straw-colored moonlight.

He moved that fist down. I swallowed past a large, dry lump in my throat. Up. I rubbed my hands, hard, against my hips to stop the uncontrollable itch. Down, up. Up, down. He fisted his cock as surely as he had tongued my clitoris, and though I could see his muscles move with the pleasure of it, he never removed his stare from me.

I saw his sack, which hung heavily in its nest of caramel hair, pull in toward his pelvis in the moment before he came. His mouth opened as the stream of thick salt spurted from his clenched hand, but no sound escaped, and I did my best to follow suit, though I had to raise my own hand to my mouth and bite to stifle the groans that pooled against my tongue.

When his cock ceased its spasms, he released it from his grip. It fell, still swollen from the attention, back against the coarse hair, and was soon hidden from sight in the worn leather of his damned subligaculum. He tied it tightly, still staring up at me, and I felt tears prick the backs of my eyes with their tiny needles, though I could not say why.

He broke that stare once he was again clothed. Leaving his training sword where it lay, he backed away slowly, until the darkness obscured him completely. I thought I saw the blurred outline of a second figure move toward Marcus in the moment before he disappeared from my sight, and wondered if we had been seen. But I blinked and the vision was gone, and so I concluded that it had been simply conjured by my mind.

I stood there, on the balcony, long after Marcus was gone. There was nothing to see, and still . . .

I could not tear myself away.

The next morning I awoke slowly, heavily, feeling weighted down as if with opium. I wanted to curl up against my sheets, to savor the memory of what I had seen in the night, but knew that to lie abed longer than usual would arouse Lucius' suspicions.

The reminder of suspicions made me wonder, again, about the male sounds of pleasure that had come from his room the night before. I dismissed them once more, however, for he was perfectly entitled to do as he wished.

But the fantasy of his flesh straining against that of Marcus again made me twitch with want.

After forcing my heavy limbs from the bed, I blearily made my way to my dressing area. Drusilla, who would have hovered outside my curtain since her own early awakening, entered silently, and urged the fine webbing of the sleeping tunic that I still wore up and over my head.

Knowing that I normally slept nude, I saw her cock her head slightly, as if questioning the presence of the tunic to herself. She did not comment, however, though from her I would have tolerated the questioning.

"You should bathe." Roughly raking her slim fingers through the sleepy snarls of my hair, I caught her eye in the reflection of the oval mirror that hung across from where I was seated.

"I do not feel like it." My response was churlish, but the purse of my girl's lips irritated me. I did not need to be judged by my closest friend, not when I was already judging myself so harshly.

Drusilla's face softened as she continued to smooth my hair, but in her eyes I saw the stubborn streak that she had possessed since girlhood.

"You smell of sex." My mouth fell open at these words, which I would not have tolerated from anyone else. "If you do not bathe, Lucius will know of your actions yesterday."

I felt an emotion that I could not quite define rising in my chest, and I stood, pushing Drusilla's hands away. "Do not judge me, Drusilla. Why are my actions so dreadful? Lucius fucks whomever he chooses, whenever he chooses. Why should I be miserable, simply because my husband has ceased to desire me?" I felt tears causing my throat to swell as I spoke, and to my mortification, I felt a hot trickle of tears spill down my cheeks.

Drusilla drew me into her arms for a hug, rubbing the flat of her palm up and down my back. I resisted the embrace momentarily, not wanting to be touched in my embarrassment, but her familiar touch relaxed me, evoking countless comforting embraces in the past.

She held me until my body relaxed, then led me back to the stool upon which I sat while being groomed. Deftly working through the length of my hair, she spoke softly, lest anyone be passing by.

"I do not judge you." I started to protest that she absolutely did, until I realized that she had voiced no such thing. "You have lived a long time without love. You have had long-held desires go unfulfilled. I do not blame you for taking happiness where you find it, though I do think that perhaps this man was not the wisest of choices."

I winced as the truth of her words struck home. She had always been the wiser of our pairing, and though she had always insisted that it was the trait of a slave—always in the background, always observing and nothing more—I had always thought that her soul was simply older than that of most.

Though I was still in no mood for a bath and allowed Drusilla only to sponge water over me, I acquiesced to this, knowing that, as always, she had only my own interests at heart. Though she may not approve of where I had slaked my desire, she would always support me, and to refuse this support would be churlish.

"Thank you." I murmured the words as the water sluiced over my skin, the words applying to more than the makeshift bath. I saw the reflection of the dark-haired woman in the mirror, nodding crisply before continuing with her task, and knew that her feelings were my own.

Lucius would not have approved of my sponge bath—he would have called this quick cleaning a whore's bath and have insisted that I use our large, expensive marble bath. But I knew that I would never again be able to immerse myself in the liquid there without thinking of my gladiator.

Still, civilized people bathed, and so I allowed the musk of sleep—and of sex—to be rinsed from my skin. Lucius would never know the difference, for all the attention that he paid me now. The droplets of water that coursed down my frame, tickling and tempting, were no better than the bath, for they teased my already heightened state of need yet again, as did the brush of the coarse fabric of my towel as Drusilla rubbed it vigorously over my exposed and freshly clean skin.

Lucius entered as Drusilla was helping me on with the loose tunic that I intended to wear that day. It was the lightest that I owned, a thin wisp that was just a few threads away from transparent, and was a defense against the insufferable heat of a Roman summer.

I winced at his entrance. I had rather hoped to hide the fact that I had slept longer than normal. I felt certain that my guilt was painted over my face.

"Alba. I thought that you would be ready for the day already." Though his words were curious, his eyes avidly sought out the pucker of my nipples against the ethereal fabric.

Knowing very well why I had chosen to lie abed, I felt my skin flush, and looked down in an attempt to hide it.

"I . . . I was not feeling at my best this morning." This was true enough.

Lucius noted the flush of my skin. "I fear that this heat is not agreeing with you." His voice was fussy, the bother that my lack of readiness for the day brought him overriding the concern of husband for wife. Though I supposed that the fact that he had noticed something was amiss was more attention than many wives received from their husbands—he was not entirely disengaged from our life together. "Still, I need you to pull yourself together and come to my office." He made to leave, but I let my curiosity overcome me.

I was never called to his office. It was a meeting place for the men.

"Just come, Alba. And quickly. We are to meet with the doctor." With those words, he pushed through my curtain and left, leaving me intensely curious and a little apprehensive.

We never had the doctor to the house, not unless it was an emergency of some sort. We employed a full-time medic and dietician, to ensure the continued health of the gladiators, and the man was quite capable of looking after most mild ailments that occurred.

Drusilla, noting my agitation, did her best to hurry as she dressed my hair. I had planned to have her bind the thick coils of night-sky black against my skull, tied tightly down with gauze, and on top of it arrange the mass of fashionable yellow hair that I had purchased a month earlier, for yellow was what the noble ladies currently deemed fashionable. Both the heat and my curiosity overcame the desire. I had Drusilla finish combing it through and bind it up simply while I stepped into the leather sandals that I wore while at home, and as soon as I was presentable, I wound my way through the halls to the corner where Lucius' office lay.

Drusilla squeezed my arm as we parted ways, a gesture

of support. With a quick glance around to make certain that we were alone, I leaned in and brushed a hot, dry kiss of appreciation over her cheek before slipping through the curtain that blocked the entrance to Lucius' office.

The room was dim, as always, with weak, pale beams of light filtering in from the small window carved out of the graveled wall. Justinus, the slave who handled the majority of our bartering, and the local doctor were seated across from Lucius, crockery cups of wine in hand. A platter of glistening, ripe red grapes sat on the table, drops of wetness glinting fatly in the straw-colored light, and a grumble low in my belly reminded me that I had yet to break my fast.

"Eat, Alba." Lucius, with a halo of agitation surrounding him, pushed the large plate of grapes close to where I took a seat, the edges of the wooden chair digging uncomfortably into my hips, but I shook my head.

"I am not hungry." If I admitted to hunger, Lucius would send for more than grapes—for bread, for meat—simply to show his ability to do so in front of the doctor. The men would then wait to talk until I had finished eating—they would wait until I had swallowed every morsel to begin the conversation, and my curiosity was too rampant for that.

As it was, I had to wait for Lucius to cease his pacing. Back, forth. Back, forth. The room was too small for it. All three men seemed somewhat agitated, actually, or at least anticipatory, and their mood dripped on top of mine, smothering it and changing it.

But it was not appropriate for me to start the meeting, so I had to wait. Finally, Lucius sat, his chair cushioned with a soft pillow, and reached across the expanse of the table between us. He took my hands in his.

The touch made me start. He so very rarely touched me anymore. There was no need to, not when I could not bear his child.

"We have very nearly secured the patronage of Baldurus."

I smiled, a real smile, as a frisson of excitement shot its fizzy way through me.

"Excellent work, husband." As a client of Baldurus, one of the wealthiest men in the city, the costs of keeping our ludus would be greatly lessened—the cost of keeping the men was a financial burden that we could, at times, just barely meet. Though they were slaves, they required food and frequent medical attention. Also, law decreed that they were entitled to a large share of their own winnings. So though Lucius' family had managed on its own for generations, the patronage of Baldurus would be more than welcome. Baldurus would, in return, receive a percentage of the money that we made, and we anticipated much coin at some point with our potential new champion, but we, too, would make more.

Patronage was not something that Lucius' father, Junius, ever would have considered, and so long as he was alive, the tradition of *patria potestas* forbade Lucius from going against his father's wishes. A man was not considered to be the pater familias until his father was dead. But Junius had passed nearly a year earlier, and ever since then Lucius had been negotiating with Baldurus. His efforts had wrought an excellent situation, and I knew that Lucius had worked hard to make it happen.

He did not look nearly as pleased as I expected he would, and I remarked upon it.

"Yes. Well." He raked a hand through his hair again and exchanged a knowing glance with Justinus. I fought to swallow a morsel of irritation that a slave would know something before I did—I, Lucius' wife—but said nothing.

Seeing that Lucius would not, or could not, speak his mind, Justinus spoke for him. "There is a condition to securing the patronage."

Lucius cast him a look of irritation, for Justinus had clearly spoken out of turn. A slave did not take charge of a conversation that involved his master, and I was surprised that Lucius let it go with little more than a raised eyebrow.

"Yes," Lucius continued as if his slave had not spoken, "Baldurus, as you know, considers himself very much a family man."

I nodded. This was true. Baldurus himself had sixteen children with his wife and had climbed many rungs on the political ladder by endorsing the strength of a large Roman familia.

It was suspected that soon he would wear the purple-edged tunic of a *senator*.

"He is very interested in the profit that his patronage to us would bring, but feels that he has a certain . . . reputation . . . that he must uphold. Politically speaking."

The pleasant expression that I had assumed while listening froze on my face. I suspected what the next words would be, and they stung like a thousand tiny needles pricking at my soul.

"He will not enter into an agreement with us unless

My Wicked Gladiators   35

you can become with child." The force of the words, though spoken flatly enough, felt like a huge blow to my stomach.

I was barren. I could not have children, though I longed to do so. It seemed cruel that Lucius would even bring this matter to my attention. If we needed a child to secure the patronage, then the deal would never be struck.

"Do not cry, Alba." Lucius knew me well enough still, despite the growing distance between us, that he recognized the shimmer of tears before they fell. "I mean no insult. It is . . . it is just that when in consult, the doctor, here, suggested a notion to me that had not before occurred." He gestured to the third man in the room, the one to whom I had paid not a whit of attention. I recognized the man, whose name I believed was Pompeius, from the time that a visiting *patrician* noble had fallen on our slick steps and twisted her ankle, and it would not have done to have her treated simply by our gladiators' medic.

The doctor cleared his throat before speaking, and he seemed to make a point of looking at me, not at my husband.

"You are aware, I believe, that your husband has . . . relations . . . with your slaves?" I flushed and nodded. This was not a topic of conversation with which I felt comfortable.

To his credit, Lucius looked uncomfortable, too, and even slightly guilty. It warmed my heart, just the smallest bit, to see that he wished me no heartache, even though he was well within his rights to sleep with our slave girls.

"In discussing matters with your husband, as we tried to find a way in which you might become pregnant, it came to my attention that . . . ahem . . . the good man Lucius has not begotten any offspring with any woman." My hand jerked violently, and knocked Lucius' cup off of the desk. It lay up-ended on the small, brightly woven rug that covered part of the stone floor, its position echoing my view of the world as it had become in the last few moments.

This was true. This was absolutely true. Why had I not ever thought of it? Possibly because I never thought, at all, about the children of my slaves, or to whom they belonged. That shamed me, even as a wild hope welled up, twining with confusion and reaching into my lungs to steal my breath.

"It is possible that it is your husband who cannot breed, madam. Not you." Seeming relieved to have the words out of his mouth, he sat back and took a long, messy, relieved chug of wine from a goblet clutched in tense fingers.

I turned to my husband and was met with a face that I had never seen. Seemingly devoid of emotion, it was as if someone I did not know had slipped into Lucius' body in the moment I had turned away. I did not know the man who was left at all.

I suspected that it was a mask he had donned to hide his shame over his barren state, but its blankness still startled me.

"This patronage is necessary for the survival of our ludus, Alba." His words were clipped, his fingers in mine tight, and I understood that he was not enjoying what he had to say. "Without it, we cannot afford to continue. We will have to sell the gladiators, and I will have to find some other means of income." This was yet another unforeseen piece of information. I had been under the impression that we were just as well-off as we had been for the entirety of our marriage.

"But . . ." I stared at the unyielding planes that made up my husband's face. I did not understand. We needed the patronage but could not have it unless I became with child. And I could not become with child if my husband was unable to provide me with one.

"You are to be mated," Justinus spoke, and Lucius again turned angry eyes on him. I stood without realizing that my limbs had moved.

"I am to be what?" So many feelings flocked through my being that I felt dizzy, and stumbled, but refused the doctor's help back into my seat. "With whom?" Anger branded each word with a crispness that threatened to crack.

My marriage vows had deemed that I could have relations with whomever my pater familias—Lucius—deemed permissible, but none had been mandatory except himself, my husband. And never had I ever imagined something like this.

"You will be mated with a slave of my choosing, and you will mate with him at every time that you are ripe, until you conceive a child." This man could not have been my husband. It simply could not have been. He may have grown distant in recent times, but never before had he sounded so calculating and cruelly certain.

As I stared at him with disbelief radiating from my very skin, I saw a crack form in the calculation.

I did not believe that he wanted to force such a situation upon me. But I also had no doubts that he would do so, if it was what was needed to provide for this family.

"With a slave? But . . . we have only one . . ." I cast my eyes to Justinus, who sat in the corner, looking pleased with himself. "With Justinus? I will not!" I had never liked the man, found him to be unscrupulous and conniving. But we had no other male slaves in the house.

"No!" The response from Lucius' lips was more forceful than I had expected. "Not Justinus." There was an unreadable glance exchanged between them again, and I did not like it, though I did not know what it meant.

"Who, then?" And as I said it, I knew. "One . . . one of the gladiators?" The thought both frightened and excited me. Repulsed and delighted.

I knew better than to expect that I would be able to select the one who appealed to me, and many of the others were wild, untamed, and would be fearsome in bed.

The odds were against it being Marcus, and even if it was, I resented not being given a choice.

"I will not!" The fingers that had held mine so sweetly only a quarter of an hour earlier suddenly seemed to belong to an animal, for they clasped my wrist so hard that I knew I would have bruises.

"You will." I tried to rise, to back away from the stranger that inhabited my husband's body. "You will do it for this family, or you will be divorced. And if I divorce you, where will you go? You will have nothing. You will be nothing. You will be no better than those that you are turning your nose up at." The fear wafting off of me like a perfume then seemed to penetrate his façade, at least a bit, and he softened, if only a smidgen.

"You have always wanted a child, Alba. Now you will have one. And he will be mine in all but conception."

I studied my husband's face. In his eyes I saw desperation. He did not want to force this indignity upon me, but he did not have a choice, not if we were to keep the ludus. Still, nausea churned in the depths of my belly, and my womb felt heavy. For all I knew, I might already be carrying the child of a gladiator, something I had not considered, for I had assumed that I was unable. And now I was expected to let anyone that my husband chose spill his seed between my thighs, to fuck me until I was pregnant, no matter how repugnant I found the process.

And unless it was Marcus, I would indeed find the entire situation vile.

"I . . ." Lucius was right. I had no choice. I had no money of my own, and was no longer considered a part of my birth family, not since I had taken vows with Lucius. They had no obligation to care for me should I be turned out of this house. I would have to become a slave, and not all slaves were treated as well as the ones under our roof.

Crushed, and yet with a tiny bird of a thrill rioting around my belly, a thrill at the thought of a child in my womb, I sank back, all fight draining out of the soles of my feet. I had no choice, not unless I ran away. And if I ran, I would be forced into slavery. There were no other options.

Taking my posture for the acquiescence that it was—*reluctant* acquiescence, Lucius released my arm, leaned back, and took his cup in hand. "You will be pleased in the end, Alba. To our new patronage with Baldurus!" His arm raised in the air with such exuberance that his fresh cup of wine slopped over the side, and Justinus and the doctor followed suit, and I found that I could not blame them, no matter how I felt.

If the ludus could grow, could thrive, it would be best for us all.

I did not raise my cup. I would not, could not, rejoice

my free will being extinguished with a few choice words. Stunned, I pulled inward, wrapped myself into a tight inner ball of emotion as the men began to discuss who would be the most likely candidate, who amongst the gladiators would have a strong seed. There was mention of a champion. One sentence penetrated my consciousness when it was asked of me, however, and I blinked, bird-like, up into the face of the doctor, who now stood over me.

"When were your last courses, lady?" I had to think before I answered.

He calculated, counting days on his fingers, before speaking words that sealed my fate.

"One night every cycle, until pregnancy occurs. It would be best to begin tonight."

Chapter Three

The mask quite literally took my breath away.

Shiny and white, a depiction of Juno, the Roman goddess of fertility, it covered most of my face, including my nose, making it difficult to draw breath. But Lucius had insisted upon it.

He had not wanted the man whom he chose to have the privilege of looking upon his wife while he fucked her.

He had given me the choice of masking my mate or leaving him barefaced. I chose the mask. I myself did not want to dwell on the identity of the brute who would force himself between my thighs.

I had no hope that it would be Marcus. There were nearly fifty men who lived and trained in our ludus. The odds were far too low to allow myself any hope.

I drank cup after cup of savory wine as Drusilla attended to my body, my hair, my skin. Though she pressed the occasional sip of water through my lips to counteract the effects of the wine, she otherwise let me be, knowing how I yearned for the blurring of the senses that the wine would bring. Every touch of her hands against me made me shudder, not because it was her touch but because I knew that my husband had ordered it. Lucius had insisted that I be rubbed with oil, scented with perfume, removed of all bodily hair but one slim, perfectly groomed stripe. He would not have one of his slaves see his wife in any state other than perfect. So I had spent my long afternoon being groomed, something that I normally would have enjoyed.

Knowing what it was for, the only way to endure the preparations was to lose myself in the oblivion of wine. I had indulged far more than I ever had before, and when I was led to the room where the event was to occur, Drusilla had to clutch my arm and guide me, to save me from bobbing and weaving my way through our home.

Normally a bit too much wine left me giddy and full of fun. I had slunk over that edge now and was feeling a full sea wave of emotion. The emotion spilled over when I saw my husband, leaning against the doorframe to the most opulent room in our house.

"You are not intending to *watch*, are you?" I was horrified, and the combination of my incredulity with the overindulgence of wine caused me to speak more freely than I ever had in our marriage. "No. No! I will do as you wish with the brute, but I will not submit to you watching." I glared, lethally sharp knives arcing out of my eyes to pierce the cool demeanor of my husband.

It worked. Though he looked like he was about to argue, he also donned a cloak of discomfiture, and it made me feel slightly, very slightly, better.

"Alba, I know of your reluctance to do this deed. And

though I beg your pardon, we must make sure that it is done." I wanted to believe that he begged my pardon for form's sake only, that he did as he wished, and would continue to do so. That he was arrogant enough, sure enough of his authority over me, that he was certain I could carry the argument no further.

But I knew that he did care. I was still angry, still furious that his duties to the ludus took priority over his duties to me, his wife, but I knew that he did not force this upon me lightly.

In my anger, I did what I had never done and carried the argument on. He needed me for something now, for the first time in our marriage, a fact that had occurred to me sometime between my third and fourth cup of wine.

I had leverage.

"Spare me my dignity, at least, husband. If you will spare me nothing else." The words hit him in his pride, exactly where I had aimed them. Lucius was proud of his ability to take care of his wife and family, had always been—another reason that securing this patronage was so important to him. That I was so upset by his decision surely kept him unsettled, though I knew it would never be enough to make him change his mind.

He closed his mouth, which had fallen open a bit with my outburst. Then it closed again, and determination settled over his features. I could not understand why he was so insistent. While it was common enough for a husband to sleep with other women, the wives of Rome were not always permitted other men. Not fair, to be sure, but it was how it was—I had always suspected, though I would never have voiced the thought, that perhaps the ego of men was simply more fragile than that of women. So why would Lucius want to watch? Would it not make him feel somewhat impotent? Should he not be relieved that I would not permit it?

Surely he would not get some kind of perverse pleasure from it.

At his elbow, Justinus schooled his lips into the smirk so characteristic of him, the one that I detested. I wondered why he had to be everywhere that Lucius was. It drove me near to insanity.

"I'm sorry, Alba. It has to be witnessed." The tone of his voice warned me that he had made up his mind, and I racked the sloshy recesses of my brain, trying to come up with an alternative that would be acceptable to us both. I did not have much hope. Lucius looked determined, even anticipatory.

"If I might speak?" I jerked as Justinus spoke, his words oozing into the hallway. The combination of my start and my spinning head nearly made me stumble, and Drusilla had to help me stay upright.

I was surprised that the man had bothered asking, since for reasons unbeknownst to me, Lucius allowed him to say far too much, and whenever he wanted.

Lucius inclined his head a fraction. "Speak."

"Perhaps Domina would be more comfortable if, in your stead, someone else that you trusted was present?" Though his lips remained in a straight line when he looked at me, the gleam in Justinus' eyes was unmistakable. The gleam, and a determination of his own.

He looked like he would stop at nothing to make certain that Lucius was not in that room, observing the sordid scene. Though oftentimes I thought that his devotion to his master went too far, ran too deep, this one time I found us in agreement.

"No." Never in the space of one conversation had I said this word so many times to my husband. "Absolutely not. I will not have that cretin witness something so private."

Lucius eyed me reprovingly, and it infuriated me. I was all for treating slaves well, but for him to support one in his wife's stead was, in my opinion, inexcusable.

"Justinus is a valued member of this family, Alba." I would have laughed if that much movement would not have made me sick. I knew some families that considered their slaves to be trusted members of the household, but it was much in the way of a dog. They were not, and could not be, equals, not with Roman society the way that it was.

I had once watched Justinus claw his way from mere household slave to become my husband's right-hand man. At the time I had approved, for I saw that the man had been trying to better his position in life through any means that he could.

Now, though, he took it too far. He spied, he pried. He used information as a commodity, and as such no one in the house trusted him—no one save my husband, who was for some reason blinded when it came to the man.

"He is a *slave*, Lucius." At my side I could feel Drusilla flinch; I would have to speak with her later. Though she knew very well that she meant so much more to me than a slave to her domina, my words would sound cruel to her ears. I wished that I could communicate that immediately, but I could not, not with Lucius and Justinus standing so close.

Justinus remained silent, remained still, but I felt a trickle of unease all the same at the manner in which he received my comment. Or maybe it was how he received Lucius' response to my comment, for my husband seemed to be considering my thoughts.

"Well then, Alba. What do you suggest, if not Justinus? Do not say Drusilla, for I know she would lie if you told her to." I bit my lip, and a trickle of sobriety entered my consciousness as I tried to find an outcome that would work. I had hoped that Drusilla would indeed be acceptable, and for the very reason that my husband would not allow her presence.

Lucius would fully trust no one but himself and Justinus. I refused to have either in the room, and did not even want my husband anywhere near the proceedings. It just felt wrong.

"Justinus may stay." My announcement was clipped, and met with a smug smile by the man. "*Outside* the room. And I would have a heavier curtain placed over the doorway."

Incredulous, Justinus turned to Lucius, as if to ask if he would possibly allow this madness. But my husband seemed to understand that if he wanted me to do this thing without being forcibly held down, then he had to give, at least a bit.

I silently thanked him for it.

"Very well." He turned to his man. "Fetch the curtain from the balcony overlooking the ludus. Replace it here." To me he nodded, and I thought that possibly—maybe—there was a tinge of regret in his eyes. "Alba, go in and make yourself ready."

This was it. Nausea churned like a storm on the charcoal-gray sea, and my feet were so unwilling to move forward that Drusilla had to tug, hard, to get me into the room. There she seated me on the chaise that had been centered on the hard floor and fetched a cup of water.

"No more wine for you." She ran a hand through my inky hair, which I had asked her to comb through and leave down, all the better to hide in.

Her touch was comforting, and brought on thought. Drusilla was a slave, something I often had to remind myself of. She was my confidante, had been my lover, was the one who cared for me. Not all slaves would welcome the opportunity for some measure of revenge in this encounter, a danger that Lucius had not seemed to have considered.

If only I could have been assured of a decent partner, one who I would not fear. One who was not likely to beat me, or to perform perfunctorily.

If the man went about it properly, I might even enjoy it, as I had enjoyed Marcus. It was so rarely that I was touched like that.

No, I had to correct myself. No matter the kind of lover that my faceless gladiator was, he would be nothing like Marcus. What had sparked between us when our skin slid on skin was something I had never before felt, and though the battle-roughened man confused me greatly, I had an inkling that he was not any more immune to it than I was.

Oh, I was confused.

"How would you be most comfortable, Alba?" Drusilla pulled lightly at my tunic, and I realized that it would be easiest if I was in some state of undress when the man arrived. But Justinus had just come back to hang the heavy curtain, and I would not disrobe in front of him, not in this situation.

Though he had seen me in my skin numerous times before,

it had not been by my choice, and it would not happen while I had a say in the matter. It would relinquish some power to him, now, and I was not willing to give it up.

After the curtain was hung by Justinus, I allowed Drusilla to strip me down to my lace sleep tunic, which I wore under the heavier tunic that I had changed into earlier. It would provide the access necessary, but I would not feel completely exposed.

And then she left, left me alone, though she cast me a sympathetic, heartfelt backward glance—and though I was not by myself for long.

The heavy fall of men's steps sounded from the other side of the curtain. "Alba?" It was the voice of Lucius, but he was not alone.

I raised a hand to my mask, then lowered my head. I did not want to look, did not want to hope that I would recognize the body that would soon cover mine.

I ran fingers gone cold and wet with nerves through the inky, scented ribbons of my hair, then twisted them so tightly in my lace that it nearly ripped. I tucked my legs beneath myself on the chaise, attempting to hide the shadowy area between my legs, though it was ridiculous, I knew.

The man would see it soon, after all.

"Alba?" Again Lucius called, and the curtain twitched. I cast my eyes down, riveted their stare to the floor so that I did not have to see. Then I cleared my throat, trying to make room for the words to escape.

"I am ready."

"Domina." The shadow stretched, longer than the man could possibly be tall, on the floor where my eyes could see. It might have been childish, and I knew that he wore a mask, but I did not want to see him, not at all.

I nodded; I would have spoken, but what was there to say? I concentrated instead on the flicker of the light cast by the fat wax candles that had been set around the room. They were to offset the dark brought by the setting sun, but the manner in which they played off of the gold, the muted stones, and the heavily textured fabrics gave the area an entirely romantic feel.

The man cleared his throat, and I realized that possibly, just possibly, this was no easier for him than it was for me. Did he have a wife outside the ludus whom he remained loyal to? Not likely, but it was a possibility. Men in debt often signed their freedom over to a ludus for a period of five years, simply to earn money that they could use to pay their debts, or that they could choose to send home to their wife and children.

At least he had not mounted me the second that he had entered the room. For that I was thankful.

"Domina, how . . . how would you prefer this to be done?"

I looked up then, startled by the uncertainty in the question.

Why did he care, so long as he rutted until his seed spilled? I was under no delusions that Lucius had instructed him to do more than not leave any marks.

But he stood across the room, and the shadow of a large urn fell over him. All I could see was skin, beautifully sculpted skin, and a face half covered by a mask sculpted in the visage of Mars, the god of war and male virility.

That skin gleamed like fresh honey in the low crimson-sunset light.

"I . . . I do not care." I still did not have much hope of this encounter being anything that I would enjoy. The men below, the gladiators, were deprived of women for such long periods that it would be over quickly, and if the man got rough, then I would be only too glad for a brief encounter.

He stepped forward then, toward me, and even as my heart clenched in my chest, a wild hope sprang from my gut.

His hair was golden. I still could not see most of him, but his hair was the color of flax, just like Marcus, though in this light I could also see threads of copper and red.

I quashed the excitement as quickly as I could. What if it was not? We owned several fair-haired men. After my first encounter with Marcus, I had noticed them all, without making any effort to do so.

There was Marcus, and there was Caius, both considered potential champions. There was Animus, and there were two more whose names I did not know.

This man could be anyone.

The uncertainty of the entire situation made me sick to my stomach. Making a snap decision, I lowered myself from the chaise to the pile of cushions on the floor, and knelt on hands and knees.

"Take me from behind." I moved so that he could see nothing of me but my ass. "I do not wish to see you." Hard words, but I meant them. If I saw him, I would dream that he was Marcus and would be sick if he was not.

This way, I could at least pretend that he was, and while

knowing all the time that it was not real, it might get me through the situation.

"As you wish." I sensed the movement more than saw it, though I did catch a glimpse of undulating shadows out of the corner of my eye as he made his way across the room. He settled behind me, and I braced myself for a rude intrusion.

Instead I heard a soft intake of breath, as if the man was staring at something beautiful. Gentle fingers teased the hem of my tunic, testing the weight. I was so bewildered by the action that when the man moved to lift it up, above my waist and over my head, I let him, and in the blink of an eye I was bare to his stare.

I could have insisted that I put the tunic back on. But that slight touch had softened me. I was curious, curious about the warrior who would take the time to lightly remove such a delicate garment.

I shivered, slightly cold, as I waited to see what he would do next. Still half-expecting a brutally hard cock to be thrust between my unprepared legs, I felt a wave of goose pimples hump my skin when fingers brushed the tender skin behind my right knee.

"What are you doing?" The question sounded harsh, even to my ears, but I could not think through the wine and the confusion to temper the words.

"There is no need for this to be unpleasant for you." My mouth fell open in surprise, then in pleasure as the hand trailed from behind my knee, tracing a seam up the back of my thigh and around to cup my hip.

I felt pleasure, just the slightest honey drip, begin to spill into my unease. Waiting for the next curiosity, I caught my breath, then huffed it out on the next touch of his fingers, dizzy from lack of oxygen.

He knelt behind me, but his skin did not press against mine. His left hand reached up to cover my naked hip, the one that was not being gently caressed, and a surge of something unidentifiable surged through me, mixing with the wine and causing me to become drunk.

It felt as when I had received my first kiss, from a young slave boy that had belonged to my family.

That boy had been brutally beaten for that very same kiss, and the memory had left a bitter taste that coated the memory still. But when that boy's innocent lips had touched my own virgin ones, it had brought an intoxicating rush, one that faded a little bit with every kiss I had received thereafter.

This touch, this man's hands on my hips, brought back the sensation. It also brought a feeling that this couldn't possibly end well, but what say did I have in the matter?

I knelt, my joints stiff with tension, afraid and unsure. But the masked man did no more than knead the soft flesh at my hips, running his fingers gently back and forth, up and down.

It felt good. I could not deny that. It was arousing, arousing enough to chip away at my nerves. Those nerves left crevices that were slowly filled up with curiosity and, I think, desire. Soon I began to rock, just the tiniest bit, with the want of something more.

"Domina?" The word hung in the viscous air, melting away into the warmth of the summer evening. He was waiting for me to tell him what to do, what would be acceptable to me. What I wanted.

What I wanted was for him to just take control, but I was afraid to let go of the upper hand. What if the heat of passion turned him into the brute that I had been expecting?

So I told him to do the first thing that came into my mind.

"Use your fingers." I thought that this might be a test of sorts. Perhaps I could judge how brutal he would be with his cock by how he played me with his fingers. Squeezing my eyes shut, I waited.

A gasp of delight slipped from my lips when one of his large, calloused hands migrated from my hip to splay, flat, over my belly. The tip of his smallest finger brushed through the shadowy curls between my legs, and suddenly my every muscle was tense, willing him to move his hand further downward.

The hard patches of his palm scraped my tender, perfumed skin as that hand slid slowly downward. I was so still, so tense that it hurt, and I could not understand how I had gone from apprehension to such anticipation with such a small touch.

Then those long, thick fingers began to comb through my newly damp curls, and I stopped wondering. Stopped thinking. A single finger moved further downward still, tracing the slit of my labia, gently massaging the fleshy petals there, and the tension in my flesh began to move, became a vibrating force.

"Is this what you want?" The words were whispered, low and deep, into the waves of shadowy hair that covered my neck. The individual strands waved gently with his breath, and caused the longer coils that hung over my breasts to tease the dark circles of my nipples.

I did not answer, not with words, at least. It was exactly

what I wanted, and yet it was not. I wanted more. But I only wanted it if I could be sure that he would not switch from this persona, a purveyor of sensual pleasure, to the heavy-handed brute that I feared.

I knew that Justinus was just on the other side of the curtain if that happened, but I was not entirely convinced that the man would come to my rescue, at least not right away.

But I was beginning to lose the capacity for rational thought. Though I did not answer his question with words, that single finger that teased my flesh pressed against the slit that divided my labia, gaining access to even more sensitive flesh. It swiped through the slickness that pooled there, moved back and forth, and then probed gently for that hard nub of my clitoris.

I exhaled when he found it. I knew that this was my last chance for rational thought. If I allowed him to touch me here, I would allow him to do as he wished with me. I would no longer have the presence of mind to stop things before they got ugly, *if* they did indeed get ugly.

It might have been stupid, it might have been irresponsible, but I wanted this. If my husband was going to force me to mate with a gladiator, then I wanted to enjoy what I could.

It seemed that this man had a respect for me, a respect for women, that I found highly arousing.

I wanted him.

With a low, guttural sound from the depths of my throat, I shifted myself backward and pressed into the figure that knelt behind me.

He let loose with a harsh noise of his own when the naked globes of my ass pressed into his lap. I had not been sure, since

I had not laid eyes upon him, but he was as nude as I was, and I felt the hard length of a cock, the coarse brush of pubic hair against my skin.

I wriggled my hips, grinding down on his lap with feverish need. He tried to hold firm, but the finger that pressed against my clitoris shook, the rough edges of his nails scratching the bundle of nerves, and a small cry escaped my lips.

Before I could blink, impossibly large arms clasped me tightly around the waist and pulled until I was no longer on all fours but seated between thighs that could have been carved from marble by an artist. I wanted to protest the removal of those fingers from my clitoris, but they returned before I could even exhale.

I no longer remembered what my concerns had been. All I cared about was the hard body that held me tightly and, ridiculously, provided a sense of security, a safe place in which I could let go.

He was not as gentle as he had been with that first touch, beginning to touch me with the strong caresses that I expected from a gladiator. He did not circle around the perimeter of my clitoris, or trace it, or touch and tease. Instead he rubbed directly on the blood-filled area, rubbing rhythmically back and forth, creating a whirlpool of bliss that circled around, closing in on the epicenter.

I writhed in his lap, seeking a way to escape the insistent press of that finger. It was too much, too intense. I needed to retreat from it, but there was nowhere to go, not with the solid flesh that encircled me, and the impending orgasm that allowed me to focus on nothing else.

The whirlpool boiled over with a handful more of those

hard, rhythmic rubs. I bit my lip, doing my best to stay quiet as I shook, but another small cry bit into the syrup of the air as a finger slid past my clitoris and right into my cunt before the tremors had ceased.

I pressed back against him, feeling the length of his cock move against my spine as I did. I still needed to escape—the sensation was too much to bear. But once again I was not permitted to go anywhere. I quivered through the overly sensitive, mind-numbing experience of yet more pleasure right after pleasure, and if Justinus had not been right outside the door, I might very well have screamed, as every nerve in my body was doing.

The lone finger in my cunt moved in and out, not slowly, not fast, but in a steady rhythm designed to again bring me to peak. I groaned, my voice thick, when he added another finger and crooked them several times in quick succession, deep inside of me.

Losing myself, I splayed my legs as far apart as they would go, urging him to drive his fingers deeper. His breath grew ragged, and the heat of it burned my cheek as he pumped his fist, the two fingers buried inside me, up and down, stretching them, crooking them, rubbing them against my tender inner walls.

The second quake was not a wave that drowned me like the first, but rather a slow melt that liquefied me from the inside out. My voice caught on one note, long and low, as I flooded into his hand, and I sprawled into his lap, a creature without bones, when the ebb ceased.

I could not speak. I had not experienced pleasure like this, ever. I had not been touched like this, ever, as if the only pleasure that mattered was my own. And yet it was not enough. Could not ever be enough.

It was impossible, but I wanted more. Just as soon as I could again move.

I lay for a long moment like that, boneless, softness melted overtop his hard heat. But soon his hands moved from my cunt to rub over the soft swells of my belly, up to play over my ribcage, and finally to cup the heavy globes that were my breasts.

"Domina?" I murmured a sleepy, very nearly contented sigh, even as I rocked my hips backward again, seeking friction.

"You know that we must . . . we must finish." I stiffened a bit, for I had very nearly forgotten. The touch of this masked gladiator, this warrior, had wiped memory from mind, filling its empty spaces with ecstasy, but now that the orgasmic haze was receding, I could recall what had put this little scenario into play.

"Yes." I lifted a shaking hand to brush the hair from my eyes. "Yes, I know." I tried to sit up, but my spent limbs would not let me.

"Would you still prefer that I take you from behind?" I would have laughed at the absurdity of the question, but there was a note in his voice that stopped me. It was a note coated with . . . I didn't know how to put it into words. But what it told me was that, given his way, we would remove our masks and make love face-to-face, eyes locked.

I could not allow that. No matter his gentleness as a lover, no matter that I was feeling warm toward him as well. This was still a forced fuck, ordered by my husband, and I still had feelings that confused me for another gladiator, for one of his brothers.

Why should we not enjoy ourselves, if we were to be forced into intimacy anyway? We were simply making the best of a difficult situation.

"Yes." Untangling myself from his arms, though I had no illusion that I could do so if he did not permit it, I slid from my splayed leg position on his lap to my hands and knees on the floor, as I had presented myself to him earlier. "Yes. Take me from behind. And do not be gentle."

As soon as the words were out of my mouth I regretted them. Though he had been considerate thus far, when his cock entered the equation he might not be, and I did not need to invite him to throw away any scruples that he might possess.

Again I was disconcerted by his movements. I felt him close the short distance between us, felt his heated skin press against my ass. But rather than grabbing his cock at the base and shoving it into my cunt—which, truth be told, I might have even enjoyed, for he had gotten me wetter than the Tiber—he took those delicious fingers and traced the crease that divided my behind.

When his fingers grazed over the pucker that lay between, I both tensed and shivered, but his fingers continued. When they again found my cleft, found me drenched and ready, he took his cock and pressed it against my opening.

I rocked impatiently. I had told him I did not want it gentle, had I not? Even if I had questioned myself moments afterward, he did not know that. And now I was being teased again, and I was beyond the point where I could enjoy it.

I wanted him to ride me, and I wanted it now.

And then I had the breath knocked out of me. In one hard thrust the head of his cock moved from the entrance of my cunt to the wall of my womb. I could not breathe, I was filled so full, and I could then understand why he had been hesitant.

He was large enough that it hurt, just a bit, and my mind flashed to the same sensation, experienced with Marcus days earlier. But I shook it out of my brain, or had it shaken out for me, as one of those ridiculously muscled arms again clamped around my waist, the other digging fingers into my breast, and I was rocked back and forth on the hardness of his cock.

He did not pull all the way out before slamming in again, as I had been accustomed to in the past with my husband. Instead he moved only the smallest bit in and out, the girth of him stretching my insides, and the incredible friction caused pleasure to build again.

It was not rough. Nor was it gentle, though, the slow movements firm and forceful. My eyes rolled back in my head when the coarse thatch of hair that surrounded his cock brushed against my clitoris, again and again. Combined with his movements, deep inside of me, I again experienced that sweetest of quakes, short and hard and intense.

As my flesh spasmed around him, clutching and pulling at the silky skin of his cock, he groaned and thrust once, hard, into me. I gasped when he pulled me back as hard as he could against him, the jut of his hipbones digging into my flesh as he emptied himself inside of me.

And then we were still, both of us sweaty and spent.

The next moments were awkward. I felt the ridiculous

urge to curl up into his side, to remove the masks and stare into his eyes. That was something I had never even done with my husband. Sex was for the purpose of begetting children, or release, and there was no point in remaining afterward.

I might have imagined it, but I thought that his hands lingered on my flesh when he pulled out of my body, leaving me empty. Again I felt the wild hope that he was Marcus, but combined with the hope was a desire for him to be no one but who he was.

And who he was, was a nameless, faceless gladiator who had possibly just made me pregnant.

The pleasure was quickly seeping away, and I was confused.

His hand splayed over the slick skin at the small of my back, rested there for a moment before falling away. I heard him stand, heard the brush of cloth over skin as he cleaned himself.

Then the padding of bare feet on stone as he walked away.

I was full of seed, full of the potential for a child, but I was very much alone.

Chapter Four

My body ached, and my heart even more so.

The sheets beneath me were bunched uncomfortably, but I could not find the energy to move. I was more conflicted than I could ever remember being.

My body was limp with satisfaction. My mind was not. My thoughts trailed, one after another, in a circle that rotated with ever-increasing speed.

How could I have found pleasure tonight? I should have found only embarrassment. Before Marcus, the only other man that I had been with was my husband, and he was the very person who had betrayed me, had sold me out.

I knew that he thought he was justified in his actions. I was more inclined to think that perhaps he should have just pursued the patronage of another, though finding another man of such high patrician status who would give us any attention was indeed unlikely. Though we were of the highest class of plebeians, plebeians we still were.

There was not anything to be done about that. A person

was born to his class—it was simply dependent upon the whims of the gods.

Still. I felt slightly akin to a common whore. My body was being used as an instrument for financial gain. And yet I also felt a wild, terrible hope that even now a new life was forming in my belly.

To add to all of this, I still felt shame over my encounter with Marcus days earlier. Shame, and yet the strong feelings that my heart held for him would not wane. I still prayed that, should I become with child, it would be his. The thought of bearing a child that would be half of some man that I did not know, much less cared for, was unappealing in its strangeness.

Oh, this was such a mess.

Lucius chose the moment in which my thoughts had sunk the lowest in which to push aside the curtain to my chamber and make his appearance. He did not even announce his presence before entering, and it made me angry.

"Well done, Alba." His jovial persona suggested that I had done something to earn his favor in the manner of performing well at a dinner full of politicians. I found it slightly incredible that he would not come to me with his head bowed and guilt hanging over him like a shroud.

I did not reply, simply stared at him balefully from eyes that stung with dry tears and a mouth pinched in upset.

"Oh, come now, do not be like that." He reached out a hand to stroke it down my arm. I flinched back, away from his touch, and could not believe that he looked affronted.

He switched tactics. "I have something for you." Holding out his palm, I saw a small silk sack, tied closed with a drawstring, resting on the damp flesh. "To thank you for tonight."

At these words I sat straight up. I could not ignore them. "Do you think my forgiveness can be bought?" I swatted at his hand, and amazement colored his features, exaggerated comically by drink, though I could not tell if it was because I had raised a hand to him, or because I thought he needed forgiveness.

"Alba. This is for our family." I let my lips curve upward, just the slightest bit, in bitter distaste. He again held out the pouch, shaking it a little with impatience. "Go on, take it."

"I will not." If he had chosen to come to me after I had had some more time in which to arrange my thoughts, or even when they had not been so dark and depressing, I might have been more receptive to his overtures. Instead I was filled with rage, rage that all of my confusion, my upset, was due to him, the man who had promised to love and cherish me for all time.

Another slight astonishment appeared on his face, then regret. Then the tiniest flash of calculation, before he released an exaggerated, comical sigh, one that spoke of a beleaguered husband dealing with his shrew of a wife.

"Very well. I will open it for you." I turned away, not caring what was in the sack, but he dangled the contents in front of my face. It was a necklace, a beautiful one with a cluster of shining indigo sapphires dripping from a thick gold chain.

It was lovely, and at any other time I would have been thrilled with the gift.

At that moment, it enraged me instead of pleasing.

"Again, husband. What makes you think that my forgiveness can be bought?" I felt sick to my stomach that this was what my husband thought of me, that I was the kind of woman who could be placated by shiny baubles.

"It cost thirty *denarii*." His words were proud as he thrust his chest forward. "I am certain that we will well be able to afford it, soon enough."

After I had been impregnated by the gladiator who had made me weak in the knees and overcome my resistance to the situation. Yes, then we would have plenty of money, and all I had to sacrifice was my pride and my morality—though I supposed that I had already thrust my morals into question the second that I had ordered Marcus to remove his leathers. Still, that had been my own choice. In my coupling with the masked warrior, the gods would be frowning down upon me for a decision that had had nothing to do with me.

"You had best save the coin." I turned away from the empty enticement of gleaming blue. "If you are to gift me every time I fuck one of your men, we will be on the streets within a month."

He waved away my words like an insect, revealing still more about his feelings toward me compared with his feelings for the ludus. He would not, perhaps could not, acknowledge my anger, for it was inconsequential to him when compared with the prospect of losing his familial legacy.

"I am confident that this man will sow his seed." His grin then became a bit silly, and my suspicions that he had been into the cups with Justinus were confirmed. "And you will be mother to a champion." He all but licked his lips as he spoke the last word, and I wondered briefly if he felt a sexual pleasure from the thought of his "child" being of such prestigious stock.

Lucius had always been attracted to power. It fed him in ways that I was only now beginning to see.

Still, my heart leapt at his words. We had no champion, not since Quintus the Large had been put to his honorable death in the arena. Rather, we had three men who were considered to have the potential to become champions.

Three men. Caius. Appius.

And Marcus.

Lucius mistook the change in my mood, and I was shocked with just how he took it. With one fumbling yet quick movement, the chain of sapphires was around my neck, the largest stone hanging heavily beneath my breasts, and those very same breasts were being roughly massaged with wine-fueled hands.

"Lucius!" My breasts had not felt the touch of my husband's hands in recent memory, and I was appalled that he would think to touch me now. Now, when the scent of sex with another man seeped from my skin, and that same man's semen stained my thighs.

"I will touch you, Alba." The scent of fermented grape was heavy on the hot breath that grazed my cheek from behind. "I will touch you everywhere he touched you, and brand you again as my own."

For a moment I was too shocked to even breathe. To brand me as his own? He may have been the head of my family, of the house in which I lived, but I was not a slave. I belonged to no one but myself.

I told him so, and tried to wrench out of the tight squeeze of his arms. He merely laughed, though his laugh sounded hollow, and raked his hands lower over my flesh.

"If I fuck you now, if I place my cock in your cunt, it will be as if I am the one impregnating you. In fact, we will never know whose child it actually is." The wine was loosening his tongue, for never would my reserved husband make such an admission under normal circumstances.

I writhed in his arms, but not in pleasure. A trickle of fear began to make its presence known, drugging me and stealing my strength.

Yes, this was my husband, but I did not want this. Not like this, and not now.

"I *will* have my wife." I was shoved unceremoniously toward the bed. "For you *are* my wife, and it is your duty."

"And it is *your* duty to honor that wife!" I fought to wrest the lace of my tunic, which still smelled of the musk of sex, from his clumsy fingers. "If you persist in this, I will scream!"

I felt as if I had received a blow to the stomach when he merely laughed. "Who would come to your aid? I am the head of this house." The fear came in a potent dose then. I did not know this man at all, had never seen this side of him.

I screamed anyway. It made him start, and I saw confusion, shame, and bitterness swim through his eyes. I thought for a moment that I had finally broken through to him, but then he continued his fumbling ministrations regardless. Tears began to leak down my cheeks, burning the tender skin that lay there.

Had I not suffered enough humiliation for one night?

"Apologies, Dominus, Domina."

I screamed again, this time because I was startled. Justinus stood in the entrance to my bed chamber, his face unreadable from that distance.

"Get gone." Lucius struggled still to rake my skirts up to my hips. "I want to fuck my wife."

I had never been happier to see Justinus, though I was appalled that he had the audacity to enter my room uninvited. Though perhaps he had taken my scream as an invitation, which I supposed that it in fact was.

"Apologies, Dominus." The words were repeated. "But I suspect that you will be unhappy in the morning if you follow this course of action." He mimed a cup lifted to his lips, and though I could not believe that Justinus would dare to advise my husband such, I was again grateful.

And it was also as I had suspected. Lucius was drunk. But I had never believed that drunkenness changed one's personality. It merely allowed inhibitions to fall away.

I thought that Lucius would ignore Justinus, or would send him away. But given the softness at the front of his tunic, one caused by the excess of drink, I suspected that he welcomed the excuse to back down.

"Very well." The full effects of the wine seemed to be hitting my husband only now. His words slurred, and he had trouble righting himself after removing his unwanted flesh from my own. "I'll go fuck someone else." The words were sharp and pierced my heart, even though I knew that that was exactly what he did most nights, and though I knew that he was in no condition to fuck anyone at all that night.

Or perhaps he already had. Even though I was shaking and still blinking back the salty sting of tears, I smelled the unmistakable scent of sex wafting off his garments with his abrupt movement.

It did not come from me, that much I knew. I had run a sponge with water that smelled of herbs over my skin before I had left the chamber in which I had rutted with the gladiator. I could still smell the oils that had coated the wash basin, transferred to my skin and masking the scent of sex.

So that same smell was coming from Lucius, and not myself. This told me even more about his current state of mind. He had not been wanting me for release, not when he had clearly had one so very recently. No, he had wanted just what he had admitted. To mix his seed with that of the masked man, so that we might not know who the child belonged to. For though the doctor had indicated that he *thought* Lucius unable to spawn a child, we had no way of knowing for sure.

I did not think I could feel any worse. Justinus cast me a guarded look that I took as a warning.

"We all do what we must to get through." He muttered the words as he took Lucius by the arm and helped him from my room. I merely blinked at him—was the man I despised offering me comfort? I decided that I did not care as I sat, frozen with shock, on the edge of my bed. His face was unreadable, unreadable with perhaps the slightest hint of anger, and he looked as if he wanted to say something to me but either could not or would not.

And then I was alone, as I had been before my husband had so very nearly raped me. There were no words to describe my feelings, no thoughts that could assimilate what had just happened with the reality of my life.

I only knew that, though I had not been perfectly happy before any of this week's events had occurred, I had never dreamed of leaving my husband.

Now, it was a possibility foremost in mind.

I refused to ponder the impossibility of it. I needed the

dream to get me through the horrific reality of the moment. And as I fingered the heavy stones that still dangled around my neck—my payment for fucking, just like a whore—I allowed myself to dream.

The necklace had cost thirty denarii. That was no small sum, assuming it could be resold for a similar value.

The thought took root and began to sprout, and I slid off of my bed and to the floor, where I stretched out a hand for the polished wooden box that was stored beneath.

It contained my jewelry, every piece that I owned.

The wood felt cold and smooth under my fevered fingertips, and I focused on the sensation, letting it take precedence over everything else that wanted to float to the surface.

The interior of the box was lined with heavy velvet, velvet that matched the curtains that had separated myself and the gladiator from Justinus tonight. It contained a dream of freedom, though it was not something that I could seriously consider. But a dream might be enough to help me through the horror, and so I let go and dreamed away.

The ring with a sanguine ruby the size of a bird's egg had been my gift from Lucius after our vows. I remembered his boast that it had cost him sixty denarii, an unheard-of sum—and really, it had cost his father that amount, for his father had still been alive and in charge of the ludus at the time. I rarely wore it, as it caught on things with ridiculous ease, but its price could support a woman in good style for months.

Then there was a bracelet, gold with a stone of pale green, the type I didn't know. And another ring, one ringed around with sparkles of all different hues.

My lips curved in bittersweet remembrance when my fingers found my childhood *bulla*. A locket given to every Roman child at birth, it contained an amulet intended to ward off evil. I had worn it until the eve of my vows with Lucius, and then had set it aside, in this very chest.

I would not sell this. Likely I could not, as they were common as rats and worth nearly nothing, but even had it contained diamonds, I'd have kept this reminder of my childhood, a more innocent time in my life.

Shaking my head to clear it of such whimsical thoughts, I returned my attention to the task at hand. There were hair combs carved from pure gold, a necklace with opals the color of cream. Even clamps for my nipples, which dangled with strings of onyx beads.

All of these could be sold at the market, or sold to a jeweler, and I knew a few. They would not support me forever, not in the style in which I was accustomed, but they could allow me freedom.

But at what cost would that freedom come? I would have to go far away, would have to change my name if I did not wish to be found. A husband had a legal right to forcibly keep his wife at home, or to retrieve her from elsewhere. That was if he did not divorce me.

And where would I go? My birth family had no obligation to take me in, and I could be found there too easily. And what of my life after the money from my jewels ran out? Even if I lived modestly, it would not last me forever. I would be forced into slavery myself, for I had no skills from which I could earn a living. I knew of no business but gladiators, and a woman could not open a ludus.

I knew, deep in my gut, that I would never be able to leave on my own. I would have to find a way to bear my circumstances here, the forced relations that I so shamefully reveled in, the unpredictable husband who saw me as a possession, the man whom I longed for and needed to forget.

If only I knew what that way was.

Chapter Five

It seemed to be just my luck that the next day, one in which I wanted nothing more than to hide in some shadowy recess of the house, I had to put on a bright smile, extend a loving hand, and support my husband in public.

I had risen early, or rather I had not slept much, and Drusilla had entered my chambers that morning to find me tucked into a small ball on the cold, hard floor, glittery baubles all around me. I had heard the gasp that had escaped her lips as she ran across the floor toward me, and had felt her arms around me as I buried my head into her lap and cried a river of bitter tears. She had held me wordlessly—what was there to say, after all? But she offered comfort where I needed it most, and I was grateful.

I had never considered that she would take any of my jewels, as I might with another slave. I trusted her completely, not needing to watch as she tidied them quickly, placing each back in its box with a reverence that showed she had never owned anything so expensive.

No, I hadn't needed to watch, but I had, again calculating

the worth of each as her fingers touched it. The baubles were my insurance, my hope, and my mind was full of them as the girl all but dragged me to the baths to wash away the stripes of my tears and to clean me for the games.

I knew she had heard of the events of the evening before, of Lucius' visit to my room, and of what had transpired. There were no secrets in a house with slaves. It was almost a relief to not have to share, to not have to formulate those words on the tongue to explain my tired eyes, my swollen face, my ragged appearance.

She already knew why I had difficulty walking. The area between my thighs had not been so tender since the night I lost my virginity.

I had urged her to rush through the bath, for it still brought memories of Marcus, of what I wanted so desperately and yet could not have. Then I sat with a poultice of chilled herbs and extracts on my eyes while she dressed my hair and fussed with the tunic that I would wear that day.

I made certain to fasten the golden necklace with its heavy eggs of sapphire around my neck. It was my payment for becoming a whore, and I would announce it to the world.

All too soon I found myself ensconced in our balcony at the arena. Though there was a canopy of striped silk overhead, and though Drusilla fanned me with a large, waxen leaf, the heat was dreadful. Two layers of cloth covered my body—my tunic and my *palla*, my woolen shawl—and sweat rolled in fat, wet drops down my spine. My toes felt swollen against the closed covering of the bright yellow shoes that I wore when I left the house. My scalp itched dreadfully beneath its covering of tight white gauze and fashionable yet damnable yellow silk hair, but it was better than it had been on our way to the arena, when I had had to cover my head. My skin felt thick, layered as it was with chalk and charcoal.

Sitting beside my husband was more dreadful still. I would have been displeased with him even if the evening had stopped with my tryst with the masked gladiator, but Lucius' forceful visit to my bed made the situation nearly unbearable. Worse, he had made no mention of it. There was certainly no apology, not that one would have made amends.

It was as if it had never happened. As if he did not remember. And, given the amount of drink he had consumed, that was a very real possibility.

I gained no small amount of pleasure from his very obvious, and very distressing, aching head. He was wan, and the smell of the wine being consumed all around us was visibly turning his stomach. And there was plenty of wine, provided by our host, a hopeful senator. This game—most of the arena games—were *munera*, or public demonstrations, provided by the wealthy or the politically hopeful, to appease and entertain the common citizens.

This senator was seeking the favor of the upper class plebeians and his patrician fellows as well as the common Roman citizen, and so we were plied with expensive honeyed wine, the freshest quinces and figs, and rare sweets.

It might have been petty, but it made me feel ever so slightly better that my husband could not partake of the bounty due to his roiling stomach. And I would take what pleasures I could, for the circumstances were dreadfully uncomfortable for me. We were surrounded by our friends, though I privately considered them no more than acquaintances, for I knew that they would turn on one another and on us for the smallest of gains. I had to smile and laugh with them, had to appear to enjoy myself and the games to the fullest, and all the while I could barely contain the anger and betrayal that being near Lucius brought.

Or the dread and delightful anticipation of what the night would bring.

"Oh, who have you put up against Corvinus' Januarius, Alba?" asked Iuliana, who was possibly my favorite of the lot that surrounded us. The wife of Sextus, a fellow businessman, she was silly and vain, certainly, but she possessed a kind heart.

I blinked. I could not remember. Corvinus was our rival, the owner of another fine Roman ludus—though Lucius daily pronounced it to be trash. After the tedium of the early matches today, in which pair after pair of inconsequential gladiators would spar and warm up the crowd, the prestigious matches would begin.

Januarius was considered to be in the running for the title of Roman champion, along with our Caius, Appius, and Marcus.

"I..." I could not think past Marcus. The thought that he might be put up against Januarius, might have to take part in a duel in which he would be very nearly matched, made me sick to the marrow.

"I have not yet decided," offered Lucius with a show of joviality, stretching an arm casually over the back of my seat and brushing my shoulders. I flinched away and was frowned at reprovingly.

I did not care. I would not have him touch me, not anymore.

With eyes narrowed to show that he would tolerate my behavior—because he needed me that evening, no doubt—but that I had best watch myself, Lucius snapped his fingers and quickly received a cup of water from Marina, one of our slave girls. His fingers lingered on hers, something he did so that I would see, and I wrinkled my nose with distaste.

He might have cared for me, but he was also a man of pride. He was clearly not happy that I had not permitted him to be in the room while I mated with the gladiator the night before—this was my punishment.

The insolent chit giggled in response to Lucius' touch, and a bitter taste coated my mouth.

I could not believe how quickly the bond with my husband had deteriorated. I had not seen it coming.

Maybe I had been fooling myself blind.

"I am waiting to see how our three perform today. Then I will decide." He winked at Iuliana, who giggled at the obvious flirtation, which was simply a way of communication amongst the well-to-do plebeians and the lower-classed patricians of Rome.

Iuliana signaled for her own cup, though it held wine instead of water. "I had heard that it would be Marcus. I do so wish to see that battle!" She wriggled her eyebrows at me lewdly, and I knew that it was not the fight that she wanted to see, but rather the straining, sweating muscles of two potential champions.

"Is this true, Lucius?" My voice was sharp and higher-pitched than usual. "Will Marcus meet Januarius?" I wanted to vomit.

With a sidelong look at Iuliana, whose attention had been

temporarily caught by the bloody spectacle below us on the sand, he spoke out of the side of his mouth to me. "No. I would not chance losing Marcus now. Appius will meet Januarius."

He would not chance losing Marcus now? Why, by the gods, would that be his reasoning? A gladiator could lose his life at any given moment in battle. That was the danger that they accepted when taking an oath to the brotherhood of their ludus.

Was it because he needed him for another purpose?

I could not deny that the thought excited me, thrilled me, in fact, and it kept me occupied throughout the long hours until the midday sun had ceased its relentless pounding, and the match in question came to a head.

Beside me, Lucius stood. After Corvinus called out his chosen man, Januarius, Lucius named ours. Appius. But it was not Appius who stalked through the barred iron gate.

It was Marcus.

My heart leapt into my throat, choking me, both at the breathtaking sight of him, rigidly militant, and in terror. Januarius was a huge brute, with long, unkempt hair, a plethora of missing teeth, and battle scars slicing his face into segments. He was not known to fight with honor, and if there was one thing I now knew about Marcus, it was that the virtue of honor was what he swore by.

Though he was a large man himself, Marcus appeared small beside him.

"What is this?" Lucius was still on his feet, agitated. "Marcus! No!"

But it was too late.

Collectively the group in our balcony drew in a breath and leaned forward. The two men were frozen on the sand, which glittered like a million miniscule jewels in the gilded light. I very nearly swallowed my tongue at the sight of Marcus, so fierce and so proud, every sharply defined muscle tensed in anticipation, his face a study in concentration.

It reminded me so much of our time in the bath, our clandestine encounter. He had had the same look on his face when he licked my cunt, that same expression of do or die.

I quivered with need even as I tensed with fear.

He couldn't defeat this giant. Could he? I had seen men beat more unlikely odds, but I had not harbored illicit feelings for those men. Ultimately, whether they lived or died had not mattered all that much to me, though I had often reflected on the tragedies of lives cut short.

This did matter to me, very much.

Beside me, Lucius was tense with rage, muttering his disbelief. But I sensed desperation beneath his anger, that the upset was mostly for show.

Could it be that he depended on Marcus for something else? Say, to bear him a child?

I wanted to cover my eyes. I could not watch. I would not have had to know what was going on, at any rate, for beside me Iuliana kept up a high-pitched running commentary.

But in the end I dropped my hands from my eyes. I could not take my eyes off of the man in front of me on the sand. I knew then that my feelings for him were getting out of control, but I could not seem to stop them.

He was bare-chested, as was traditional. Gladiators did not cover their chests in the arena, the bare skin seen as a sign of virility. *Manicae*, wraps fashioned from leather and cloth, wound around the large trunks of his arms and wrists, and his *balteus*—the band of leather that held his weapons—made a singular stripe over his chest.

He was not wearing his *cingulum*, which protected his midsection from fatal blows, and that worried me greatly.

Still, even through the worry, it was impossible not to notice that the way he fought was a thing of beauty. Hard ridges stood up on his arms as he sliced toward Januarius with his sword. He managed to slash through the flesh of the giant's upper arm, and blood, thick crimson blood, sluiced down through the air and mixed with the granules of sand, boiling in the heat of the day.

The giant, whose arms were unprotected, roared and charged. He got his meaty hands around Marcus' arm, yanked him close, and bit. As blood spurted, Marcus pulled back with an unimaginable strength and then retreated, just a slight bit, before slashing again.

He moved as if he was uninjured, and his focus amazed me.

I knew that this could not end well. Knew that one of them would die before this match was over. They were too evenly paired, despite the advantage that Januarius had in size.

I kept my eyes on Marcus, praying to Fortuna, the goddess of good fortune, that it would not be the last time I saw him alive. Knowing that, despite the wrongness of it, despite my enforced mating with a warrior who might or might not be him, I would make certain to see him again, would make certain to feel him again, if only he lived.

As he moved below on the sand, thrusting his sword out, cutting through flesh more than once, and retreating from the bitter kiss of the other man's weapon, I thought I might be sick. I distracted myself by studying his frame, looking for similarities to the man who had used me so well the night before.

It could have been him. And then again it might not have been. I had done my best to not look, to not make that kind of contact. And I had not studied this man's body when I had had him the time before, had focused more on the bliss of the joining than on the details of his flesh.

And now I might never again feel that flesh against mine.

The tension was unbearable. Beside me, Lucius was transfixed by the sight as much as I was. Januarius had been injured, and so had Marcus. He did not wear a helmet, and I feared for his head, which was so exposed. So easily cleaved from its neck.

Then Marcus fell, and I felt tears prick the backs of my eyes as I jumped to my feet and screamed. The scream was noted by no one, for the entire arena was standing, screaming, and cheering, caught in the throes of bloodlust. Women flashed their breasts in a show of support for their favorites, and the entire spectacle seemed suddenly like a warped scene straight out of my worst nightmare.

This was it, then. Marcus was going to die.

As Januarius charged, I focused on that lean golden body and prayed to the gods. Prayed to Fortuna to let him live.

The very moment before Januarius would have thrust his sword into the exposed ribs of my gladiator, Marcus thrust up and out with his shield. It sent the larger man to the ground with an impact that raised a storm of dust and sand. Using muscles that had to be exhausted, he staggered to his feet, clearly weary but not defeated.

Before Januarius could react, the metal battle sword of Marcus cleaved the tension-thick air in two and separated the head of Corvinus' potential champion from his body. Blood spurted as if from a fountain, spewing in a wide circle, staining the sand with florid markings.

I gasped. The sight was gruesome, one that I never became accustomed to, no matter how many times I had seen it. But all that mattered to me in that moment was that it was not the head of Marcus rolling on the ground. No, Marcus was standing tall, bloody, clearly weary, but alive.

I shook, swamped with an onslaught of emotions, ones that had been bottled up since the day before, and fresh ones releasing their tension, spewing out into the day as the blood did onto the sand.

"Champion!"

Beside me, Lucius was riotous with excitement. Never mind that this was not how he had intended the match to go; he would reap the rewards. And it was true enough, we now had the champion in our fold, having defeated the only other potential outside our school.

I should have been exuberant.

Lucius would not now pair either Caius or Appius against Marcus. Marcus was champion.

I cared little for that. Instead I reveled in the fact that he was alive, alive and the most sinful thing I had ever laid eyes on, even covered in dirt, sweat, and viscous red blood. As he raised his arms to the sky, his face a study in solemnity and so different from the celebratory expressions of many, I felt need begin to grow.

I did not want to fuck the masked gladiator that night. Not unless he was Marcus. No matter that he had brought me such pleasure the night before.

My heart had spoken, and it wanted Marcus. It should not have, but it did.

He had given no indication that he wanted me in return. Yet even as the thought permeated my mind, he turned and faced the balcony where we sat. He gestured toward us, giving the gladiator's standard dedication of his win to the house that held his vow.

But my heart lurched. There was something in his expression that made me believe he was dedicating it to me. And the thump in my chest, the clenching in my gut as I wondered if I could possibly be right, had me vowing to myself that I would unmask the golden-haired gladiator that night.

I would see if I was right.

"Where did you get that stunning necklace, Alba?" Iuliana was easily bored, and she had moved past the excitement of Marcus' win. She reached out to stroke a small, thin finger over the largest of the blue stones, an expression of envy on her face, and the movement attracted Lucius' attention. He must have been puzzled, for if he could not remember the previous night clearly, then he could not remember the circumstances in which he had given me the gift.

I smiled, melting the bitterness that wanted to play out across my face. I made sure that Lucius was listening when I replied.

"It is payment for being a good wife."

"Have you ever fucked one of them?"

Hilaria was an acquaintance, one of many who had gathered at the impromptu party to help us celebrate our new champion. Her words were spoken with the smug amusement of a woman who enjoyed shocking others, and I provided exactly what she was looking for.

Wine, much finer wine than we usually drank, slopped out of my cup as I started, staring at the other woman incredulously. I fought a telltale flush.

"No!" I knew without looking in the direction she was pointing that she spoke of the gladiators, who were lined up on the far side of the room. "Hilaria! I am a married woman!"

"What does that have to do with anything?" She laughed, the sound low and as rich as she was. "It certainly did not stop me." Snapping her fingers, she gestured for Drusilla to bring her the platter of glistening sliced figs that she could easily have reached herself.

I busied myself with my wine, pouring myself more since I had slopped mine on the floor. I could have had Drusilla do it, but wanted the time to calm myself. When I looked up, I hoped that my face was more composed.

"I will be with no man but my husband." I felt shame for the lie, but what could I do? I certainly could not confide in the woman. Not only were we not close enough for me to feel comfortable doing so, but I had no doubt that by the next day the entire patrician class would know not only that I had had a tryst with a slave, but that my husband was using one to try to impregnate me.

"How dull." Popping a fat green grape and a slice of fig

that was dripping with juice into her mouth, Hilaria rose to her feet with the sinuous laziness of a woman with both money and freedom. She held out a hand for me, which I had no choice but to accept.

I did not want to go look at the gladiators. I had spent the better part of the evening trying to ignore them.

But Hilaria had never liked the word *no*. Though my feet dragged on the cool marble floor, I found myself being pulled through the thick crowd of revelers to the line of hard male flesh.

The gladiators stood in a line against one wall, clean yet dressed in the leather subligaculum of battle. They had nicer garments, short tunics of light cloth that we provided them for formal occasions, but at a party like this their near nakedness was expected.

More, it was appreciated.

"Oh, do relax, Alba." I kept my stare trained on my feet as Hilaria spoke, noting a slight scuff on the dyed leather of my left sandal. After a tense moment she placed one of her long fingers under my chin and tilted my face up. "Surely Lucius will not divorce you for appreciating the . . . talent . . . of your livelihood."

I looked nowhere but at Hilaria, though I was aware of the cliff of a naked chest directly to my left. I could not think of what to say, and so remained silent.

My stiffness merely made the other woman laugh. She reached out with her soft hand and ran a finger down the nearest hard chest.

I looked up involuntarily, jealousy rearing its head before I could even think. But it was not Marcus. It was Caius, one of the men who had been considered a potential champion until that afternoon's games.

He did not respond to Hilaria's caress, at least not to the eyes of most. He was not permitted to. The men were allowed to do nothing but stand rigidly in formation, decorations at the party.

I, however, saw the shiver roll over his skin, perhaps because I was watching so intently for it. It was not, I thought, a reaction caused by desire.

No, I rather thought that the man wanted to step back, to remove his body from the touch of the woman.

"Mmm." The expression on Hilaria's face suggested that she had tasted something delicious and sweet and was savoring the sensation on her tongue. "How delightful." Her fingers trailed down, down, coming to rest lightly on the top of the leathers that saved Caius from indecency.

Caius' jaw clenched, just the slightest bit. That small movement was all that it took for me to understand much about this man's temperament, and he certainly had one, one that was held in check in a manner much less firm than Marcus'.

He was angry at the unwanted caress. Being a gladiator, he had no choice but to bite back the words that surely wanted to spring forth from his lips.

I was not sure what to do. Certainly Lucius would not mind Hilaria's actions, but they did not sit properly with me. I knew it was most likely because Caius had golden hair, just like the mystery gladiator who had given me such pleasure.

In the lights of the torches that were set into the walls of the room, that gold held a sheen of ruddiness, just as the hair of my masked warrior had.

Had it been Caius, then? Oh, I was so dreadfully confused.

Watching her fingers on his taut skin caused a tightening in my abdomen, similar to the sensation brought on by thinking of her touching Marcus.

What was *wrong* with me? I had no reason to be upset.

"Do you ever hire your warriors out, Alba?" Hilaria's hand stayed where it was, and I marveled that Caius' cock did not rise under her touch. "I would dearly love to fuck one."

I felt as though something heavy had fallen on my head. "Hilaria!"

She laughed, squeezed Caius' cock through the thin cow's skin lightly and moved her hand to my waist. I thought I saw the man's eyes flick toward my face, thought I saw the faintest hint of a sneer on his lips, but his face became stony and still again so quickly that I thought I must have imagined it.

I did not feel that his disgust had been for me.

"Alba, do not be so shocked." I knew I should not have been. Hilaria enjoyed a sexual freedom that married women and young innocents did not.

But still . . . to pay us to fuck one of our men? I knew that such things happened at the other ludi in Rome, but it had never happened in ours.

Yet.

"What are you two desirable women laughing about?" Lucius' arm was around my waist without warning, and I steeled myself to not flinch from his touch. He toyed with Hilaria's fingers, and she giggled.

Like his flirtation with Iuliana, this had never bothered

me before. But knowing the things I now did about my husband, the seemingly innocent gesture made my skin crawl.

"I have a query." Hilaria smiled beguilingly at my husband, the glance more intimate that I thought proper.

I gulped past the lump in my throat and willed myself to relax into Lucius' embrace, even as words spilled from my lips rather desperately. "Oh, let us not bother the man with such girlish affairs." Though my every muscle urged me to yank myself out of my husband's embrace, I quieted them. It would not do for me to remove myself from his touch abruptly, at least not in public.

"Do tell." Lucius cocked an eyebrow at the other woman and added a lascivious smile.

Hilaria leaned in close, and I was not sure if I should take offense at her overt flirtation with my husband, or if it was light and innocent as it had always been.

"I wondered if you could be convinced to hire out one of your men. For . . . special services." She smiled then, the smile of a woman who knew she would get what she wanted.

I looked at Caius. I could not help it. What did he think, I wondered, at his "services" being bartered like this?

His eyes met my own, but that was the only acknowledgment of me, and it struck me what a true blue they were, a pure blue that contained no hint of any other color, as the eyes of many did. They flickered away again before I could but blink, but somehow the man had managed to convey to me an attitude of defiance, as if he would die before showing that any of this bothered him. I thought that I saw his hands clench into fists, as well, but then he was again as if carved from stone.

He knew the trouble he would be in if Lucius caught him doing anything but standing stoically.

I turned my head and saw Marcus standing seven men farther down the line, at the very end.

He, too, was still, a golden statue.

"Did you have a man in mind?" I could practically see the greed oozing out of the pores in Lucius' skin. If he could get Hilaria to agree to a high-enough sum, it would pay for this party, this celebration of something that had occurred simply by chance. This party that, by my husband's own admission, we could not actually afford.

"I would love to have a go at your champion." She slid her gaze down the line of men, and I was reminded of a serpent, slick and sinuous. "But I suspect you would say no."

"True enough." Lucius sipped at his cup, which from my vantage point I could see was filled with water and not wine.

He had likely had more than enough of the latter the night before.

"You know that a gladiator needs his seed for strength in the arena." Hilaria pouted at Lucius' words, but she seemed resigned to the fact that she could not have Marcus, and the knowledge made me weak in the knees with relief.

I may not have been able to have him again, but it did not mean that I wanted his cock sold to the highest bidder.

"This one shall do just fine." Hilaria again reached out to caress Caius' hard pectoral muscles. Her touch made me feel sick, though I could not have said exactly why.

I was sure that Lucius would agree. Was sure that a sum could be agreed upon.

Why did I care?

"No!" My husband spoke with such vehemence that I jumped. I looked at him with puzzlement, and Hilaria with astonishment and annoyance.

"Why ever not? You have your champion." The woman gestured with her head to the end of the line, where Marcus stood. "I am sure I can afford whatever you would charge for this one." Her eyes raked over Caius, lingering on the little that was hidden beneath his leathers.

"And if our champion is killed?" I wondered if Hilaria had heard the same pause before Lucius spoke again, as if he had needed to make up a reason that she could not purchase Caius. "Caius is our next hope. No, no, you may choose from any man, except those two."

"Hmm." Hilaria stepped back, and studied Lucius. I was sure that she suspected what I did, that he had another reason.

"Why don't I let you think on it?" I had already known that Hilaria was used to getting her own way—she no longer had a husband to answer to, after all.

What I did not know was why I cared so much about whether it was Caius or not.

"I can assure you that my mind will not change on those two." Lucius smiled apologetically, but I could feel the tension in the arm that was wrapped around my waist.

This was risky, refusing the woman her desire. She was higher class than we were, and she could make Orcus' hell seem pleasant in comparison with our lives, if she so chose.

"Let me appease you." Quick as the snake that Hilaria had reminded me of earlier, Lucius moved his arm from around my waist to hers. "A mock battle!"

He repeated the words, louder, until everyone in the room had heard and had stopped their chatter, giving him their attention.

"Marcus, our champion!" Lucius gestured, and my onetime lover stepped forward out of the line. "And Caius, his closest match!" From behind me, the second man moved out of line, and the naked skin of his arm brushed against my own. Our eyes caught, and he dared to let his face relax into a smile, one both wicked and fierce.

I shivered involuntarily, heat suffusing the area that had been touched, as my husband turned to Hilaria, who stood with pursed lips.

"Will you accept my offering, lady?" He lifted her hand to his lips, a gesture I had seen him perform a million times before. Only now did it look unctuous.

"Very well." She finally, reluctantly, acquiesced, and allowed herself to be pulled to one side, to make room for the men to fight. As she brushed past me, however, she squeezed my arm and giggled in a whisper. "We will convince him yet, will we not, Alba?"

It might have been only a mock battle, a game for fun and entertainment, but our guests smelled blood.

"Oh, use real swords! Do!" Hilaria pouted as she spoke, the sight of the fake swords obviously offending her bloodlust.

Doctore, the former arena fighter who trained our men, had given Marcus and Caius wooden training swords to use in the game, but Hilaria was having none of it. "It is not exciting if it is not real."

I could see that Lucius was about to argue—it was just a game, after all, so what should it matter, but the pout on Hilaria's lips reminded us both that we had refused her once already, and as such must tread carefully. She could influence Baldurus in a way that would not be beneficial for us, if she so chose.

"Very well." Lucius gestured for Doctore to replace the wooden swords with lethal metal ones. "But everyone must stand clear. It would not do for someone to get hurt on such a wonderful occasion."

The crowd that had clustered around the perimeter of the room tittered, though the words were true enough. In a space so small, someone, anyone, could easily get hurt, something that I reminded Lucius of in a whisper.

He shook me off impatiently. "What would you suggest, then? If she cannot have Caius, then we must appease her with someone." Then he was off, speaking to his two top gladiators, leaving me to stand beside the smirking Hilaria, wondering why he was so adamant that Caius' services not be sold.

My thoughts were distracted when the two men entered the empty space from opposite sides of the room. Everyone was distracted from their conversations, it seemed, because the room fell instantly silent, all eyes trained on the men who stood facing each other on the veined marble of the floor.

Even if I had not had reason to look closely at the pair, I would not have been able to help myself. They were spectacular—breathtaking. Two golden demigods, skin darkened from the sun, muscles honed to rock solidity by incessant training. Both had flaxen hair shorn close to the head, though Caius' contained a hint of red, and Marcus' was solid gold. Both were tall and intimidating. If I did not pay attention, I could easily have gotten confused, wondering who was who. But after a few minutes of intense scrutiny, they were easily identified.

Marcus had features as sharp as the blade in his hand. His eyes were dark as tar, and he looked as dangerous as he was.

Caius, on the other hand, could have passed for a full god himself, with an innocent face and eyes as blue as the sea. It was misleading, I knew, for he was nearly as formidable a gladiator as Marcus, though more reckless and hot-headed, it seemed, especially when compared with Marcus' stern control. I knew I had not imagined his anger minutes before, though he now seemed eager to work out his rage in the fight.

I found heat pooling between my legs as I compared the two. I knew Marcus' body, knew how his hands felt on my skin. Knew the sensation of his cock between my legs.

Did I know Caius as well? Was that why Lucius has been so adamant that Hilaria not have him?

I found myself wishing so, wanting both of them, though I knew that my masked man could have been either of the duo, or any of another handful of fair-haired gladiators.

But watching the two as they began their demonstration, as they began to parry and thrust with steely intent, I was caught up in the fight, as much as any of the others who stood around me cheering.

They were beautiful to watch, specimens equal in form to the gods. They fought differently—Caius was quicker to react and therefore made more mistakes, but he was stronger, and Marcus evaluated before moving, leading to less movement and less energy spent—but they were very nearly matched in skill.

It was like watching a dance, a dance that drew me to them. I fisted my fingers around my cup, for fear that I might actually reach out and touch one of them.

For the first time, I found myself wishing that Caius was the masked man, if only because then I would have had them both. But I knew that if that was true, then I would have to try very hard not to summon Marcus to me again.

My thoughts made me feel shameful. Marcus had not had a choice, and the man I was mating with did not, either.

I was so deep in my thoughts that I did not see what had happened, did not know that anything had until the people around me, our guests, gasped as one. Startled, and with some emotion punching me low in my belly, I stepped forward to see.

Caius knelt on the ground, his hand clutched to his abdomen. Blood leaked out from between his fingers, a crimson trickle that scented the air with copper.

Dressed for display at the party, not for a battle, neither had been wearing a cingulum. Now Caius had a wound that the thick leather belt could have protected him from.

I was at his side before I could even think of what I was doing, kneeling beside him. Ever anticipating my needs, Drusilla followed quickly, a coarse towel in her hand, which I took with gratitude.

Before I could touch the man's skin, he released his wound and swung out briefly with the flat of his sword, striking

Marcus across the shins and causing the surprised warrior to stumble, then fall to the floor. To my astonishment, both men laughed, in rollicking gales, even as Caius pressed his hands again to his side, wincing with pain.

Nudging them aside, I placed the towel that Drusilla had handed me over the wound. I caught the eye of the man as I did, and jerked back when I saw him leaning toward me, his lips barely open.

I stared at the red that was spreading over the wound, doing my best to appear nonchalant. The man had been a whisper away from kissing me, I was certain. Kissing me, in front of everyone here.

I had wanted him to.

"Alba." Lucius tugged on my arm, pulling me to my feet. On his face was barely masked anger and embarrassment. As usual, Justinus stood just behind him, his lips schooled in that detestable smirk.

I saw Marcus and Caius both over my husband's shoulder, both crouched on the floor. Caius looked startled at his actions, even angry at himself.

Marcus' expression was unreadable, as it so very often was.

"Let me go!" I spoke quietly enough that none of our guests could hear. If I embarrassed my husband in public, he was well within his rights to punish me. "This is ridiculous. Arena swords at a party? We are lucky that this is all that happened!"

I turned back to look again at the injured man, who had the towel pressed to his gash tightly. He nodded at me, his face now a studied blank. "Gratitude, Domina."

"Yes, gratitude." Marcus bent and placed his large, scarred hand on his comrade's shoulder, while looking up at me. His eyes revealed nothing of our tryst, but still sent a jolt through my body when his stare met my own. His look was penetrating enough that it took a full moment before I noted the tenderness with which he touched his fellow gladiator.

And then I was permitted to look no more. Lucius pulled on my arm again. "This is not appropriate, Alba." Straightening, I looked up into his angry face and bit my tongue. He spoke to me as if were a petulant child, and I did not like it.

"Fine." But Lucius was already moving away. Doctore and Marcus helped Caius to his feet, and they left the room. Lucius consoled Hilaria, who was not happy to have her entertainment thwarted yet again, by ordering Marina, one of our slave girls, to straddle a gladiator whose name I did not know on a table in the middle of the room, for everyone to watch.

The gladiator untied his subligaculum quickly, letting it fall to the floor. He laid on his back eagerly enough, pulling Marina atop him roughly. With strong arms he ripped her thin serving tunic in two. It fluttered to the floor, leaving her skin bare.

Those who gathered around her roared with appreciation. They had been promised excitement, with blood and with swords, and this was nearly as good.

The man clasped Marina around the waist and roughly lowered her onto his already erect cock. She gasped at the intrusion—he had spent not even a moment preparing her—but after several thrusts I saw her skin begin to flush and a haze of lustful enjoyment begin to cloud her eyes.

There were women, I knew, who enjoyed their sex rough. It seemed as if Marina counted herself among them.

Though I was repulsed by the events, I could not look away.

The gladiator's skin began to shine with a sheen of sweat, and the moisture picked up light from the torches that the slaves had just begun to light. His grunts echoed through the cavernous room, cutting through the murmurs of our entranced guests like a scalding blade through flesh.

Beside me, Hilaria let out a small noise of excitement before lowering her hand discreetly to the shadowy cleft between her legs.

I was not sure why she bothered being coy. Everyone in the room appeared to be coming under the spell of arousal as they watched the scene unfold before us, as the gladiator pushed Marina off of his cock and onto her hands and knees before thrusting into her again, though by cunt or ass I could not see.

The wild look in the slave girl's eyes said that, whatever the method, it aroused her.

I supposed I felt the same as our guests, aroused by the sight before me. But though heat pooled between my legs, I no more would have reached between them for release than I would have fucked my husband in public.

I merely watched with the others, sick with knowing that Lucius had made this happen, and as drunk with lust as everyone else.

The gladiator began to thrust faster, harder, and Marina began to moan low and loud. With a hoarse shout he came, thick liquid spilling down Marina's fair skin as she whimpered.

She was not given her own release, the gladiator pushing out from beneath her as soon as he had spilled his seed, and this broke the spell for me. Disgusted with my own behavior, for I knew I should have left, or at least tried to leave, before this had even started, I turned away, leaving a horde of people swimming in a soup of lust.

I was sickened at the whole evening, but as far as Lucius was concerned, he had told me how to behave, and that was that. In the past it certainly would have been.

I disagreed.

Chapter Six

I had never been down into the gladiators' quarters before. I was not forbidden to go, I just had never had a reason to. I knew where the skeleton key to the great iron gate that separated them from the upstairs house was—it had never been hidden.

I studied the key now, its metal worn and scarred from generations of use. One of Lucius' ancestors had installed this gate, with its lock, to protect those who lived upstairs from the brutes and beasts who roamed below. Did I dare defy both Lucius and tradition and head into the bowels of our home, simply to make certain that a slave was all right?

It was reason enough for me, but I knew with certainty that it would *not* be reason enough for my husband. That alone should have made up my mind, for Lucius was my pater familias, and as such deserved my unswerving loyalty and obedience.

I was starting to wonder if that unquestioning obedience was right, if it was deserved. Did I have any rights at all? Did being my pater familias give Lucius the right to mate me with whomever he chose?

If he felt guilt, did that exonerate his actions?

Would I soon be expected to entertain his friends, his associates, in the way that our slaves were? The notion did not sit easily.

My hand reached unerringly for the key, even as nerves made my muscles clench. I had never defied Lucius, and though he had not specifically told me not to visit Caius this evening, it had been explicitly implied in his chastisement of my behavior earlier.

I glowered back up the stairs that I had descended at the reminder. Overhead I could still hear the revelers, loud and full of mirth. No doubt they had all already forgotten about the man who had been injured for their entertainment.

In the end, that was why I fit the key into the lock, turned it until the latch gave way. I simply wanted to make sure that the man had received proper care, given that our medic was upstairs and hip deep in the cups.

As I clutched my ornately embroidered silk tunic tight in sweaty fists, I knew that that was not true at all. I wanted to look closely at Caius, and at Marcus, if I could.

I wanted to know which man had been wearing the mask.

My pulse fluttered in my temples and my wrists as I reached the bottom of the stairs and entered the long stone corridor that was lit by torches. I was not afraid, not really.

Most of the men were still upstairs, and if perchance I came across one who was not, I was their domina, and they owed me respect.

The slave who did not show that respect would be brutally punished by Lucius. Yes, they would be punished. That was the benefit of my obedience to my pater familias, I supposed, that others were to treat me with nearly the respect that Lucius was afforded.

And after they were punished for disrespecting me, I would be beaten as well, for causing the incident in the first place. Lucius had never yet had cause to beat me, as I had always been a model wife, but given what I had learned of his character in the past few days, I absolutely believed that he would not hesitate to do so, if he felt within his rights.

Shaking away the thought, I continued down the hallway. The bitter aroma of sulphur stung the insides of my nose, strengthening as I moved cautiously through the corridor. Steam became visible in the thickening underground air, and the thin webbing of my tunic clung damply to my skin.

The hall opened to a large room before continuing down the snakelike quarters. The blast of mineral-tinted moisture in the air made my eyes tear up, and I blinked several times before my vision again became clear.

When I was again able to see, I found the source of the moisture. A row of wooden tubs, the rich grain swollen with ages of wet, was set back against the wall, and all were filled with steaming water, now pumped in by aqueduct, though in years past the tubs would have been filled and heated by hand, by the men themselves, before they reaped the benefits.

In front of the tubs were benches, long stone benches that were cracked and worn by the decades that they had stood watch in the steam.

On first glance I saw that the room was empty, and thought to continue across and into the continuing hallway, where the men's small cells were, I suspected. But out of the corner of my eye I saw movement, and turned my head quickly to find the leftmost corner tub occupied.

My night-sky hair, already tangled from the evening's festivities, whipped across my cheek and became stuck with the damp. Impatiently, I batted it away with scrabbling fingers, wanting to know if what I thought I had seen had indeed been so.

I knew from hearing Lucius speak that the soaking tubs were the size to fit a single man, designed to soothe muscles that were raw and aching from training and from the arena. I was therefore perplexed to see two heads and two sets of broad shoulders occupying the one corner bath.

But as I looked, I knew even from across the room to whom those heads belonged. Hair the color of burnt honey glistened in the torchlight, and my own wetness began to pool, in my mouth and elsewhere.

Marcus sat with his taut back, roped across with sinewy muscle, against the side of the tub, facing away from me. I recognized the pattern of scars that crisscrossed his skin. Snugly between his legs was Caius, who leaned forward to expose the tightly arched column of his back.

Marcus' hands were rubbing over the exposed flesh, his touch as tender as I had seen it upstairs when he had been checking on his fallen comrade. His hands might have been large and scarred from battle, but they were sure as he smoothed water over Caius' skin, soothing the injured man.

An ache began between my legs, even as I wondered what, exactly, it was about. The sight of my lover's hands touching another man so softly, so *intimately*, softened my insides like wax left too long in the midday sun. I thought that I should be jealous, that I should feel sick. That I should stop my intrusion on this obviously private moment, both for their sake and for my own. I should say something, should announce my presence, but all words and sounds were frozen in my throat.

Instead I stood still, frozen in place in the very entrance of the room. I bit my lip and clenched my fists, and above all else I watched.

"You must learn to control yourself." Marcus continued to massage Caius as he spoke, his thumbs pressing down the length of the other man's spine, tracing the wings of his shoulder blades with strength. "You are lucky that Dominus did not see."

I wondered what Marcus spoke of as a sound of pleasure from the injured man broke through the steam. He turned until his face was in profile to me, and I saw him grin rakishly at the other man, who still bore a stern countenance. He murmured something that I could not make out, winked at the larger man, and Marcus finally, reluctantly, broke into a smile.

It took me a moment to identify it, but I realized that Caius' sigh had not been borne of sexual pleasure, or at least, not entirely—rather it was a noise of contentment.

Through the arousal that drenched my skin like the mist of steam, arousal caused by watching the hands of a warrior soothe so gently, I wondered again what their relationship was. And I wondered why I was not disquieted by the suddenly sure knowledge that there was one. They seemed to fit so well, the devilish Caius, who appeared to follow no rules, and the rigid, formal Marcus. They provided a delicious foil for one another.

Should I not have been mad with jealousy? Should I not have felt hurt, though I had no legitimate reason to?

I was not, and I did not. Instead I felt arousal, and almost a sensation of greed as I watched, watched and wanted.

Marcus' hands finished their work, finished kneading the tough knots from his gladiator brother's back. Caius leaned back, his back to Marcus' chest. Though the steam had thickened while I watched, I could tell that Marcus' groin was snug against the hard planes of Caius' ass, and the thought made me quiver.

How I wished to be in there, tucked so snugly into that little tub with them, and not simply to feel the surely incredible sensation of two men's bodies pressing against my own.

How content would I feel, how safe, surrounded by such strength? Surely there, circled by two warriors of their caliber, I would not, could not, be forced to do anything that I did not want to do.

But I was not a part of that scene, no matter how I suddenly longed to be. As they lay in the ancient tub, spooned together as two halves of one whole, I actually began to feel like an intruder, a voyeur in an ultimately tender moment. I felt worse than if I had happened upon them mid-fuck, as if I had seen something that no one should know about but those involved. Slowly I began to back away, out of the room and back down the hallway from which I had come. I moved slowly, so as not to alert them to my presence, though scalding tears began to prickle at the backs of my eyes in accompaniment to a horrible yearning, a great hole in my chest that had suddenly been torn open.

Thus occupied with my feelings, it did not occur to me until I was back at the iron gate that I had not accomplished what I had entered the men's quarters to do. Yes, I had looked long and hard at both men, but I had been distracted by questions about their relationship with each other. Distracted by my own reaction to something that I could never have.

I was no closer to knowing which, if either, was the man I would not again meet until my next courses had come.

If they came at all.

I supposed that I could already be with child, and it was an odd sensation, one that shocked away the thin film of streaming tears that I had not been able to prevent. I pondered it as I opened the gate just far enough to slip through, and closed and locked it again behind me.

At least I was not pregnant with my husband's child. Once that very thing had been my dearest wish, but I no longer wished to create a baby with the man I now knew Lucius to be, a man who would stop at nothing to acquire what he wanted.

True, my husband had admirable qualities. But the very fact that he had chosen to hide them in favor of his ruthless business practices had changed my feelings toward the man entirely.

And while the thought of a champion growing in my womb thrilled me to the tips of my toes, I knew that that baby would still be raised by Lucius, would be influenced by him, and that made me sick to my stomach.

The noises of the party were lighter as I reached the top

of the stone stairway than they had been when I descended, though I could not have been downstairs for all that long. The moon was not yet waning, the dawn and blistering sun not yet on the horizon. Only some drunkards and heavy revelers remained, I was sure, but the majority of our guests would have departed for their own homes.

That meant that I could retire to my own chambers and likely still not be missed.

"Where have you been?"

I shrieked at the words that sounded, close to my ear and from behind me. Frantically I looked around, but the speaker kept just out of sight for a full minute, deliberately, it seemed, just to irritate me and cause me worry. It worked. When finally I spun around and saw that it was Justinus, I was well and truly irked, even while my heart hammered a fierce staccato in my chest.

I was no longer standing right at the top of the stairs to the gladiator's quarters—I had crossed the room that led to the great hall, filled with statues of our house's past champions, as I had contemplated the hour—but I was still fairly close to the stairs that led to the great iron gate. How long had Justinus been standing there? Had he seen me ascend?

I hoped that my thoughts were not displayed on my face, that they were hidden in the shadows cast by the busts with exaggerated cocks as I thought frantically about what to say.

If Justinus were to detect my confusion, my guilt, and my arousal, then I would be in a sorry state.

"Who are you to question me?" I deliberately raised my chin, the heavy scorn in my voice something that I felt for no slave but Justinus, though society would say that I had every right to it and more. I gave in to a keen frustration for the man, whose desire to better himself had given way to unscrupulous dealings in a manner that I could not condone. I knew that he provided the men below, and the women above, with whores, with drugs, with access to gambling. If he had not been so close to my husband, I could have used my own knowledge as leverage against anything he might discover about me, but as Lucius' right-hand man, I knew that his shady practices would more than likely be overlooked. "I will not be questioned by a slave!"

The small smile that had been playing over the man's lips faded, to be replaced by anger and defiance. As quickly as I could blink, though, that too was gone, and overtop it a mask of false reverence.

"Of course, Domina. Apologies." He lowered to his knees at my feet. I saw a moment too late that my leather house sandals were covered in the fine, dry white dust that lined the corridors below.

Perhaps the man was too caught in his little scene to notice, for the entire situation, his reverence, seemed like a mockery.

Failing that, perhaps the shadows were dark enough.

Though, in society's mind, I should not have had to hide my whereabouts from a slave. I should not have had to wonder if his respect was real or false. What did he know that made him so certain he was exempt from punishment? He might have been Lucius' right-hand man, but surely if I was to complain to my husband, then the man would be punished.

But what if he had seen where I had been? Would he tell?

Uncertain of what I do, I hid behind my own mask, this

time one made of my will, not molded shiny and white. Tilting my head in acceptance, I took a step back.

"Ensure that it does not happen again." I did not feel the haughtiness that I layered into my voice. Instead I moved down the hall, toward my own room, trying not to move any faster than I would have had I not been feeling so anxious.

I did not look back.

I was not sure that I would like what I saw, if I did.

Shortly after dawn, I lay in my bed, as awake as if I had never tried to sleep at all. I watched the colors of the rising morning as they played out over the stone walls—pale rose, brilliant saffron, and the pale gold of straw, washing over the veined white in a cascade of brilliance.

I could not stop thinking about what I had seen below. Could not stop fantasizing about it.

I had worried momentarily about Justinus, and about what he had seen, as I had removed my false yellow hair and unwound the strips of gauze that bound my own dark coils to my skull. Drusilla normally performed the task for me, but I had wanted to be alone, so I had dismissed her to the women's quarters, where she, no doubt, was soundly sleeping away the aftermath of our celebration.

As soon as my hair had been blessedly released from the stifling cloth, and my skin from my tunic, I had lain atop my sheets, restless.

Trying to forget.

Unable to do so.

And now it was early morning. Rome would be rising,

preparing for its day. So would the gladiators, though they had been at the party as late as the last guest.

I needed sleep. Needed rest of some sort to face the day. As I tossed and turned, the sheets of my bed tangling around me, pulling at the delicate strands of my hair, the first sheen of the day's sweat broke over my skin in small drops.

Frustrated, I sat up straight, reaching for the jug of rich, honeyed wine that sat on the tray next to my bed. Without bothering to pour it into a cup, I lifted it to my lips and drank deeply, gulping until I had drained the clay pitcher and rivulets of ruby ran down my chin and across my breasts.

The wine made me dizzy. Hopefully it would make me dizzy enough to fall asleep, even if just for a few hours.

Even after the wine took effect and my head started to swim, I was tense. My muscles were stiff with stress, with the upset of the past few days.

With the image in my mind of two golden heads, one defiant, one proud, both damp from the steam, I moved my hand from where it rested over my head, down between my legs.

With my left hand I held myself open; I found my clitoris with my right. Without preamble I used my finger to circle the hardening nub, just the way I knew worked the best. Around and around, over and over, until I felt the familiar tension between my thighs.

I fisted my left hand tightly against my pelvis as the shock waves rolled over me, and bit at the softly woven fabric of my pillow to stifle my cries. I rode out the storm, coming back to dry land only after the last ripple had ridden through my flesh.

Relaxed, finally relaxed, I began to drift to sleep, an odd

sensation with the early morning sun beaming in gilded blocks through my window. But I willed each of my muscles, one by one, to submit to the languor brought by the wine and the release. The sweat of sex clung to my skin, rolled off of my breasts onto my bed. Its musk hung heavily in the air.

I slept, finally. And while I slept, I dreamt of gladiators.

Chapter Seven

I sat on a bench covered with plush cushions, a tray of the freshest fruit at my side. I had only to ask for a cup of sweet wine, or for someone to massage my temples, or to rub my feet. I had every comfort within arm's reach, and yet I felt sick inside, as if some plague was rotting away the flesh of my gut.

Hilaria was due to appear at our home at any moment. The purpose of the visit was to decide which gladiator she would purchase the services of, and I knew that she still felt entitled to Caius. To Marcus, too, for that matter, and if the sum she named was high enough, I knew without doubt that Lucius would overlook his rules and allow her whatever she wished.

Hilaria's late husband had left her very, very rich. He had also left her all of those riches several years earlier. Enough time had passed for her to become used to the opulence and freedom that her lifestyle afforded her. As far as she was concerned, she could do as she wished, and her piles of denarii granted her the means.

Though I constantly reminded myself that I had no right,

no claim, to either Caius or Marcus, I could not stop the growth of jealousy's green leaves and twining vines as she sprouted throughout my entire body, piercing my flesh, my veins.

"Alba!" Though I had been waiting, I still felt unprepared for the reality of the woman. Hilaria sauntered into the room as if she owned it, as if *she* was domina here, her every step measured and deliberate. She paused several steps from me, waiting, I knew, for words of praise.

"You look . . . lovely." And she did. Though her features were somewhat angular and her figure thinner than current fashions appreciated, she was a very attractive woman. Today she wore a shimmering tunic of brilliant azure blue, embroidered with the palest of gold, and it set off the shimmer of her naturally pale yellow hair.

I shifted uncomfortably before forcing myself to still, aware of my own dark tresses coiled tightly against my skull so that I, too, could have waxen ringlets the color of sunshine. I was incredibly aware that my hair, however, was not my own—it had once belonged to a slave girl, and was attached to my own skull tightly with pins.

"You do indeed look lovely." Lucius followed several steps behind Hilaria, with Justinus as always a few paces behind him, and stopped to press lips moistly on Hilaria's hand. She giggled, then swept a hand over her brow.

"I am parched from the journey." She batted her long, silken eyelashes at my husband, who snapped his fingers sharply for Drusilla.

"Why does our guest not have wine yet?" His tone was harsh, his scowl fiercer than I thought the situation warranted. And Drusilla was *my* girl, after all. Not Hilaria's, not Lucius'.

"It is hard to find slaves who will be more than lazy layabouts, these days." Hilaria spoke as she sauntered over to sit beside me on the plush, cushioned bench. I saw a shadow cross Drusilla's face as she hurried to press a cup filled to the brim with spiced wine into the richer woman's hand.

The shadow made me mad. Drusilla was more to me than a common slave girl, and Lucius knew it. Why did he not speak? I did not appreciate insults flung her way.

"Well, you did just arrive." I kept my tone jovial, teasing, though I felt neither emotion. The journey that had left Hilaria "parched" had taken perhaps twenty minutes at most, carried as she was in her *litter*, that bed hoisted by her slaves. And wine did need to be poured, after all, before it could be drunk—it did not appear magically if one snapped one's fingers.

Lucius looked stunned at my words and then ferociously angry. I had dared to mock him in front of our guest, and as such he was well within his rights to punish me. In the past, I would never have feared that he would, but greed had so overtaken the man whom I had loved that I no longer could anticipate his actions. I gulped at my wine, swallowing past the lump of—surely that could not be fear—that had suddenly congealed in my throat. I realized that I did not know this man at all, not anymore. And he appeared fierce enough to cause very real fear to begin skittering through my veins.

When Hilaria turned to face him, however, he morphed into another man completely—a jovial host, a charming flirt.

I watched, sickened, as he smoothed a hand through his

dark hair. He looked none the worse for wear from the celebration the night before, and I suspected that he had imbibed water only, no wine, for as had been proven once again the night I had been mated, wine left him with a terrible head and no memory of his doings while under the influence.

"Have you made your choice, Hilaria?" I could practically see the denarii dancing in front of my husband's eyes, and I hid a grimace in my cup and tried, very hard, to quash my jealousy and possessiveness.

This was going to happen, whether I liked it or not. Hilaria *would* purchase one of the men for her pleasure, and chances were very good that it would be one of the ones that I cared about.

It would be best for me to align my desires with Lucius'. After all, he was thinking of our familia when he acted as he did. The money from Hilaria was needed, and I would benefit from it.

The knowledge did not much help.

Hilaria leaned back on the lounge, reclined at an angle that she must have known accentuated her small but pert breasts. Her nipples, round and dark, were very clearly visible through the thin cloth, and I watched Lucius' eyes rake over them.

Slowly, enjoying making us wait, she pulled a dusky red grape from the platter that Drusilla, now standing still behind the lounge, held. Lifting it to her glossy lips, Hilaria bit into it, licking up the juice that dribbled out before chewing and swallowing.

My nerves felt grated at her deliberate movements, at the knowledge that she acted as she did out of a sense of superior-ity. Perhaps I was alone in my feelings that denarii and social class did not make a person worthy of a pleasurable afterlife, but it was how I felt, and it was something that I thought of often when in Hilaria's company.

"I have thought on it." She paused again, this time to sip at her wine and arch her back ever so slightly. Damn her, she knew that my husband was looking at her breasts through her tunic, and she was doing this on purpose. Likely she had even worn such thin cloth by calculation, as well.

Was she so insecure that she needed the constant praise of others? Or was she truly that horrid a woman?

"I have thought," she repeated her words and sipped more wine. "I have decided that I do not know enough to make my decision."

"My lady?" Lucius stepped forward, confusion and a trace of panic echoing out through the room. I was right, then.

We needed the money, and he would allow Hilaria to do as she wished with our men, so long as the price was high enough.

"Calm yourself, Lucius." Raising herself up, with her weight balanced on her elbows, she placed a hand lazily on my knee. It felt heavy and wrong where it rested, but I knew that I could not shrug it off. "I merely wish for a demonstration."

Lucius' brow furrowed. "Surely you don't expect to . . . sample . . . the wares before an agreement has been made?" His words were cautious, and the panic he had shown on his face leaked through them, though I could see that he was trying to hide it.

I understood his feelings. Had Hilaria crossed us? Was she intending to demand the services of one of our men for free, knowing as well as we did that she could ruin our alliance with Baldurus?

Did she even know of our potential patronage?

Had Lucius sunk into depths far over our heads?

She must, of course, know of our potential deal with Baldurus. Just as there were no secrets in a house with slaves, neither were there amongst those who flitted about in society in Rome.

I did not like the thought. Might I have to endure her possession of Marcus or Caius while receiving nothing with which to comfort myself in return?

Hilaria laughed then, her laugh sounding to my ears like shards of glass scraping on stone. "Oh, you should see the faces on the pair of you!" Lucius and I exchanged a glance, our expressions stony. Though it had been a very long time since we had agreed on anything, in this instance our desires snapped into alignment. "We will come to an agreement, fear not. A *financial* agreement. But I want to inspect the goods before purchase." In the blink of an eye, the lazy languor that she had so carefully displayed moments before vanished, replaced with brisk, business-like acumen. Who *was* this woman? Nothing in her silly, flirtatious attitudes had ever before suggested to me that she had a brain, as well. She continued, "Bring me your champion, and the other one that I desired last night. Bring me two others as well, two of your best."

As Hilaria's demeanor had changed quickly, so too did Lucius'. He shifted from stunned underling to sly businessman in the beat of a heart.

This was business. This was something that he could understand.

He would leave the silly women's games to me, of that I was certain.

"Hilaria, we have discussed this." He smiled then, that unctuous turn of the lips that I only recently found so revolting. "Our champion, and the next in line, are not available. We simply cannot risk weakening them."

Hilaria returned my husband's smile, but beneath the seemingly innocuous expression was metal, forged in fire. I wondered if perhaps there were two people in her one body. "I will see them, Lucius. After all, I need something to compare the others to, do I not?"

This time Lucius did not look to me, his wife. Rather he turned to Justinus, who had been standing quietly—for once—just inside the doorway.

They communicated silently, which I found odd, for the understanding pulsing between them seemed far deeper than that normally found between a slave and his master. It irked me that Lucius would consult his man before his wife, but I bit my tongue.

"Justinus will fetch the men." With this announcement, the charming, flirtatious man reappeared in my husband's demeanor. "Marcus and Caius, Appius and I think perhaps . . . Christus. You will like Christus." He winked once and mimed length with his hands, and Hilaria again spilled over with mirth, the forcefulness of her attitude again receding as the silly flirt returned.

The games these two were playing were hurting my head. And at the same time, my insides clenched at the thought of seeing Caius and Marcus.

I was not happy imagining what Hilaria considered a demonstration, however. No, I was not happy at all.

The chamber, full with the bright light of the early afternoon's sun, was full. Hilaria still sat beside me on the soft chaise, and she had nestled in close, as if we were the best of girlfriends. Lucius stood behind me, and Justinus and Drusilla behind him.

In front of us, in a rigidly formed line, were the gladiators. Caius, Marcus. Appius, Christus.

I cared nothing for the latter two. My eyes were firmly fixed on the two former, who appeared like two gods, two statues of sculpted muscle and bronzed skin.

I wanted to run my hands over that sun-bronzed skin, that taut, sinewy muscle. And I wanted my hands on them both. No longer did my loyalty lay with just Marcus. No, in my mind they had become entwined, one unable to exist without the other, though both were very clearly still individuals.

Two gladiators whom I cared about. Two whom I desired. Two whom I wanted to do with as I wished: Caius, who entered the room with a defiant swagger, and who managed to suggest a wink and a smirk without his face changing at all, and Marcus, the soldier, his face expressionless, his eyes dark as a summer storm.

I could do as I wished with neither, no matter how I longed to. They were here at Hilaria's bequest. They were here to do as *she* commanded.

To be at her service.

So, too, it seemed, were the members of my husband's household, for Hilaria turned to Lucius and fluttered a hand. "Leave us now, Lucius. This is a women's matter." She smiled at me then, a conspiratorial smile that alarmed me, and I looked to Lucius for an answer.

He appeared to be in pain. He started to speak, then stopped, and I knew very well what he was thinking. If he was not here to control the situation, what might Hilaria do? It would be up to me to monitor things, and confrontation was not something that I enjoyed.

"Very well." What could he do, after all? The damned woman had wrapped us all in her sticky web, and we could do naught but as she wished, for fear of the consequences. "I shall just kiss my wife farewell."

I watched with foreboding as he crossed the small space between us, placed hands firmly on my waist, and, lowering his head, kissed me thoroughly, the kind of kiss a man gives to the woman he craves more than anything.

I did not know how to react. My husband had not kissed me in this manner in years, and I could not imagine why he was doing it now. My whole body stiffened involuntarily with displeasure at the lie.

Trailing his lips from my mouth, over my jaw, to brush in the silken hair by my ear, he whispered, and his words managed to sound harsh even in that quiet tone.

"Keep her under control. Do you understand?" His fingers dug into my hips as he spoke, a loving squeeze to any observing, but I felt pain under the brutal force of his fingers on my tender flesh.

Tears pricked the backs of my eyes. Had all of his love for me gone, then, all of it replaced with greed?

When he moved back, away from me, he was again jovial, and gestured grandly with his left arm. "Well, you heard the lady. We shall all remove ourselves, but for my wife." He stressed the last two words, and I understood something then that I had never quite seen before.

I was his property, just as much as the gladiators were, as Justinus was.

I caught Justinus' eye as he moved to follow my husband, and he cast me a look of loathing. This was nothing new, but it was still not pleasant. I dared not look at Hilaria until my features were composed, so I turned instead to the row of gladiators.

A quick punch of adrenaline shot straight through my flesh when I saw that both Caius and Marcus had moved. Neither was staring straight ahead, eyes distant, in formation, as they were meant to be. No, both had shifted just enough to look at me, and I wondered what they saw that interested them both so.

Distaste, just the slightest hint of it, was apparent in the features of each, though Marcus sowed it in the crinkles around his raven dark eyes, and Caius in a tightening of the lips. I saw that Marcus was stiff, his muscles tensed, while Caius looked liable to fly into a rage at any moment, to strike Lucius down.

I did not think that their distaste was directed at me. It could have been toward the situation, but something told me that that wasn't it, either.

Could it be . . . could it be that they had understood how my husband had just made me feel?

No. No, that could not be it. For even if they had seen, their loyalty lay with Lucius, not me.

"Alba." Hilaria snapped her fingers, and I blinked in irritation, not so much at being abruptly brought out of my ruminations, but at being snapped at as if I was a servant girl. "Come now. Stop dreaming while awake and let us have our fun."

Reluctantly, I walked the short distance that lay between Hilaria and myself. She cooed as she drew me down to sit beside her on the lounge.

"Before we start to enjoy these luscious men, I have a treat for us." The polite smile froze on my face as I watched the woman pull a vial from between her breasts. It was attached to a leather thong around her neck, and was too small to hold anything troublesome that I could think of.

"Give me your cup." Warily I handed her my clay cup, which did not yet contain any wine. I watched her pull the stopper from her vial, then upend a viscous splash of liquid into the vessel.

"Drink it." Her words held certainty that I would do as she said. I watched as she drained the rest of the vial into her cup, which was full of wine.

"What is it?" I looked into my cup. The liquid contained within looked oily, thick, and dark. I had no more desire to drink it than I would to drink my own urine.

Hilaria lowered the cup that had been raised halfway to her lips to grin at me with delight. "It is a special mixture of opium and belladonna and it has traveled halfway across the empire to my hands." Lifting the cup the rest of the way to her lips, she took a long drink of the wine and opiate mixture, then licked her lips.

"Mmm." Narrowing her eyes at me, her expression became suspicious. "I expect you to drink this with me. It cost a pile of denarii, and many patrician women would quite literally die for the taste that you are about to have."

I thought that perhaps the opium would help me through the ordeal that lay before me, but when I lifted the cup to my lips found that I could not swallow. Now that I knew it was opium that had been in the vial, I also knew that it had been mixed with flax oil and honey, and though some, I knew, considered this combination to be a rare treat, I found the very idea repulsive.

In parties held by my husband, I had seen many a Roman become slobbering and foolish under the influence of such substances, whether they were the common varieties available in the marketplace, or special ones imported from across the Empire, like the mixture that now swirled in my cup.

I knew that I would need all of my wits about me to deal with Hilaria in the next few hours. And though I was loath to even allow the thought to surface, I did not wish for Caius or Marcus to see me so.

"Let me add some wine, at least, as you have." I stood before the other woman could protest, rounding the chaise and approaching the standing tray that Drusilla had left with cups and a large pitcher of our most expensive wine.

My hands shook as I poured wine into the cup that held the opium and also splashed some into the cup directly next to it. I needed to distract the woman while I switched them.

"Tell me, Hilaria, you have seen both Marcus and Caius, but what is your first impression of Christus and Appius?" As I had hoped, she turned from me to survey the men, and I took in hand the cup that held only wine.

"I do not yet know." Her voice was fretful as I again approached the chaise. "I suppose they look well enough, but I must see their cocks to know for certain." Her attention returned to my cup as I again sat, and she smiled at the sight of the liquid within.

I noted that her mood had again changed. She had been angry and forceful when directing me to drink the opium, and now she seemed as a little girl, a child whose treat has not lived up to expectation.

"Let us toast to the cocks of men!" I narrowly managed to turn my grimace into a gay smile as we both lifted our cups in her toast, which I found distasteful. I took a deep, fortifying sip from my cup, which I alone knew contained nothing but wine.

Satisfied that I was indulging in her "treat" along with her, Hilaria turned her attention to the men who stood before us.

"Remove your . . . what are they called, Alba? Their leather garments." She had replaced her hand on my leg, and her thumb rubbed absently over my knee as she spoke to the men. Though it still felt wrong to have her hand upon me, the excitement of being near the two men whom I wanted so badly made any touch thrill.

"Subligaculum." My voice was quiet, and I remembered telling Marcus nearly the same thing. I also knew that Hilaria knew very well what the garment was called, but from the glassiness of her eyes and the flush of her skin, I could see that the drugs and the wine were beginning to take effect upon the woman.

I was aware of all four men reaching for the ties at their waists, of strong fingers loosening garments until each man's worn leather fell to the hard stones at their feet, slapping against the floor with the sound of a palm slapping flesh.

The men returned to attention, their cocks at half-mast under our stares.

"Fist your cocks." I sucked in a breath at Hilaria's command. I half expected the men to refuse, though I knew that they could not.

Instead they all did as told. I watched Marcus close his large hand around the cock that had been inside me, hilted inside of me, and felt liquid pool and trickle down the insides of my thighs.

I bit my lower lip as Hilaria inhaled deeply, and my vision narrowed to include just Marcus, Marcus and his brother gladiator Caius, who stood beside him. So similar, and yet so different, they stood frozen, their erections clasped tightly in their work-roughened hands.

"Pleasure yourselves. All of you." I could not believe the audacity of Hilaria, though I was as transfixed by the sight before us as she. I would not dare to tell these men to do such a thing, and they belonged to my familia.

Though I supposed I actually had told one of them to do something very similar, and in fact worse. Though it had been so very out of character for me, ordering Marcus to fuck me made me no better than the spoiled, wealthy woman at my side, and I would do well to remember it.

"Stop."

"They have not done anything yet, Hilaria." I turned to look quizzically at the other woman, whose eyes were now bright and glassy.

"I know." She rose, moved toward the line of men, who all stood with their hands wrapped around their cocks.

I could scarcely catch my breath. This was so depraved, and yet I could not deny that it was arousing beyond measure.

"What . . . what are you doing?" Hilaria stood by Christus, who showed no sign of noticing her presence, save for the quivering of his planes of muscles as she drew near and leaned in.

The woman did not reply with words, letting nothing but a breathless laugh fall from her lips. She was affected by being so close to one of the mountainous men, and it showed in her shortness of breath, the flush on her cheeks.

"I am inspecting the merchandise." As she had the evening before, Hilaria reached out with curious fingers and splayed a hand across Christus' naked chest. Apart from a subtle intake of breath, one that I noticed only because I was watching so intently, he gave no sign of even noticing.

I think his lack of response excited her.

With a wicked grin tossed back over her shoulder at me, she slid those fingers down, trailing surprisingly gentle, feather-light touches over chest and belly that seemed as if carved from stone. When she reached the springy thatch of dark curls, she leaned in until her lips brushed over his jaw.

I watched as Christus' lips quivered.

In a change as startling as a candle being extinguished, Hilaria abandoned the teasing play and grabbed hold of Christus' cock, twining her fingers with his own. She began to pump, moving her fist roughly up and down the length of his shaft, forcing him to do the same with her, and I marveled at the man's ability to stay composed.

I myself was not composed, not at all. I was breathless and hot, and I ached—my breasts, my cunt. My skin felt too tight, as though the guilt at finding pleasure in this debauched spectacle wanted to punch its way free.

A groan finally escaped Christus' lips, and the muscles in his thighs bunched tightly. Hilaria noticed the same, and, with a mocking laugh, she wrenched her hand free from the base of his cock. It leaked just the slightest bit at the tip, but otherwise remained swollen, a bruised shade of purple, as if it had been beaten.

I could not believe the cruelty. She had deliberately brought the man to the brink of finishing, then had stopped. I could not see the point, and said so, though inside I was trembling with the thought of having that much power over a man, any man.

Gods knew that I did not.

"I have to see if they will give me my money's worth." With another of those depraved grins, Hilaria left Christus, with his cock pointing toward the heavens, and slithered her perfumed body in close to Appius, who stood next in line. With the new man, she did not bother with the teasing trail of touches down his torso. Instead she simply pulled his fingers away from where they were clamped on his erection, lowered her head, and placed her mouth over the bulbous head.

"Hilaria!" She paid me no heed, and in that moment I wondered if she was entirely sane. Perhaps the loss of her husband had driven her mad.

Perhaps it was the effects of the opium.

Perhaps she was just a heartless harpy with no thought but of herself.

Lucius had told me to stay in control of the situation. It was evident that I had not, but how was I to control a madwoman?

Did I even want to take control? Did I not wish, at least to my most secret self, that I could shove Hilaria aside and place my own mouth around the next man's cock? That I could suck the seed out of Caius, while fisting the shaft of Marcus, the man I now was convinced was his lover?

Who was I to cast stones at Hilaria, when clearly I was no better?

"Oh, dear." Hilaria's tone was sweet as honey and yet terrible, directed as it was at Appius, who was losing control of his stony demeanor, and fast. Hilaria found it amusing, if the upward turn of her lips even as they rhythmically sucked his cock was an indication.

The man was rapidly approaching release. Instead of pulling back, as she had with Christus, she added her hands, one spreading his thighs and allowing her to stroke the sensitive seam that lay hidden between them, and the other to cup the heavy orbs that dangled below his erect cock.

A harsh moan grated against the otherwise silent air in the room. Hilaria laughed as Appius lost control, threading his fingers through her hair and thrusting between her shimmering lips.

The smell of salt saturated my sense of smell, and Appius lost his seed in Hilaria's mouth. She continued to laugh as the thick liquid filled her mouth, her throat, and trickled down her chin.

When he had finished, when his hands disentangled themselves from her hair and dropped limply to his sides, Hilaria wiped the back of her hand over mouth and stood. She smiled at Appius, a smile jagged with ice, and then slapped him across the cheek with the flat of her palm.

"That will not do, not at all." Her words were thick with desire. "*You* will not do." When she turned to look at me, I could see clearly that her pupils were dilated, the black nearly swallowing the blue that was the color of the skies. The rosy flush of arousal had spread from her cheeks and flowed down her neck and into the deep vee shown by her tunic.

"It is your turn, Alba." She again wiped her mouth, this time with her palm, and then held that hand out to me. "It is not fair for me to have all of the fun."

I went to her like a woman under a spell. I knew that this was not fair to the men, that it was not right, but the ambrosia of desire hung heavily in the air, and I was drugged with it as surely as I would have been drugged if I had ingested the opium mix.

Hilaria wiped her hands on the folds of her tunic before placing them on my shoulders and rubbing slowly, languorously before positioning me in front of Caius. I swallowed past my distaste at the touch as I looked up, up the long golden length of his body until I was looking straight into the sea-colored depths of his eyes.

I wanted to think that if I had seen anger there, or shame, that I would have stopped. That I would have had the strength of character, the morality to draw back. But what I saw was desire, matching my own in intensity. Whatever his relationship with the man to his right, he wanted my touch.

I wanted to touch him.

I took my eyes from Caius' only long enough to glance at Marcus. His dark eyes were hooded, his breath coming short and fast.

He, too, wanted. I would think about what that meant later.

Slowly, tentatively, I reached out and placed fingers on Caius' erection. It quivered under my touch, and I heard his rapid intake of breath.

I looked up to his face sharply. Something in that breath had sounded familiar.

Still tentative, I reached out with both hands. Placing them on his chest, palms flat and fingers splayed, I paused for a moment and simply reveled in the sensation of skin on skin.

It was so awkward with Hilaria there, watching my every move. But need overcame nerves, and I shut her from my mind.

I let my palms trail down, down, until my fingers tickled Caius' hipbones. They were so familiar. But were they actually, or did I simply want them to be?

I brushed across from his hipbones and through a gilded nest until I reached my goal. Softly, slowly, I twined my fingers around the rigid column.

The shape, the hardness. The scent. It took me straight to that dusky chamber where I had met my masked warrior.

Senses collided as the very real possibility that Caius was the man who had been given the job of impregnating me penetrated my mind.

But my senses were fogged, and I could not be sure.

From behind me, Hilaria's breathing grew louder and more ragged, as if she, too, was waiting to see what I would do next. The noise was all that it took to break the spell for me, and within the merest of moments I felt disgust wash over me like frigid rain.

I forced my fingers to release their hold, one by one, and though I knew it was the right thing to do, it made me ache.

Who knew when I would again touch these men who made me feel so much? Who made me feel so safe and yet wild? I reminded myself yet again that it was the right thing to do.

"Hilaria, this is ridiculous." I stiffened my spine and turned, jutting my chin out in a display of confidence that I certainly did not feel. "You already know what you want. Let us finish with the games."

The other woman started as if she had been slapped, and I watched, shaking inside, as the languor of desire and perhaps a shade of insanity faded from her eyes. They again became cold and calculating, cold as the depths of the sea.

"I rather thought you were enjoying the games, my dear." Her voice was flat, and I was terrified that I had overstepped. Would she complain to Lucius? Would she make trouble for us with Baldurus? I shuddered to think what would happen to me if that was the case.

I kept my stance rigid, even a bit annoyed. "I am not, Hilaria. I am a married woman." I tilted my head to the side, waiting for her reply, determined not to let her see my nerves.

She considered me for a long moment, and I had not a clue what was going through her head. It was a completely valid excuse, though like a wild animal around a wounded one, she seemed to sense weakness and was determined to sniff it out.

She did not. Instead, she drew herself up tall and nodded in my direction.

"Of course you are. Apologies, Alba. I did not consider that this would be uncomfortable for you." Her words said the right thing, but I still sensed that she was not completely appeased.

I did not know if it was the drug speaking, or her.

I would have to take her apology at face value; it would simply have to do for now. I called for Drusilla, who I knew would be waiting on the other side of the door, and told her to escort the men back down to their quarters.

I steadfastly refused to look at Caius or Marcus as they walked by me. No matter that I had seen desire in their eyes, as well.

I was ashamed.

"Farewell, Hilaria." I walked with my guest to the door of our home. I had expected to find Lucius and Justinus hovering outside of the chamber, anxious to know of Hilaria's decision, but they were nowhere to be scene.

I wanted to know, myself, however.

As I was steeling myself to ask, Hilaria stopped unexpectedly in her tracks. Turning, she grasped my hands with a fervor that startled me.

"Alba, we are friends, are we not?"

"Yes." I replied cautiously, for though I knew that that was the answer expected of me, I considered us nothing of the sort.

Hilaria nodded, satisfied at my response. Her stare fixed in the distance, behind me, and she was silent for a long moment before she spoke.

"Did you know my husband?" She still stared beyond me, and I wondered why she would not meet my eyes.

I had not been expecting the question. "I met him on several occasions, yes." Where was this leading?

"What was your impression of him?" Still she would not look at me.

I hesitated before replying. My acquaintance with her husband had been brief, true, but I had not liked the man. I had sensed a cruel streak in him, visible in the way he delighted in the games, in the quickening of his breath with a particularly harsh coupling demonstrated between slaves.

"I fear I did not know him well enough to form an impression. He . . . he seemed to be an honorable man." This was the highest compliment that could be paid to a member of Roman society.

"Honorable." Hilaria's eyes sharpened momentarily, and I saw something dark swim through their depths. "The word covers so many things." She paused, long enough that when she again spoke I was not certain if she still spoke of her husband, or was simply speaking in generalities.

"Tell me, does a man who rapes his wife, who makes her wear chains, who beats her with a whip have honor?" She finally pinned me with her stare, and I found all words fleeing my mind.

Surely she was not speaking of herself, of her married life? Surely a true Roman man would not perform such atrocities?

But Hilaria did have that streak of . . . well, very nearly of madness, that I had witnessed in her moments of lessened control.

When I did not respond, Hilaria shook her head, her eyes clearing. "No matter. I will take my leave."

As I stepped back to allow Drusilla space to open the large wooden door to our home—no easy feat, as it swelled in the insufferable heat—I gathered my strength and asked.

"Have you made your decision then, Hilaria? Will you have one of our men? Which one?" I tried to make my voice sound as if we were girlfriends, sharing secrets, but I heard the undercurrent of desperation in the words and hoped that she did not.

The noble woman stepped out into the late afternoon sun, then turned on the heel of her expensive leather shoe, which was dyed the color of an emerald.

"I will make my decision soon." And then she was gone, lying lazily atop her litter, swept away by her slaves, who had been waiting for hours in the heat.

Her reply brought me no peace. But it was better, I supposed, than what her decision could have been. And still I wondered at her final question. An uncomfortable thought had occurred to me.

Was the silly, flirtatious woman simply a persona that Hilaria had adopted in public to hide the shame of her husband's actions?

Was the sharp businesswoman the real Hilaria? Had she been humiliated and tortured by her own husband?

Had it driven her partially mad? My mind flitted to past occasions in which my path had crossed with Hilaria's. I realized that I had never paid the woman much mind before her husband had passed. Surely if she had been the same person then that she was now I would have noticed her more.

She was the kind of woman who commanded attention. Who *demanded* it.

Regardless of how she had been in the past, or how she came to be as she was, the woman that she was now was dangerous indeed. Though the thought of a woman with such emotions made me ill, and I felt sick at the idea that it might be true. And, selfishly, I was worried: What would a woman such as Hilaria do with my Marcus and my Caius?

Chapter Eight

I did not send for him because I was bored.

I did not send for him because I knew that I could.

The day after Lucius and Justinus left for business on the coast, I had Drusilla fetch Marcus up to my chambers because I simply could not stand the loneliness.

The decision had been hastily made. I had selected Marcus because, well, because he had already proven that he desired me. And now I waited, nerves combined with something equally potent skittering over my skin.

"Domina." And there he was, pushing aside the curtain to my room.

I had planned to speak, to tell him that he truly did not have to do this, not unless he wanted to. To apologize for giving him no choice the last time.

I had no opportunity to speak. Marcus crossed the room, placed his hands so that they spanned my waist, and lifted me off of my feet. He was so strong, so certain in his movements, so sure that I would reciprocate.

"What are you about?" My voice when I spoke was breathless.

I was lowered to the bed as if I weighed no more than air. My tunic twisted around my legs, hampering movement. With one quick movement, Marcus had the fragile cloth grasped in his large hand, and the next moment it was rent in two.

Whatever my next words would have been, they caught in my throat at the action, causing me to choke. His strength, his dominance, aroused me beyond measure.

Marcus froze in the act of ranging his body over top of my own. His expression serious, he swept away the downy dark strand of hair that had fallen across my eyes.

"Is this not what you want, Domina?" His eyes were deep, starless pools, and to have them focused so intently on me gave me a small clutch in the stomach.

He made to remove himself from the bed, to take away the glorious sensation of his feverishly hot skin pressed against my own. I clutched at the huge, hard mass of his upper arms with suddenly clammy fingers, urging him to stay with a nearly frantic grip.

"No! No." I licked suddenly dry lips as he hesitated. "I . . . I just . . ." I sounded like a half-wit. Closing my eyes momentarily, I tried to solidify my thoughts.

"I merely do not wish you to do this, to be here, with me, if it is not what you want. I would not impose my will upon yours." I eyed him cautiously. This was not the normal way one treated a slave, that I well knew. But I no longer cared how "one" was to treat slaves. It was not how I would treat mine.

Marcus smiled then, just the barest ghost of a smile that curled the corners of his mouth. I had never seen him smile before, and it warmed me to the core.

"I think you would find it difficult to make me do something I truly did not wish to do, Domina." And then he placed his hands again at my waist, tugging me down until my silk-covered center pressed against the heat of him, heat that seeped through his thin leathers.

I wanted to ask him about Caius, about their relationship. I wanted to know if he was my masked warrior, and if he was not, if he knew who was.

Instead my powers of rational thought were swept away, licked away in a hot, open-mouthed kiss.

I groaned. I had convinced myself that our first time together had been the only time. That I could not call upon him to be with me again. That I did not want to be, not when I knew in my deepest self that he would likely be forced to be with Hilaria.

I was wrong, so wrong, on all counts. This, *this* felt more right than anything I had ever felt before.

Though I writhed beneath him, desperate to feel him, *all* of him, all at once, he did no more than kiss.

But oh, how he kissed.

Soft presses of the mouth turned to long, slow licks with his tongue after he teased my own mouth open. The soft sucking sound of mouth on mouth became frantic faster than I had ever thought that it could, and it was not simply from my own urging.

The heat between my legs was unbearable. My breasts felt swollen, and they ached. My skin was so sensitive that the merest brush against it made me moan out loud, into the moistness of Marcus' mouth.

He pulled back to look at me. I frowned at the loss of his lips.

"I would be gentle with you, Domina." His words were solemn, and I detected a meaning slightly deeper than surface value. "I have no wish to hurt you, to degrade you. No man ever should."

Those night-sky eyes searched my face, as if he was trying to impart some deep meaning to me that he would not speak aloud. My memory flashed to the day earlier, and the odd expressions that I had found on his face and on Caius'. The ones that had appeared after Lucius had dug his fingers into my skin so hard that I had nearly cried out.

Understanding dawned. I was in awe that this man, this big, glorious warrior, would care to be so gentle.

To show him that I understood his meaning, I reached up and entwined my fingers with his. He settled his weight on the elbow of his free hand, which allowed him to look down my body, to look where I was leading him.

Our entwined fingers found the jagged rip down the middle of my tunic. I tugged it aside, slowly, and brought our touch to the bruises on the gentle curves of my hips, saying nothing.

Loosening his grip on my hand, he traced his fingers over the marks, which did not hurt all that much, but which were an ugly blemish on my otherwise smooth skin. After tracing each one, he looked back into my face, and I saw anger in his eyes.

Whatever this was between us, and however forbidden it

might have been, it gave me deep pleasure to know, to understand that I had a champion. With both arms I hugged his head with its prickles of pure spun gold, and pulled him down to rest against my breast.

And then I pulled my tunic, rent down the front, wide open, and pressed my hips against his pelvis in a manner that could not be interpreted as anything other than what it was.

I knew that my champion would not hurt me. And so I did not want him to be gentle. I could have gentle, had had it before. I wanted rough hands upon me. Large fingers in me. An unschooled mouth between my legs. I told him so.

In a moment of bravery, I told him the secret fantasy that I had had for years, that I had never dreamed of broaching with my husband.

"Will you . . . will you bind me?" My face suffused with heat as the words escaped my lips, and I buried my face against the weave of my sheet. I wished that I could take back the request as soon as I had said it.

Marcus would now think me strange, perverse, much as Lucius would have if I had asked the same thing. I would not have a chance to explain that my desire had nothing to do with perversion. No, it was concerned only with the relief of the pressure to please being stripped from me, so that all I had to do was enjoy.

When I had been with Lucius, I had never been permitted to just enjoy. A wife was responsible for her husband's pleasure. This was my duty.

Marcus inhaled sharply at my words, and I felt shame wash over me, assuming that I had shocked him. I could not turn and meet his eyes, but when he drew me in his arms and rolled me I had no choice but to move where he put me.

Still, I avoided his stare, but he tucked a finger under my chin and turned my face until I was forced to look straight at him.

"You truly wish for me to bind you?" He did not ask why, which puzzled me momentarily. But I saw no judgment in his stare, only . . . could it truly be excitement?

I nodded, again trying to turn away. His grip on me held firm.

"You trust me this much?" There was wonder on his face, and I cocked my head as best I could while in his grip.

He answered my silent question. "I am a gladiator. My life is death. And yet you trust me."

Slowly I nodded, then, simply because I felt moved to, leaned forward until our lips met in a tender kiss.

This great man made me feel as if I had given him a gift, even as I felt relief as his acceptance of me, of the true me.

What had I done to deserve such wonder?

Clasping his face in both hands, I continued to kiss the man, my lips slanting over his until we were both panting.

Slowly, slowly he lowered his frame overtop of me, then sucked in a breath when the centers of our heat met. Then, with that bare hint of a smile again appearing on his lips, he loosened his subligaculum as quickly as a man was able, and pressed against me with bare skin.

I closed my eyes against the sensation, the indescribable sensation of that hottest, softest skin on skin. The feel of his coarse lower hair against the tender folds of my sex.

Wrapping my legs tightly around his waist, I rocked my hips.

He hissed through his teeth, then reached down and guided his cock inside of me.

As he hilted I cried out, then bit my lip. With Justinus gone with my husband, there was no one in the house who would tell tales on me, but still, there were no secrets in a house with slaves. So I bit down upon my tongue until I tasted blood, and all the while I ground myself frantically on the shaft that was imbedded in my hot, wet flesh.

It felt better than anything I had ever experienced. I was full, and the heat burnt away all traces of residual guilt.

And still it was not enough. Though Marcus began to move within me at a slow, steady pace, slamming against the wall of my womb with every thrust, it was not fast enough, was not hard enough or deep enough.

I writhed beneath him, caught in a frenzy born of too many nights alone and untouched while my husband fucked a slave girl in the other room.

I wanted more.

I had no idea how to ask for it.

As if amused by my impatience, Marcus slowed his movements, deliberately, I knew. I cried out again, another stifled sound, and fisted my hands in the sheets.

He chuckled then, and I found myself astounded, even through the heady cloud of arousal. I had never seen a gladiator laugh before, had never seen any sign of mirth from one—and rightly so, for their lives and deaths were so very closely linked.

But I apparently amused this one, and though I was agitated at the removal of his cock from my cunt, I was somewhat gratified that I had been the one to make him smile.

But I could not wait much longer, and I communicated that without words. Slowly, agonizingly so, Marcus slid his hands from my knees to my inner thighs, then moved them apart, far apart, with his rough palms. Pushing me back farther on the bed at the same time, he placed one of my knees on his shoulder, and then the other on his other, until my legs were wrapped around his neck and my center was open for him to drink like honeyed wine.

Supporting himself on impossibly strong arms, he dipped his head and nuzzled at my amber curls. They were wet, I knew they were wet, and he inhaled their scent, his hot breath tickling the tender skin. His tongue stroked through those curls then, just as it had stroked my mouth earlier. He murmured as if he had tasted something especially fine before tasting again.

My world became centered on the sensation of his rough tongue sliding through my lower lips. Occasionally he would stray from the rhythmic licks to rasp his teeth against the swollen nub of my clitoris, or to push his tongue inside of me, but always he returned to the tasting.

I felt the heavens begin to descend, and forgot to keep quiet as the swirling sensation began.

Before I could shatter like pottery dashed on the ground, he stopped. I nearly screamed aloud with the sudden sensory deprivation, but then found myself straddling the big man's lap, his cock delving deeper even than it had before.

When I overcame the shock of sitting astride a man—something I had never before done—I saw with dazed eyes that my slickness shone on his mouth.

It seemed to me a mark of possession, and I adored seeing it on him.

With my juices on his lips, it seemed silly to be embarrassed at the position that I was in. But it seemed so exposed, sitting astride him, with him able to see every inch of me as I moved.

Yet it felt so good to let him thrust so deep. When he placed his hands on my hips and urged me to ride him, I was unsure of how to go about it.

He solved the problem by taking the length of my tattered tunic, which lay tangled beneath us on the bedding, and wrapping it around my hips like a scarf. With an end in both hands, he pulled, forcing my hips to move as well.

His cock rubbed inside of me, and my clitoris pressed down against him with a pressure I had never felt before.

I was still stiff and unsure, so he pulled again, then released, and again. Once I had been shown the exquisite sensations that the position wrought, he no longer needed to pull with the silk—I moved on my own.

But nonetheless, he wrapped the length of fabric around his hands once, and then twice, forcing me to lean down over his chest, bracing my weight on either side of him.

He kissed me then, our mouths perfectly aligned. Pulled tight against his body, anchored by his cock and his tongue, I was the happiest that I thought I had ever been.

When he tangled one of his hands in my hair and pulled,

emitting a hoarse, guttural sound from his throat that told me his end was near, it made my own ending come into sharp focus.

"Do not hold back. You are safe with me." His words pushed me over the edge as together we moved, skin glued together by sweat and sex, and I felt ripples beginning in my toes and fingers and moving inward to my very center.

I shattered, and moments later he yelled, though he tried to smother the noise in the inky ribbons of my hair. And as the bliss washed over me, I nearly forgot that this was not real, could not be real.

We might steal moments from time to time, but this could never be my life.

Though the thoughts swirling through my mind when Marcus bade his farewell were dark and depressing, they lifted as a bubble blown in water, comforting me as I luxuriated on the sheets that contained the smell of our lovemaking.

No, this could never be my life. I might dream, I might contemplate selling my jewels and running away. But at least I had this to get me through the hell that my life with Lucius had become. And hell it was, for though I knew that if he had a choice, he would not submit me to the indignities that he had, the fact remained that he had chosen money over me.

A temporary respite from time to time would save my sanity. That realization also helped to lift my guilt, which I now realized was not from my lack of loyalty to my husband. No, it had been guilt brought about by the feeling that I had forced Marcus' hand. Now that I knew he felt the same, a great pressure within me had eased. I also suspected that, strong-willed as he was, there was not much that Marcus did that he did not wish to do.

I had made vows to my husband, yes. But so, too, had he made them to me, and he had not honored them. As I thought of my enforced mating with the gladiator whose identity I still did not know, I realized that Lucius had, in fact, made a mockery of those sacred vows.

So I would do as I needed to pull the shreds of my life together. I smiled, though there was no one there to see, and if the smile held the taint of sadness, I thought that it could be understood.

I wished, more than anything, that my marriage was strong and true, that my husband was noble, embodying those traits of a true Roman.

If that was not to be, however, then I would take my joy where it came.

Stretching hugely, I wished that Marcus had been able to stay longer. The sensation of lying within his arms, a safe cocoon, was one that I wanted to prolong. I had been so comfortable that I once again had passed by the opportunity to question him about Caius, about the masked gladiator.

Did it matter, really? I suspected that I already knew the answer. After the past hours, I was certain that my masked man was not Marcus. And though only days earlier I had longed so very much for the two to be one and the same, I no longer felt that way.

If that other man was not Marcus, then perhaps, just

perhaps, he might be Caius. I wondered if I would find the strength to find out for certain in the days after my next courses.

I stretched again, then forced myself to rise from the bed. My lips pursed together tightly as I looked down at the tatters of what had once been my silk tunic.

I should have Drusilla remove it, dispose of it before Lucius could see it and question its condition.

Remembering how Marcus had rent it in two, how he had wrapped it around my body, however, I knew that I would keep it. Bending, I pulled my chest of jewels from beneath my bed and carefully placed the shreds of silk inside, piling the glittering stones on top of them.

It was not the wisest action, I knew, but when things were difficult with Lucius, I would be able to pull them out and remember.

I yawned, a sense of languor and relaxation having fallen over me. I was so rarely free from Lucius' shadow. Though I had felt abandoned by him for a very long time, he had always been near. He simply had chosen not to be in my immediate vicinity.

What should I do? I could do as I wished with him gone. With Justinus gone, as well, I did not fear any of the slaves telling tales on me.

Pulling a new tunic over my head, this one a simple shift of crisp cloth that I adored for its simplicity and comfort and that Lucius hated for the very same reason, I decided to enter that most sacred of Lucius' inner sanctums, that place where I had never been alone: his office, that tiny room where I had been informed that I was to lie with a stranger. That room where he entertained politicians and nobles, where he did all of his business, and where he directed my life.

Smoothing the cool cloth of my tunic over skin that was still flushed, I left my room and made my way across the great hall where the celebration had been days earlier. Lucius' office lay on the other side.

It was dim in the late afternoon light, and already a fine layer of dust had gathered on the surface of the large wooden desk that had first belonged to his great grandfather, Tiberius. This desk, I knew, was a symbol of Lucius' duty to honor the traditions of his ancestors, and for a moment my anger lessened.

It was not an easy position that he was in.

Pursing my lips, I shook away the thought, focusing instead on the motes of dust dancing through the air. Lucius had been gone for only a day, but his presence, which normally saturated the very air of our home, seemed to have faded just the barest whisper.

Or perhaps it was that mine was growing stronger, with my decision to please myself as I would. Either way, not feeling as if the walls were drenched with his omnipotence gave me the courage to make my way behind the grand desk, to sit on the plushly cushioned chair.

I saw that the other chairs were still arranged as they had been during our meeting with the doctor, and scowled. The anger that the reminder of that scene brought out in my very core, the memory of the three men sitting here so smugly, knowing that I would do as I was told, knowing that I had no choice, infuriated me.

I had not intended to do more than enter the room, to sit in this very chair. But fueled by resentment, I pulled the meticulously arranged stack of papers that sat nearest to me on the desk closer still.

As the freeborn daughter of a centurion, a Roman soldier, I had been schooled as a child alongside both boys and girls. As such I could read and write as well as my husband, and even had a fair talent for figures, though I was not sure that my husband knew it. So when I opened the heavy, leather-bound book that sat beneath the loose papers on Lucius' desk, I saw quite quickly that it was a ledger, an accounting of our household.

The numbers seemed very low. Thinking that I had misread, I rubbed at my eyes, attempting to obtain clearer vision in the dim light. But no, the numbers were indeed very low—well, the numbers pertaining to what we had.

Lucius had told me that we needed Baldurus' patronage to continue to run our ludus, but I had not thought that we were in such a fragile position. We earned a great sum of money every time one of our men won an arena match, and Marcus' win against Januarius at the munera weeks earlier must have brought a sizeable pile of denarii.

It seemed that that did not matter. The expenditures noted in the book were high, much higher than I could have imagined. Granted, I had not ever had to run a household, so I did not have a good idea of what things cost.

I did know that if we were so short on funds that we needed to secure a patronage, though, that the purchase of a length of imported cerulean silk seemed to be quite an unnecessary expense.

There were other purchases such as this, ones not pertaining to the running of the house or the ludus, meticulously noted in Lucius' neat hand. I was puzzled, for though I recognized some, such as the extravagant necklace that I had been presented with after being forced to fuck a gladiator, others, a unique cask of wine, a fine pair of leather sandals, and the silk, seemed odd.

I had not been given a length of silk that matched that description. Lucius did not wear it, either. Perhaps he had ordered it as a gift for some future occasion.

We did not drink that kind of wine, either. And Lucius did not spend much on the leather sandals that were worn around the house, preferring instead to invest coin where outside eyes could see it—sandals were not worn out of doors.

The thought of what I might be forced to do to deserve such an extravagant gift as any of these things turned my stomach. I shoved the ledger away, disgusted, and leaned back in the chair. The parts of the wooden frame that were not covered with cushioning dug uncomfortably into my hips, and I wondered at Lucius, sitting for hours in the thing. Then again, my hips were more generous than his, hips given to me by Juno, goddess of fertility.

Hips needed to birth the child that I might carry.

Biting my lip, confused and still agitated, I pondered the mess that I had made of the desk. I had to tidy it, I knew, and meticulously, or Lucius would know that someone had been into his things. I doubted that he would suspect it was me, for I had never shown any interest in such matters, and because he had never questioned me on my ability to read and write and figure, but I would not have one of our slaves punished in my stead.

With a sigh so loud it very nearly reverberated off the walls of the small room, I pulled the ledger close again, intending to close it, to return it to the neat stack that I had first found on the desk. My eyes wandered over the open page again before I did so, and I noticed two things that I had not the first time, when my attention had been caught on the entries that looked as if they pertained to me.

First, I saw the addition of four hundred denarii made the day before. It was an unheard-of sum, a fortune greater than most Roman citizens saw in three lifetimes, and it had been, as was neatly noted, a payment from Hilaria.

So she had made her decision, then. And I had not yet been informed of it. With a sinking sensation, I somehow knew that she would be given access to fuck Marcus or Caius, or maybe even both.

The amount was so staggering that there was no way it could have been anyone else. Only a champion, or a potential champion, could fetch such a price for their stud services.

Right beneath the entry detailing payment from Hilaria, written with the same pressure and same thickness of ink, was the removal of nearly half that amount. The similarity in the appearance of the entries told me that they had been made at the same time, but unlike the clear labeling that told me where the money had come from, it did not say where it had gone, merely that it was indeed no longer ours.

It was all very odd. Perhaps I could find a way to weave the money from Hilaria into the conversation when Lucius returned in a few days. There very well could be a simple explanation for the fact that a large portion of that money had already been spent.

It was hard to focus on that fact when the book had just informed me that my lover could very well be expected to service a woman whom I detested.

With that thought uppermost in my mind, I slowly closed the book, then replaced it beneath the miscellaneous papers. I returned the whole mass to the corner of the desk where I had found it, lining the edges up just so.

I was confident that Lucius would not notice anything amiss.

I was not nearly as confident that he would hold steady to his vow that a champion gladiator must not sap his strength by spilling seed. No, I knew with every fiber of my being that his morals and convictions had been swayed by the immense amount of denarii given to our hands from Hilaria's.

It had been less than an hour since I had parted company with Marcus. Still, I craved the sight of him, wanted to look at him and know that he had been with me through choice, and would be with Hilaria, if he was indeed the one she had chosen, because he had no other option.

I wondered if the men were training that night.

The velvet curtain that had shielded the balcony overlooking the ludus had not been replaced. It was a reminder that in just over a week's time I would again meet with my masked gladiator.

If I bled, that was. There was a chance that I was already with child, and I laid my hands flat over my belly, searching for a sign at the idea, some sign to accompany the tingle of excitement.

No sign came. Still, the sensation of my palms running over the softly mounded flesh there was pleasant, and so I kept them in place as I moved through the now-open archway that led to the balcony.

Darkness had not yet fallen, though the sky had faded from the brilliance of its afternoon blue to a paler hue that I found calming. The air had cooled as well, a rare occurrence in our city, and I drew in a crisp lungful, savoring the refreshment of the slight chill.

There were many men below, though they did not appear to be training. I could see into the open area of their dining hall, and it looked as if they were finishing their evening meal. Barley and oatmeal fortified with ash, boiled beans and sundried figs and grapes, no doubt. The house dietician kept them on a regime that was low in fat and contained no meat.

My eyes continued to scan the area, searching. I did not see Marcus, but after a moment Caius appeared, entering from the hall that housed their rooms, if that was the word for the small, dank cells in which they were quartered.

He looked angry.

Striding furiously to the large leather bag that I knew was filled with pound upon pound of dry sand, he began to beat upon it, fury raining down from his blows.

I was distressed that he was so upset, though I had no

real reason to be. And more than that, I was curious as to the cause.

Several men left the dining hall then, wandering into the gated yard. Most took up their wooden training swords, their nets, and their shields and began to spar, but one, a foreign-looking man with dark skin and a ponytail, circled around Caius and the punching bag.

I thought perhaps that the large, mean-looking man was enticing Caius to spar with him, but his manner was aggressive, taunting. They were on the far side of the yard, and so were too far away for me to hear clearly, but I thought I heard the words "mask," "domina," and "whore."

Without warning, Caius spun, charged, and rammed his fist into the leaner man's face. Blood spurted into the air, a shower of bright crimson, and the man fell to the ground, dust and sand rising around him like a halo.

The other men in the yard stopped what they were doing to watch, but none interfered. I suspected that none wanted to challenge one so skilled as he, not unless they were certain of a win. I stepped back, intending to fade back inside the house.

For some reason, I felt as though I had witnessed something that I should not have. I wanted to leave before Caius saw I was there.

But before I could retreat more than a step, the amber-haired warrior turned and looked right at me, those intense blue eyes visible despite the difference. With a nod, he raised his arm to me, as the men did after a fight.

As the men did after a fight, when they were dedicating a win.

My mouth opened to say something, then closed. And while I fumbled for words, though he would not have been able to hear them at that distance, he disappeared back inside.

Had I just discovered what I had so desperately wanted to know?

Chapter Nine

It seemed that the freedom I had felt when Lucius was gone had not been because of him alone. Back from his trip to the coast, he was nonetheless away from our home again that evening. Even with him gone, I felt none of the abandon that I had felt during the few days in which I had been alone with no one but our slaves.

It was because of Justinus, that damnable man. For once he was not accompanying my husband on his every move. When I had questioned Lucius as to why Justinus would not be with him at the dinner that he was attending that evening—I would highly have preferred a night alone to a night with the male slave lurking about—I had been informed in cold tones that Justinus was sick.

I was expected to attend social dinners with my husband, but to business matters he brought no one but his slave—and he *always* brought the man.

I had bitten my tongue at my husband's churlishness, swallowing the response that had leapt to my mouth. Every other slave in our household was expected to perform their duties no matter the circumstances. Not that I agreed with the policy, but I was astonished that Justinus was permitted by Lucius to stay behind, and not only that, but to lie abed with the girl Marina waiting on him.

The man had far too much power in our household. I did not like it, I did not like it at all, but I had no idea how to broach the matter with my husband. He was my pater familias, and I was supposed to defer to his superior judgment.

Even when I thought that that so-called "superior" judgment was absolutely ridiculous.

I had been sitting on the balcony overlooking the ludus for most of the evening, a cup of wine at my side. As far as our slaves were concerned, I was bored and simply passing the time, though I of course knew better. Both Marcus and Caius had been out in the yard sparring, not with each other but with new recruits.

I saw quite clearly why Marcus was champion and Caius was not, though both were strong and able. Marcus observed, attacking with a reserve born of skill and discipline. Caius, however, fought like the gods' own thunder, a whirling storm of anger and unbridled energy. He lacked the restraint that made Marcus the superior warrior. Still, the stoic Marcus was the only man that Caius could not defeat.

I had been watching intently, searching for more clues as to the identity of my masked warrior.

My courses had started that day. I was not with child, at least not yet. That meant that I could expect another visit from the hugely muscled man who had treated me with such unexpected tenderness and joy.

Though it should have been shameful, I found myself excited by the prospect, much as I had been thrilled to my very soul by the secret visits that Marcus had paid to my chambers while Lucius had been absent. It had always been Marcus, for though I wanted Caius very nearly as much, Marcus had given me permission, of sorts. He had shown me that his desire matched my own.

I did not have the same with Caius.

Watching the two men sparring together, watching the slightest hint of honeyed gold from the setting sun gilding their sweating skin, their hair, I felt as needy as I had before Marcus had ever come to me. As I sat on the balcony, I wanted more than anything to slip a hand between my legs, to rub fingers over the center of my desire, to release some of the pressure that being in the presence of the two warriors built in me.

Instead I sat stiff, every muscle tensed, gulping at my wine to ease the lump in my throat. When it became too much, I rose abruptly and left the balcony, leaving my cup of wine behind, not caring for the moment if Lucius found it when he returned home, though I was sure that Drusilla would tidy the area before she retired for the evening.

Stalking through the halls of our home, I did not know what to do. I could hardly summon Marcus upstairs to ease my ache, not with Justinus here, lying abed or not.

I could pleasure myself, and likely would, but it seemed a pale substitute for what I craved, a ghost of my real desire.

Perhaps I would have Drusilla draw me a bath. I did not know where she was, however—I had dismissed her to her own time when I had seated myself outside, not wanting company. She would be found easily enough, though, I knew—

she always spent any spare time that she had in her own tiny room, reading anything that she could get her hands on.

Lucius would think it ridiculous for a slave to know how to read. His attitude was not cruel—it was common thinking. I, however, liked to slip books to Drusilla whenever I could. She had learned to read alongside me, studying with me in the evenings of my girlhood, though the passion for words had never taken me as it had her.

Her room was next to that of Justinus. Thank the heavens that Lucius had not lost his last grain of sense and given the detestable man more elaborate quarters, though the way that things were going, surely it was just a matter of time. I had to pass by Justinus' room to get to Drusilla's, though, and since none of the rooms that the slaves lived in had curtains over the arched doorways, I would have to see the man.

He would no doubt have something to say to me, some little barb to throw my way that was veiled enough that I could not complain to my husband about it. The little imp was clever, I would give him that.

It was still more than he deserved.

I detected a noise coming from his room, and it grew louder the closer I approached. Grimacing, I realized that he was having relations, the telltale slap of flesh on flesh and grunts of pleasure a sure sign.

I pressed myself against the far side of the wall, the marble cool at my back, hoping to slide by without him noticing.

Like someone who cannot take their eyes from a horrific spectacle, however, I could not help but look.

Justinus lay on his back, his arms pillowing his head. His tunic was racked up around his waist, the material bunching thickly, and I wondered fleetingly where he had obtained something so fine as the blue cloth.

Marina, the slave that my husband favored the most—or at least favored *fucking* the most—sat astride him, riding him hard and fast. She did not seem to be under any sort of duress, and as far as I was concerned our slaves could sleep with whomever they chose, no matter how poor I thought that choice to be. The scene forced a slightly bitter taste into my mouth, and with puckered lips I made to continue past the open doorway.

My sandal caught on the sleek stone of the floor and squeaked, and both Justinus and Marina snapped their heads around to source out the noise. My heart jumped into my throat—why, I was not sure, for though it was a bit of an awkward situation, I was the mistress of this house, and as such could be wherever I pleased.

Marina acted as I expected, simply returning her attention to the task at hand. Her face showed no embarrassment, no emotion at all, really—she might have been polishing the floor for all the excitement that she displayed.

I found a slight enjoyment from what that indicated of Justinus' prowess.

Justinus, however—Justinus paled as if he had seen a ghost. He sat straight up, pushing Marina to the side and off of his erect cock, on which his tunic caught comically. I grimaced as the sight of his pale, straining member slapped itself across my field of vision—it was not something that I had ever wanted to see.

I could not think what had scared the man so. Slowly I turned, looking behind me, searching for the thing that had cause the man to react so. I saw nothing, and as such concluded that it was me that had frightened him. But why would he be so concerned about me catching him having relations with another slave? He was well within his rights to do so.

I did not care enough about the man to find out. I continued on my way, but before I could travel more than a few steps, a grasping hand was on my shoulder, pulling me back, turning me around.

"Alba." Never had I seen Justinus so upset. His face was pallid and ravaged with worry.

"Remove your hand from me." I had very nearly had enough of this man, of this contemptible slave. "And you will address me as Domina." My words were cold as the ice of the north, frosted and hard.

Over his shoulder I saw Marina storm away, down the hall to her own room, her naked body sweaty and tense. Her face finally displayed emotion and it showed that she was angry. I did not pity Justinus the job of calming her, if he bothered to do so.

Justinus looked taken aback, but quickly nodded. "Very well. Apologies . . . Domina."

I waited for him to speak, to tell me what the fuss was about. He did not. By this point Drusilla had emerged from her room and stood behind me reassuringly.

"Drusilla, will you draw me a bath?" I could scarcely remember the reason that I had come down here, to the overly dramatic slaves' quarters, in the first place. "I will be along in a moment."

"Yes, Domina." Had Drusilla called me by my first name—and she often did, given our past—I would have thought nothing of it. She meant no disrespect by using my first name instead of my title.

Justinus, I knew, did.

Once alone, I raised an eyebrow, again pulling the haughty manner that I seemed to need to deal with the man around myself like an impenetrable shield.

"Well?" I was through with waiting. "What do you want?"

Justinus started to speak, then stopped. Started, and choked on the words. I could see his mind churning, trying to fabricate some sort of explanation for what I had just witnessed, though why he thought I would care, I still did not know.

Tired of the game, I sighed and made to move past him.

"Please." He again touched my shoulder, then, remembering my words, removed his hand as if burned. Fussing with his tunic—and something about that garment pulled at something in my mind, but I could not think what—he finally spat out what it was he wanted to say.

"I would be very grateful if you were to not tell Lucius . . . Dominus . . . about this." He looked at the sandals on his feet as he spoke, his jaw set. I noted absently that the foot coverings looked to be new.

I was not sure what I had been expecting him to say, but this was not it.

"Why?" My words were sharp as a sword, and I did not care to soften them.

His head snapped up, and he looked me straight in the eye, a trace of a challenge swirling through the pale storm-sky depths.

"I simply would rather he not know." Gone was the humility he had shown the moment before, in its place a thick layer of arrogance.

I cocked my head to the side. I was not intimidated by him, though I think that was how he meant to make me feel. It would be a calculated move, for Justinus did nothing unless it bettered his position in life, and since I had not been born a slave as he had, I supposed that I had no right to judge. Instead of playing into his hands, however, the curiosity that I had felt for so long, the wondering of why he felt permitted to act as he did, finally boiled over.

"And what makes you think that I would keep something from my husband?"

He smiled then, and the transformation from panicked hothead to his normal, calculating self was complete. No longer was he caught in the moment; he knew what he was about to say, and why he was saying it.

"Perhaps because I know that you did not tell him that you visited the gladiators' quarters the other night."

My breath caught in my throat, though I schooled my face to remain expressionless. He had seen me, then. Or had he? Was he attempting to call my bluff? To see if I would admit it? I would have to tread carefully here, because I was no longer entirely certain that Lucius held me in as high esteem as he did this man.

"And if I agreed to keep your . . . intimacy . . . with Marina to myself? What then?" I would admit nothing, would speak only hypothetically.

"Then I will keep your visit below to myself, as well." He smiled again, certain that he had won.

I did not like the feeling that he had gotten one up on

me, and in any household that did not contain such a conniving person, I would not be made to feel that way at all, ever. I could not be certain that he had seen me ascending those stairs from below, while I had absolutely seen him with Marina.

"Then I will also require you make yourself absent from the . . . the times that I am to be mated." Again I held my breath, wondering what my secrecy was worth to him, wondering if I had pushed him too far.

What I wanted more than anything was to question him about the books, the suspicious entries in the ledger, but I could not be certain that he would know anything, and as such it was not worth risking the possibility that he might tell my husband that I had been in them.

Looking as if he had swallowed something particularly unpleasant, he considered before finally nodding, slowly.

"Fine. *If* I am able." Oh, no. I was not going to let him weasel out of this condition, not when I finally had leverage over him.

"You will make yourself able." Adrenaline was starting to course through my veins. I had never been one for confrontation, but this, confronting someone I truly despised, was strangely exhilarating. I was fairly certain that my secret would be safe, so long as his was, as well.

Justinus looked pained. "Alba . . . apologies, *Domina* . . . I cannot promise to make myself absent when your *husband* is at home. If he is away, I will fulfill your request, but otherwise . . ." He let his voice trail away, waving his hand in a dismissive motion, as if his attention had already moved on.

"You will convince him." Again, the man did not look

happy, for the gamble to improve his position yet more had not paid off. As he weighed the odds I became certain that he had not seen me ascending the stairs—he merely suspected that I had paid an illicit visit below. For when weighing my certain knowledge of his clandestine activities against his possible knowledge of my secret, he seemed to finally understand that he must do as I wished.

I could see his thoughts playing over his face—an opportunity lost. What would it be like, I wondered, to live with the constant need to thrive, not just survive? Had Justinus been born a patrician, I had no doubt that he would have made a fine addition to Roman politics. Perhaps he knew that, as well. Perhaps the frustration over his social standing was what drove him to act as he did.

As for this matter? I assumed that Justinus' concern was because he had fucked the slave girl that my husband liked to do the same to. Lucius would not take kindly to sharing with a slave, even Justinus.

"Very well." He nodded sharply, then turned on his heel to walk away, possibly to follow Marina and finish what I had interrupted. After he had gone down half of the hallway, I remembered something and called after him.

He spun around, clearly annoyed, with a questioning eyebrow raised.

"Do feel better, Justinus." My voice was as sweet as the honeyed wine that I intended to imbibe while relaxing in the bath that should have been ready right at that moment. "I know you must have been very ill indeed to need to lie abed this evening."

The man blanched, then moved as quickly as he seemed

able into the nearest room, which belonged to no one, simply to be away from me, I thought. I could not help but laugh to myself as I made my way out of the slaves' quarters and toward the room where the large marble bath lay. It was not often that I obtained a victory such as this, and it made me very happy, indeed.

As luck—*my* luck—would have it, Lucius was indeed away on the evening of my next mating. I had not taken in the details of his whereabouts, knew only that it was some sort of meeting with another of the city's ludus owners.

I was too excited. Apprehensive. Resentful. Aroused.

Instead of consuming pitcher after pitcher of wine as I had while preparing for this moment during my last cycle, I sat as Drusilla brushed through my hair, sat with muscles tensed, bursting and overly full of emotions.

"Are you quite all right?" Drusilla knew me better, perhaps, than anyone. I had never been able to hide anything from her.

"I am." I longed to confide in her, and I knew that she would keep my darkest secrets entirely to herself. Somehow the words would not pass my lips. I was not even sure that there were words to describe how I was feeling.

I was still angry at Lucius for forcing this upon me again. I felt pity for the warrior man who had no choice in the matter ... and I also felt lust for him, lust matched in intensity only by what I felt for Marcus.

I was excited, anticipatory. I was also nervous.

What if the magic had gone?

Oh gods, what if it was not even the same man this time?

My stomach clenched at the thought, which had not before occurred to me. My body jerked in response to the sensations, and Drusilla accidentally tugged at my hair.

"Apologies." She muttered curses that turned the air blue as she smoothed out the tangles of my hair. I pulled away, intending to tell her that I was ready.

Justinus pushed aside the curtain to my room before I could speak. I nearly scolded him for entering without knocking, but I had no desire to irritate him before the evening's events, for fear he would renege on our bargain.

I would have my time with my gladiator, have my time *alone*. Oh, if only he was the same man.

"It is time. I want this to end long before Lucius is due home." Gesturing grumpily, he again disappeared, expecting us to follow.

Drusilla looked stunned at the audacity of his words. "Domina? What is this?"

I wished she would call me Alba. "Domina" was a reminder that I was the mistress of the man I was about to bed.

I shook my head at her. I did not want to take the time to explain. Instead I followed Justinus, who stalked across the great hall as if he owned the place. Drusilla made to follow me in turn, but I again shook my head.

"I am fine." I smiled, attempting to make the expression reassuring. "I have no fear, this time. Go. I will summon you afterward, when I need you." She still seemed unsure, uneasy to not have a chore during this important event. Seeing that she would not enjoy time to herself, not now, I thought of something that she could do that would be truly beneficial.

"Drusilla . . . see to it that Justinus stays away from the chamber." I would not put it past the little imp to go back on his word.

She smiled with genuine amusement. "As you wish."

My slave girl did not like the man any more than I did.

And so, alone, I followed Justinus. He stopped in front of the heavy velvet curtain that belonged on our balcony, pulling it aside for me.

"Thank you." I, at least, would be polite. To a point. "Now leave."

The look that he cast me was anything but complimentary, but he did go. It would not benefit him to go back on his word. I heaved a sigh of relief as he retreated, to fetch the gladiator, I assumed.

I had a few more moments in which to compose myself, countered by a few more minutes in which to fret that perhaps my gladiator would not be the same one as last time. That I would be prostituted out to someone new, made to share my body with another man.

I could barely stomach the idea, and as such looked ill, or at least I suspected that I did, when I pushed through the heavy velvet curtain and entered the chamber.

Perhaps I would indulge in just one cup of wine, after all.

When I was free of the heavy cloth, I looked around the room, and stopped, stunned, when I saw that my gladiator was already in the room, standing defiant, fists clenched, in a dim corner.

Suddenly unsure of myself, I ran a hand up to smooth my hair, then down to fidget with my tunic. I did not like this, did not like having no time to become settled before the man made his appearance. I was certain that Justinus had suspected this, had known that I would need time to compose myself, and that was why he had done it.

I had made him promise that he would not "guard" the curtain, but he would have his little victory.

"Domina." The man stepped forward, and as the palest glow of light from the candles washed over him I saw that he was indeed the same man as before—the same rusty yellow hair, the same hard build. He was already naked, but for the mask of Mars, the god's fierce features, cast in glossy white, cast overtop those of the flesh-and-blood man. I swept my stare over him from top to bottom. It reaffirmed what I had been suspecting, though I would not know for certain unless I asked him to remove his mask.

Still, I thought, very much thought, that it was Caius.

"I . . ." I did not know what to say. My thoughts flashed to Marcus, then to the image of Marcus and Caius in the baths.

Heat suffused me from the inside out, a molten core liquefying. Still, I did not know how to handle this situation, how to work through the awkwardness that I felt.

This time, I could not rely upon disgust and anger to carry me through. This time, though I did indeed feel both of those emotions, they were tempered by lust and confusion.

Silently, with his eyes upon my own, the masked man walked toward me, shadows throwing his musculature into sharp relief. I remained as I was, frozen in time and space and, I could admit, somewhat spellbound by the man's beauty.

His hair was golden, as I already knew. His body was a

thing of beauty, and sculpted of hard ridges and planes where mine was soft. His cock had risen, suffusing with blood, at the sight of me, and the sight of it made my mouth water.

When he came close enough that I could see clearly in the flickering candlelight, I could see that his eyes were the blue of a spring pool. Not the stormy clouds of Marcus'.

I knew for certain, then, who the masked man was not.

Did I have the courage to discover who he was?

"Take . . . take off your mask." My voice shook as I spoke. What if it was someone else entirely? I was already torn between my need for two forbidden men.

The only sound in the room was that of our breath, which grew somewhat harsher and shorter with every moment that passed. The sunset glow of the fat wax candles infused everything with an air of sensuality, and the smells of candle smoke and herbs seduced me with their wafting tendrils.

Slowly, he reached behind his head, untied the strings. His movements were sure, and he did not question my order. My husband had given me the choice of masking my mate, after all. I was going against Lucius' wishes only by not wearing my own mask.

I watched the man as he lifted his hands to the sides of his head, and removed the covering of glossy white.

It was Caius.

Of course it was Caius.

In my deepest of hearts, I had already known this. Still, to have it confirmed sent relief paired with desire through every fiber of my body. I sighed, audibly, with gratification.

This explained why Lucius was so adamant that *both*

Marcus and Caius not be given to Hilaria. Marcus needed his seed for strength in the arena.

Caius needed his to impregnate me.

Knowing after weeks of wonder was an immense relief. Now I had only to understand my feelings for two separate men ... two men who seemed to have feelings for each other, as well.

Caius remained still, his muscles telling me of the tension that rode him. I thought of what I had seen pass between him and the other men in the ludus, and the anger that he had lashed out with—anger that seemed to have been in my behalf. His manner with me was so very different from that with others—he had never shown me anger, or rashness. With me he had ... respect. Yes, respect.

It was more than that, though. I thought almost that he was calmer in my presence, though I could not have said why. Perhaps it was all in my mind—he was a gladiator, after all, and when it came to honor and order, all gladiators were bound by the same code.

I ran my tongue over dry, swollen lips, trying to force the words out of my throat.

"Come. Come to me." My words trembled, as did my hands.

When he reached me, he still said not a word. With a light but firm touch at my waist, he turned me round until my back just barely kissed the heated skin of his wide chest.

I had been completely unprepared for this, had thought that, as with Marcus, I would have to give permission for each act. Not so with Caius, it seemed.

I had already consented, and so he would do as he would. I wondered if he had the control to do otherwise.

I thought to protest—now that I knew who he was, knew that he was one of the men that I wanted so badly, I wanted to look upon him, to take in his raw beauty. But it felt too good, causing shivers to rain over my skin, so I permitted him to move my body as he would.

His hands moved from my waist up the sides of my torso with a touch so light that if I inhaled too deeply I would not feel it. Traveling his way up, his hands came to rest on my shoulders, where he tugged on the cloth that hung there.

One pull, two, and my thin tunic fell down to pool around my feet. I wore nothing underneath, knowing that nothing would be needed.

And so I stood naked in front of him, waiting for ... I was not sure, precisely, what I was waiting for, until it came.

It came in the form of his finger, tracing my spine from between the wings of my shoulder blades until the cleft of my rear began. I thought that he would begin again, trace that same path again, but instead that finger continued lower, and I shivered against the decadent sensation.

He traced through the cleft, pausing for only the briefest of moments on the pucker that lay hidden between. He continued the touch through to my lower lips, pressing his finger inside of my waiting cunt just the barest hint before withdrawing.

With just those slight touches I was ready. Ready, drenched, aching for his cock. I marveled that I had gone so long without sensual touch, before that first time with Marcus, for it now seemed that I was an addict. Instead of satiating me, satisfying my cravings, each touch with either Marcus or Caius had me dying for more.

As such, I was ready for roughness, to be ridden fast and hard. I wanted to be bent over the chaise and taken from behind like a beast, to hear the slap of flesh as he thrust inside me, hilting every time.

Instead I felt something rough, something textured trailing along the path that the man had just traced with his finger. Something braided, though I could not imagine what.

My spine stiffened even as I gasped when that roughness was threaded through my cleft, when it brushed through my moist labia and against my clitoris. Some kind of string, then, some kind of cord.

No. I understood when my hands were drawn together behind my back, when the textured string was looped loosely around them.

Rope. It was rope. I did not know where he had obtained it from, but found that I did not much care, either. What I wondered was how he had tapped into my mind, how he had known my darkest desire.

But I thought back to the conversation I'd had with Marcus, the one in which I had admitted my hunger to be restrained, to have the pressure to please removed from me.

Marcus had told Caius. And Caius was trying to please me.

I could not speak. Knowing that my dark dream was about to come to fruition rendered me mute.

I bowed my head in acquiescence, shivering with anticipation.

Though I barely knew this man, though I had not, in fact,

known his name in certainty until a moment earlier, I felt safe. I trusted him like I realized now I had never trusted my husband.

This man could bind my hands behind me, could tie me wide open and expose me. I would not feel fear.

Large hands slipped beneath my own bound ones and nudged at the small of my back. I let myself be guided to the wall adjoining the one that contained the entrance. There, in one swift move, I was turned, my back pressed against chilly marble that quickly warmed beneath my skin.

I looked into eyes so blue, so pure that their gaze sent a shock wave through me.

How could I have ever doubted that it was Caius?

Slowly, slowly, he drew my loosely bound hands up my sides and above my head. He looped the rope over the sconce carved into the wall, then pulled the rope taut, securing my arms above my head, as if I was his prisoner. Being so much taller than I, he could reach the sconce without effort, and so kept his stare fastened onto my own as he bound me.

As Caius slipped a finger between the rope and my skin, to ensure that it was snug but not too tight, I discovered that my secret desire to be bound had indeed sprung from a deep need. I did indeed like things being out of my hands, out of my control. With my hands bound, I could focus fully on my pleasure.

When my arms were bound to his satisfaction, he lowered his head as if to kiss me. In the moment before his lips would have brushed my own, however, he turned away, choosing instead to place his kiss on the tender skin over my pulse, just below my jaw.

I shivered.

When he fastened his teeth there, just a light bite over that throbbing point, I was glad that I had the support of the rope, for my knees went weak. My nipples contracted, begging for touch, and my cleft became even slicker than it had been, anticipating this meeting.

He continued down the length of my body, kissing with light strokes of dry lips, pausing to tease but not fully pleasure each of the most sensitive places—the tips of my breasts, the curve of my waist, the glove soft skin of my inner thigh and the equally tender area behind my knee.

Now he knelt at my feet, and though he wrapped rope around my ankles with the same firm but tender touch that he had used on my wrists, I felt like a queen. Never before had I had such a man kneel before me. Even in the dark shadows of the room I could see the handsome features of his face, but it was not all because of his looks.

This man had such strength, strength sculpted in every fiber of every muscle, that he could do exactly as he pleased with me. And yet he treated me with respect. No, with more than respect . . . with reverence.

It warmed me to my soul, and I felt freer to be as I wanted, to do as I wanted.

To explore every erotic fantasy that I had ever had.

When he had finished fastening the ropes at my ankles, he reached for the rope above my head and, grasping it in firm hands, lifted until my feet left the ground. It was an odd sensation, dangling as I was, and it should have been uncomfortable, but he kept me in the air only long enough to spin me back around, facing the wall.

I was awed at his strength. I was not a slight woman, and yet he had suspended my weight with seemingly no effort at all.

Now I could see nothing but the cool expanse of veined stone right before my eyes. I turned my head to the side, desperate for a glimpse of my breathtaking warrior, but he stayed out of sight.

There was a long pause, and to bear the suspense I tried to focus on the stripes that veined the wall before me. Pale green, sky blue, and rust, they threaded their way through the charcoal stone and blurred before my eyes.

My hair was swept to the side, over one shoulder so that my neck was exposed. Hot lips pressed against my nape, and I closed my eyes against the feeling.

Finally, *finally* I felt the press of skin on skin that I had been craving. Caius aligned the hard range of his body against mine, his front to my back, and pressed until I was layered between him and the wall. The warring sensations of his heat and the frigidity of the wall nearly drove me mad.

He slipped a hand between the wall and my stomach, a streak of heat through the ice. He let his splayed fingers rest there, just for a minute, before they continued downward to the soft curls below. A single finger worked its way through folds that were already wet and found my clitoris. One touch and it was engorged, desperate for touch. He began to work that finger over my clitoris, that tender bud, circling around and pressing over. At the same time, his other hand moved from where it rested lightly at my waist, curving around to my back, then lower to stroke at that very soft spot where my back began to divide.

My skin heated as my blood began to flow, hot and fizzy. I was rising up, floating on the very edge of a whirlpool of bliss when the finger behind me began to stroke lower.

Pressing my forehead against the cold stone, I contemplated the sensation of pressure against the pucker of my ass. I had never been touched there before I had met my gladiators—never wanted to be touched there—and the sensation was still as foreign to me as this feeling of safety in intimacy was.

But it felt . . . pleasurable. Decadent. Hesitantly I pressed back, allowing his thick finger to impale me, just the barest bit.

The whirlpool overflowed, sending me into cascades of pleasure that seemed as if they might never stop. When I could again breathe normally, Caius turned me around yet again, though this time I stayed on my feet.

Squatting easily, he undid the ropes at my ankles and let them fall away. As he stood, he pulled my legs around his waist until the heat of our centers was pressed together.

I looked down. The head of his engorged erection was visible, pressed against the soft, flushed skin of my belly. The tip wept, and I longed to place my mouth over it and taste.

But my control had been taken away. I could do only what he let me.

Taking his cock in his fist, he angled it toward the wet entrance of my cunt. I longed for him to thrust, to slam home, but instead he moved slowly, surely, in a manner designed to drive me insane.

He slid inside my wet channel so slowly that I felt every ridge, every vein of his skin as it was submerged deep inside of me. He began to move, his hips supporting my waist. I clung to him like a child to a mother, my face buried in his neck.

I wiggled with impatience at his slow, methodical movement. Every glide of his thick cock on my inner walls was pleasure beyond words, but I wanted more. Needed to lose myself in the sensation. His thrusts started to quicken in response, tunneling in and out, my clitoris hitting his pelvis on every one and beginning to store bliss again.

Taking away from my satisfaction were the ropes that still bound my arms. My hands were beginning to tingle with the start of numbness, sensation starting to flee from being so long above my head. I tugged at them fretfully, and found it both irritating and exciting that I could not free myself.

Bracing me against the wall so that he need not stop his motions, the gladiator reached above our heads and, grasping the rope in one hand, tugged once, sharply. The rope snapped and fell, tangling in my hair.

I did not care. I used my newly freed arms to wrap around his broad shoulders, massaging sensation back into them by stroking over the jut of his shoulder blades.

I felt my thighs begin to tremble, and knew that another release was close for me, but before it could take flight he stopped, suddenly, and with one hand turned my chin until I had no choice but to stare directly into those intense eyes.

"Is this what you truly want?" Thinking that he meant the orgasm, that he was teasing me, I replied in the affirmative frantically, rubbing myself against him with no shame.

"No." The seriousness in his tone made me stop, though it pained me to do so. I searched his face, then cocked my head in confusion.

"I do not have to finish inside of you, if a child is not what you want." His expression was solemn, even with the shadows obscuring his face. "No one should be forced to bear children, if that is not their wish. I would go against my dominus in this."

There was a vehemence in his voice that startled me, but I overlooked it as the meaning of his words set in. My insides melted, and the sensation overcame the nagging need to push against him until his cock was embedded as deeply inside of me as it would go.

Pressing my face against his, so that our eyes aligned, I kissed him once, softly, so close to him that his features became blurred, but I wanted the nearness.

"Thank you." I meant it, more than I had meant anything in my life. "Thank you for giving me the choice."

He still did not move. I had made my decision, and with my back braced against the wall pressed against him as hard as I could, which forced his hard length into me as deeply as it could go. I gasped when he hilted, for his length pressed against my womb. But it was my answer.

I wanted a child. And if it was his child, it would be a blessing from Juno, from the gods.

He stayed hilted in me for a moment, a long moment, as if taking in what I had said. And then I had to use my arms to hang on for my life, as he began again to move. His thrusts increased in tempo, and a groan slipped from his lips. The pressure began again to build in me, as well. Soon I was all but lost, my face buried in his neck, my nose inhaling the hardworking, male smell of him—sweat and sand.

This release was not gradual like the first had been. Rather it was an explosion, short and hard, and I screamed before I could stifle it. A few thrusts more and he collapsed against me, pressing me into the wall with his weight, a shout escaping from his own throat.

Trembling, I clung to him, arms and legs twining around him, waiting for him to come back to himself. When he did, he again looked into my eyes, that deep blue burning bright, then pressed a kiss to my forehead.

There was a sharp knock outside the heavily curtained door, and then Justinus was in the room. I screamed. I was mortified that the little weasel of a man was in front of me while I was in such a position, and even more so that he had intruded upon such an intimate moment.

Before I could say or do anything, I found myself empty, set on my feet, and Caius had the smaller man by the throat, dangling inches above the ground. My mouth fell open a bit as I scrabbled for my discarded tunic. Caius looked magnificent, completely unabashed in his nudity. Like a statue, he stood sculpted, a vision of strength and fury.

In comparison, Justinus looked small and weak.

"You do not dishonor your domina with such behavior without consequences," Caius continued. I was astounded and hurried to pull my tunic over my head so that I did not miss a thing.

Caius shook the smaller man, who started gasping for air. After letting him struggle frantically for a long minute—just long enough to prove who was in control—Caius set him on his feet. Justinus puffed up like an angry bird, clutching at his throat and glaring at the gladiator.

"How dare you." Never had I heard a voice filled with such venom as Justinus' at that moment. "Do you know who I am?"

"Yes." Caius was frightening in his stillness. "You are a slave. As am I. She is your domina. You will apologize."

Disgusted, Justinus opened his mouth, to argue, I think. But as he stared up at the huge warrior who could grind him into arena sand, he seemed to think twice. Turning to me—and I was now again clothed, though still mortified—he grimaced, though I think he meant it as an apologetic smile.

"Apologies, *Domina*." A sense of foreboding began to grow in my gut.

Justinus would find a way to make Caius pay for this humiliation, I was certain. But for now he had no choice.

"Your husband is due at any moment." His words were stiff, angry. "It would be best if I were to escort this . . . man . . . back to the quarters now."

He seemed only then to realize that Caius was not wearing his mask. Dread filled me as I saw realization dawn, but he said nothing, simply stood, waiting for Caius to don the subligaculum that he had removed on the far side of the room, before I had even been in it.

I noticed that he watched Caius very closely, almost . . . feverishly . . . as he dressed. But then the moment was broken, and both men stood at the curtain that separated this room from the rest of the world.

With the cretin present, I would not have a chance for a farewell, then.

Justinus pushed through the curtain. Caius made to follow, then hesitated a moment. I knew that what we had just shared had been something more than what it should have been, but I did not know what to say to address it. So I clasped my hands and looked at him, eyes large, drinking in the sight of him.

"Domina." His voice was soft, and he nodded once. Then he pushed through the curtain and was gone.

It was not until after he had left that I realized I still had not asked either him or Marcus about their relationship with each other.

I resolved to ask first thing, the very next time that I had one of them alone.

Chapter Ten

It had been nearly four full weeks since I had been with Caius. In that time I had not been able to see more than a glimpse of him from afar, or of Marcus. Lucius was around, always around, and it restricted my actions until I was nearly out of my mind with need.

The only thing that kept me sane was the knowledge that my bleeding would finish today—I had never veered in pattern since my courses had first started as a girl. That meant that I would see Caius tonight, and I thought that the minutes seemed interminable as they swam slowly throughout the day. Now I was summoned to Lucius' office, and more than wondering why, I dreaded going.

I was afraid that my emotions would reveal themselves on my face.

I was afraid that Justinus would not have held to his end of our bargain.

So as I entered the office of my husband, that small dim room where I had spent an illicit half hour, it was with a heavy weight in my belly.

"You asked to see me?" I hovered in the arched entrance, scanning the room as I did for signs that I had been there. I knew that Lucius had been in the room countless times since that day, and yet I looked anyway.

Lucius did not even look up from what he was doing, which was writing in the very same book that I had scoured so closely. I was afraid anew, afraid that I had left some trace of my presence, though I knew that I had not.

"Your courses are due to finish today, are they not?" I nodded hesitantly, though I did not for a moment think that he was keeping track of them himself. No, that would be too mundane a chore. He would be paying the doctor, Pompeius, to chart my cycle, and I found it slightly distasteful to have a near stranger know such intimate details of my life.

"If you do not become with child this time, we will have to reconsider our plan." *Our* plan. My lips wanted to curl with distaste. This had not been *our* plan. I had not had any say in the matter at all. He continued, not noticing—or caring, I supposed—what my stony silence meant. "Perhaps the slave we have paired you with does not have strong seed, as we supposed. Perhaps I should choose a Gaul, or a Dacian." This got my attention, in a gut-clenching way.

"You . . . you mean to change him? To mate me with a different man?" I was proud that my voice did not shake too much.

"Yes, Alba, that is what I mean." His tone was irritable, the one he reserved for the slightly addle-brained. When, I wondered, had I become equivalent to the slow of mind in my husband's attentions? Had his love for me truly disappeared?

He might have been forced to make me go against my wishes at first, but was it now simply second nature to him?

Still, I waited, waited for him to tell me what he had summoned me here for. I could not think that that had been it, unless the words he had already spoken had been meant to impart a sense of guilt.

"Lucius?" He had returned to writing in his book, working as if I had not entered the room at all.

"What?" His voice was sharp, as if I was bothering him. It caused anger to flare, an anger much larger than the situation probably warranted. *He* had summoned *me* here. How dare he treat me so when I was here only because he wanted it so?

I was not sure what he would do if I spoke to him with all of the rage that I had been keeping inside. I was tempted, very sorely tempted, but in the end slipped back into my role as gracious wife. It was what I had been trained to do for my entire life, after all, no matter how I felt about it. My own secret rebellion was enough, for now at least.

"Is that all you wanted?" I doubt that he heard the jagged knife beneath the honey of my tone, but I certainly did. He shook his head, ran hands through his hair. I watched, bewildered that he could have already forgotten that I was still in the room. I was also confused that now, when I looked at him tousle his hair, I felt nothing. Once the sight of his pale, lean fingers in the mess of his raven locks had set my pulse racing, had sent tremors between my thighs.

Now I wanted no part of him. No part of us.

"No, I also wanted to tell you that you are not to be mated tonight." I blinked against a sudden prickle of tears at the backs of my eyes. I was frustrated by the sudden surge of emotion—I had rather thought that I'd grown stronger in the last weeks. Tonight, the anticipation of it, was the only thing that had gotten me through the last weeks.

"Why?" I tried to make my voice merely curious, instead of devastated.

"Hilaria has made her choice. She also has decided that tonight is the only night that will work in her schedule." His voice was amused rather than angry, if a bit dry, but then I supposed that a sum of money as large as the one she had given us would soothe all manner of irritations.

"Will I be mated at all, this cycle?" The idea of losing my time with Caius because of the spoiled patrician woman made me sick.

"I had not thought." Lucius smoothed hands over his tunic—a deep blue, his favored color—and leaned back in his cushioned chair.

"Well, you had best think!" The words burst forth from my mouth before I could stop them. Lucius appeared startled more than angry, however, so I continued, anxious to speak before he cut me off. "Do you want that patronage of Baldurus or not? We cannot afford to miss an opportunity for me to conceive."

This was true enough, I supposed.

Lucius merely chuckled, seeming pleased at my enthusiasm for his plan. For *our* plan, in his mind. "I appreciate your support, wife, but you need not worry. Leave that to me, for I have a head for it. And we actually are in a decent spot, financially, at the moment." I thought of Hilaria's payment, then of the withdrawal at the same time. He was lying, though of course he had no way of knowing that I possessed the knowledge to call him on it.

Why would he lie to me about our money?

"How much has Hilaria paid us?" I was overstepping my bounds, but the demon inside of me would not stop the flow of words. "Is it enough to last? We have been spending quite lavishly." By *we* I meant *he*. Quite apart from the items that I had seen in the book, the largest being the length of blue silk that I had never seen, the quality of our wine, our food had improved. I was certain that he was spending beyond our means. We needed the patronage, I was certain.

The only reason I cared to convince him of that, however, was so that he would allow me to again see a gladiator. I would have to find some way to assure him that Caius had strong enough seed.

Perhaps I could tell him that the goddess Juno had visited me in a dream, had told me that Caius would do his duty. I quaked at the thought of using a goddess to tell a false tale, but I did not see what other choice I had.

My husband studied me for a long moment, and I felt as though he was trying to look right inside every crevice of my mind. I schooled my face into what I hoped was the mask of a dutiful wife, concerned only with the welfare of her familia.

"The patronage would be a blessing." He finally conceded the point, and I felt victorious. "But I cannot stop Hilaria. She can make too much trouble for us, and for some reason she has fixated on your friendship. You will have to be mated tomorrow. I cannot imagine that one day will make a difference."

Relief that I had not lost my time with Caius was foremost in my mind, but it still did not drown all of my concerns.

"Do you know who Hilaria has chosen?" I fiddled with a fold in my tunic, though I tried to appear nonchalant.

It was one question too many. Lucius again shook his head, then waved a dismissive hand at me while pulling his book close again. His mind had moved on without me, moved on to the next thing he deemed of importance—and I knew that that thing was not the concern of his wife. "Do not worry yourself, Alba. Hilaria will be here tonight, and you will be a gracious hostess, as I know that you can be. I will be at a meeting, and Justinus will be with me. That is all that you need to know." And with that I was dismissed.

Slowly I got to my feet, aware that I was no more than a shadow in the room now, as far as Lucius was concerned. Though I kept my eyes on my husband as I moved, backward, to the door, the desired confidence did not come.

"Lucius?" I paused a moment at the door, though I was not sure what to say. I wanted to ask him how our marriage had deteriorated to this state, wanted to ask him when I had changed in his eyes, when I had become an afterthought instead of cherished wife.

He did not reply. I supposed that was answer enough.

I was using my chamber pot at the precise moment that Hilaria arrived. Marina had shown her to the room where she was to be with her gladiator, and since no one had bothered to inform me which room that would be, I had to search when I was finished with my ablutions. I became flustered that I had not been able to greet the woman at the door.

I found her in the chamber where Caius and I met. I was not happy, not at all happy, that this was where Lucius had decided that the event would take place.

"Alba." The other woman stood as I entered, pushing my way through the heavy velvet that I resentfully ruminated was for my benefit. She held out a hand to me as if welcoming me to *her* home, and I nearly slapped the patrician woman for the arrogance that she showed.

I had an excess of anger lately, it seemed, wrought by my increasing dissatisfaction with my circumstances. Unfortunately, those very circumstances were what prevented me from ridding myself of the toxic emotion. Then I remembered her hypothetical question about men who raped their wives. I felt a pang of pity, and suddenly felt awkward.

Who knew what pain, what memories the woman carried?

Nonetheless, I knew my role. I crossed to her, a wide smile pasted to my lips. "Hilaria." I suppressed a sneeze as the overwhelming aroma of her perfumed body oils reached my nose. "Are you excited?"

She yawned deliberately, then toyed with an impeccably coiffed yellow curl. "I suppose this will break the tedium for tonight."

I gritted my teeth. She had me sick with worry, with jealousy to "break the tedium"? I told myself to remember, just to hold onto the thought that she might have a harder time of things than she let on.

"And who have you selected?" I reached out to straighten one of her curls myself, as if we were close friends. Not at all as if I was dying to hear the answer.

"Oh, you will see for yourself in a moment." With lazy motions she pulled at the shoulders of her tunic, pushing it down until it fell to the floor. "I sent your girl to fetch him."

She was treating not just our home, but our slaves as her own, as well. I hoped, very much hoped, that the denarii she had paid Lucius would be worth it.

I did not try to avert my gaze from the woman's nudity, for I knew that if she were modest, she would not have disrobed in front of me. No, she was searching for compliments, for admiration. Perhaps she needed them to feel happy about herself.

I let my gaze wander up and down her muscled body. I noted again that she was leaner than was considered fashionable, but it suited her tall frame, which could easily have belonged to Diana, goddess of the hunt. Her waist was narrow, as were her hips, and her skin was unmarred and the color of rich cream. She had removed every single hair on her body, barring those of her brows and head. She also looked to have been rubbed with an expensive oil, which I supposed was what I was smelling. Regardless, it made her skin gleam.

"You look lovely." It was the truth, and I was again struck with jealousy.

If it was Marcus or Caius who appeared through that velvet curtain, would they prefer her to me? She was an extraordinarily attractive woman, and she looked far younger than her years, of which she had lived several more than I.

She nodded, having expected the compliment. Tucking a shining yellow curl behind one ear, she seated herself primly on the very chaise on which I myself had waited for Caius the first time.

She looked more like the mistress of this home than I had ever felt, sitting there wearing her confidence like a fine garment. A heavy necklace and matching bracelet with milky white stones the size of bird's eggs would have looked ridiculous on me in the same situation, but suited her perfectly.

She, I was certain, did not question her wants, her needs. She took what she wanted, and felt no shame.

I supposed that I could learn something from her.

"I have something for you, Alba." I did not like her superior tone, but smiled anyway and moved to sit beside her when she patted the seat next to her.

I was very uncomfortable at the thought of sitting next to her while she was completely nude. It was very odd that she expected it, and not entirely appropriate. She was so very unaware of my discomfort, so totally unaffected by the fact that she was bare while I was fully clothed that I had to wonder again at her mental state.

Cautiously I perched beside her. As soon as I was seated she reached up into the highly glossed curls of her yellow hair and removed a carved silver comb. My mouth began to fall open, for surely she would not gift me with something so extravagant. I would surely not be able to accept it, not when I could not even like the woman.

Then I saw that she was removing something that she had attached to the comb. It was a ring, a thin twist of metal and beads, and she clutched it between her thumb and forefinger before replacing the comb in her hair.

"Here. This is for you." She held the ring with its glittering sparkles of blue, green, yellow, and red, and as she did, I saw the polished woman's façade crack open the slightest bit, revealing a hint of . . . surely that was not vulnerability? Somewhat shocked, I accepted the ring, clutched it tightly in numb fingers.

"A friendship ring?" Such tokens were common among Roman women of a certain class, but I had never been close enough to another freeborn female citizen to exchange such things. Drusilla had once exchanged rings made of twine on one of my family's visits to our home by the sea, a place that still held a special place in my heart.

I still did not think myself close enough to any other, and Hilaria's gesture seemed to me to make a mockery of the sweet gesture between Drusilla and me so many years earlier, but I remembered Lucius' words that morning: *She can make too much trouble for us, and for some reason she has fixated on your friendship.*

"Thank you." I hoped that she would take the quiet tone of my voice for pleasure, and not for the strain that the strange situation had placed upon me. Accepting the extravagant piece from the naked woman, I slipped the ring onto the middle finger of my left hand and was confused. I was strangely touched by the gesture, though as I still could not stand the woman I also wanted to rip the ring off and fling it over the gates of ludus, never to be found again.

It was a sweet, if completely unexpected, gesture, but I knew that I would never be able to move past the amorality, the selfishness that I had seen in her character. True, I now suspected that she had suffered greatly in the years that she had been with her husband. I would not blame her for taking delight in base pleasures.

But the hint of cruelty that I often saw while she was partaking of these joys—that I had difficulty with. We all had struggles—my mind skimmed over Lucius and the burden of his ancestral loyalty; Justinus and his need to climb high; even myself and my supposed barrenness and the grief that it had caused—but how we dealt with them, how we lived our lives, was a choice.

But for the moment it would cause only excess trouble to refuse the small twist of beads, so I tucked my hand under a fold of my tunic and tried to forget about it.

Satisfied that I had accepted the gift, Hilaria nodded, seamlessly sewing up the crack that had allowed me to see that hint of neediness.

"They were a very good deal at the market." Her voice was brisk, and in direct contrast to her manner in the moments before. "You needed something pretty."

I bit my lip as I thought of the many fine pieces of jewelry that Lucius had bestowed upon me and that I wore frequently. This was clearly how Hilaria had justified the strange gesture in her own mind, and it was so strange that I did not wish to question any further.

"I would have some wine, Alba." The woman's voice broke through my thoughts. She waved her hand at me, and I saw a ring identical to the one that I had just been given glinting on her finger. I rose from my seat automatically but stood still for a moment. Marina had, apparently, gone to fetch the gladiator. Drusilla was cleaning my chambers.

Apparently I was to fetch the wine myself.

With eyebrows slightly raised in annoyance, I moved to the standing tray that rested behind the chaise. There was a pitcher of spiced wine there, and I was tempted to pour it over

Hilaria's head instead of into one of the clay cups. There the woman sat, completely naked in my home, having just gifted me something extravagant and strange, and yet I was now to serve her. I was saved from either action that I had contemplated when Marina entered the room through the curtain, her hips deliberately swaying.

Behind her was Christus. My knees buckled, and I nearly fell as relief poured over me like a warm blessing of rain. My hands trembled as I set the pitcher back down on the tray, and the harsh noise of clay smacking against wood reverberated through the room.

"Ah." Hilaria all but purred with pleasure at the sight of the man. "Leave us." This was directed at the scarlet-haired Marina and, I assumed, myself. Though I bristled with the rudeness with which she spoke, I bit my tongue, thought of the unexpectedly sweet gesture of the ring, and moved from behind the chaise.

"Oh, not you, Alba. Just the slave girl." Hilaria reached a hand out for me, and I took it before I could think.

She wanted me to stay? Why ever would she want that?

Sensing my hesitancy, she pouted. "Come now. Surely you would not leave me alone with a man who could hurt me?"

I had no response to that. Christus had the strength to overpower her, certainly. He could overpower the both of us at once, truth be told, and Marina and Drusilla as well, without breaking a sweat.

I was not concerned. He knew what the repercussions would be if he was to step out of line. Also, I had seen nothing volatile in his character, nothing to suggest that he would behave in such a manner. He subscribed to the same gladiatorial sense of honor as Marcus and Caius. No, I was not worried.

Still, if Hilaria was nervous—or even if she simply professed to be nervous, as I suspected she was doing—the matter had to be attended to. Had he been home, I would have fetched Justinus, but had he and my husband been home, I would not be in this situation.

Still. "Surely you want to be alone?" There was a gleam in Hilaria's eye, one that took a moment for me to put my finger on.

Thinking back on her past behavior, on the manner in which she had behaved when she had been sampling the gladiators weeks earlier, the manner that had nothing to do with the opium that she had ingested, I understood. Half of the woman's excitement came from exhibition. She needed to be admired, desired.

I shuddered to think of where that need had been born.

Though I wrestled with it, I could not see what choice I had. I still did not entirely trust Justinus not to tell my husband about my visit to the gladiators' quarters, and if I upset Lucius by refusing something to Hilaria, it would be just the circumstance that would prompt Justinus to tell.

Silently, I seated myself on the edge of the chaise, my body stiff and uncertain. I would have preferred a seat farther away, but since Hilaria still had hold of my hand, shiny ring and all, I could sit nowhere else.

Hilaria stayed seated beside me, languid, lazy.

Christus stood in the center of the room, still and silent. He reminded me so much of Caius in that moment that it made me uneasy. Strong and silent, still and watchful. Waiting for instruction, as he had no choice but to do. Just as I had no choice in much that I did. Oh, he looked nothing like the other man, with his short spikes of ink-black hair, his eyes of honey. But his manner . . . it was the cloak of the gladiator. Donned when the oath to their dominus was sworn, I suspected it would linger, a part of them, until death.

I doubted that Hilaria noticed or, had she done so, cared. Instead she stood, arrogance ripe in every movement, and circled the unyielding man.

"I think I have chosen well, this first time." This first time? I dared not interrupt, but I did wonder what she meant. "Hard body. I have seen that your cock gets hard, as well." She paused directly in front of the warrior, placed a hand on his chest. "What would you do to me, gladiator?"

"Whatever your lady wishes." He could say nothing else. Pity washed over me like rain, though I did not know his thoughts on the situation. Perhaps he was pleased to have the chance to fuck a woman as beautiful as Hilaria.

But he should have had the opportunity to say yes or no. On that I was certain.

"I'll tell you what I wish, gladiator." The air in the room began to grow thick, perfumed with Hilaria's rising lust. She slithered her way to Christus' back, her hand trailing over his skin.

Her hands slid up to his shoulders, which she squeezed once, hard. Then one finger, just one, traced down the length of his spine, all the way to the cleft of his naked ass. When she reached the hidden pucker, she pressed, hard enough that her finger must have moved past the tight ring of muscles and entered.

Christus did not flinch. He stood stoic, his face expressionless. His cock had risen at the touch of Hilaria's hands on his skin, but I knew that that did not necessarily mean that he liked what she had just done.

"I will tell you what I wish." She repeated the words, withdrew her finger, and finished circling the man. Retreating to the chaise where I still sat, she fondled the ornate carvings at one end, then leaned over it, the cool bronze pressing into the taut skin of her waist.

I could see the heavy globes of her breasts, dangling between the arms that supported her weight like ripe fruit on a branch. The egg-sized stones of her necklace looked luminous, catching rays of light, and I could not look away. Still I felt a slithering sensation inside of me, like olive oil spreading in water, which was not entirely pleasant.

I could not help but be aroused, be just the slightest bit wet, by the sight of so much skin, both his and hers, and by the brazen way that Hilaria spoke. But it was not a clean arousal. That was the only way that I could describe it. I felt as if I needed a bath.

"I want you to take me from behind, gladiator." Hilaria's eyes had begun to glaze over with that lustful fog that I had seen when she had first inspected the choice group of our men, and it was accentuated by the charcoal and saffron that she had ringed dramatically around her eyes. "I want you to fuck me in the ass, and I want you to do it as hard as you can."

I stood, quick and abrupt, at Hilaria's words. They were tainted with a desire so dark, so . . . warped . . . that I was not at all comfortable where I was seated. In fact, I was not at all comfortable with this situation. I did not want to watch this.

Perhaps it made me prudish, but the patrician woman receiving a cock up her ass in a manner that would hurt, that would be next to abuse, was entirely too much.

"Hilaria, please. Don't... would you not prefer that I leave you two alone?" I tried to keep my voice reasonable, tried not to plead, and tried not to resent the fact that I had to even consider pleading to another woman in the house in which I was mistress. "I can assure you, you will be perfectly safe."

Her eyes now on Christus, she waved an irritable hand in my general direction. "Oh, go then, if you are so intent on it." The way she watched Christus reminded me of a predator and its prey, a hunter with a wild boar.

I again felt sorry for the man. But I could do no more, and I comforted myself with the knowledge that perhaps he was not as upset by the entire matter. I retreated even as Hilaria ordered Christus to take his place behind her. I heard the slither of flesh on flesh behind my retreating back, and then a grunt of pain—or of pleasure, it was hard to say.

Perhaps they were the same in her view. And I found that sad, for though I was sure that some of one could enhance the other, somehow, in Hilaria's case, I thought one might be dependent on the other.

At least I was free of it. I would go for a bath, go try to cleanse some of the unctuous sensation from my skin before they finished and I had to escort her to the door. And while I bathed, I knew very well that I would slip my hand between my own legs.

I would remove the friendship ring first and the twisted relationship that it signified.

I needed to see Marcus, needed to see Caius.

The next night could not come soon enough.

Hilaria left before I could be summoned, slipping out of our home like a thief hours after she had arrived in it. I could only begin to wonder at the mental state she would be in after what she had just demanded, but in the end it was none of my business.

Marina was to tidy the chamber, as per Lucius' instructions. Drusilla was meant to escort Christus back down the stairs, back to the men's quarters, but could not be found.

"She is ill." Marina told me this with a careless shrug of her shoulder, the long tail of her hennaed hair flipping through the air with the explanation for Drusilla's lack of appearance. The two women had never been friends. "Shall I go get her?"

She sounded as if she would rather scrub out my chamber pot. I started to roll my eyes at the silly girl but stopped myself from performing the childish gesture.

"No, no." Surely if Justinus was permitted to lie abed when he was sick, then the slave who held equal position could do the same. "Let her rest. I will take him down."

Marina goggled at me as if I had suggested escorting the man to Orcus' hell. "That is not appropriate, Domina."

I raised my eyebrows, angry at the silly girl for contradicting me, which was very much not appropriate. "I will decide what is appropriate, thank you, Marina. And what I think is appropriate is for Drusilla to rest, for you to clean this room, and for me to escort Christus below."

The chit looked as if she still might argue, but I schooled myself into a glare that I only partially felt. She was right, and the second angry flip of her hair told me that she knew it. It was not appropriate for me to take the man below. It would be best for me, if I could not bring myself to rouse Drusilla, to send Marina below, and have her clean the room after.

There were two reasons that I did not like that course of action. First, the silly girl was so loose with her . . . affections . . . that sending her amongst scores of hard-bodied men was akin to waving honeyed fruit under the nose of someone who needed to become less thick in the middle. Chances were good that I would not see her for hours and would have to fetch her myself anyway, since neither Lucius nor Justinus was home.

Second, I was dying inside, needing to catch even a glimpse of Marcus or Caius. I knew that I would see Caius the next day, but I had come to have deep enough feelings for both men that the anticipation filled but half of my soul.

The realization of those feelings staggered me. I tucked it away to examine later, when I was alone.

Gesturing to Christus, who was still naked, I stalked across the floor of the main hall. I knew that he would follow. Truthfully, I wanted to walk behind *him*, for though I had no particular feelings for the man, it was a rare gladiator who was not built like a god.

I was not entirely immune to the way that his muscles, with their sheen of sex sweat, glimmered in the early evening light. It would not be an unpleasant thing to run my fingers through those inky spikes of hair, either, or to look into the honeyed depths of his eyes. I could smell the aroma of hard sex on his skin, and it made my nipples peak. I forced myself to swallow the lust down. The man had been through enough this evening, servicing Hilaria. I would be appropriate, no matter how starved I was for touch. And with Christus, that was all that it would be—touch. My feelings for him did not extend beyond physical appreciation, unlike what I'd felt for the two other men who occupied my thoughts.

The skeleton key was where I had found it last time. This meant that Justinus could not have told Lucius that I had ventured below before. If he had, not only would I have been punished, but the key would have been moved, hidden, or likely carried on Lucius' person, along with the key to the wine cellar. But it was there, free for me to take, to use. It fit in the lock just the same, too.

I should have let Christus slip through the gate, then locked it back up and gone to check on Drusilla. That would have been the appropriate thing to do. The prudent thing. Instead, I waited until the man who had been forced to be Hilaria's plaything had moved halfway to the baths and then slipped through the fence of iron myself. It creaked slightly as I closed it behind me, and I winced at the noise, which grated through the air. I knew that the baths were straight ahead— that was where I had found Marcus and Caius before, and I could see steam and smell the tang of minerals in the air that wafted from that direction.

Through the baths, on the other side, were the men's quarters, the small, cell-like rooms that they were allowed to consider their own. That was where many of the men would be right now, I knew. They would be playing games of chance, betting their winnings, or perhaps touching each other, those who favored the touch of men. Some might be sleeping, some might be awake. I could go there, could look for Caius. The fact that all of the men were locked down here, however, made me slightly more cautious than I had been last time.

Yes, they all knew what their punishment would be for touching me, harming me. However, a lifetime at the arena games had well taught me that when in a group, the lust for blood, for . . . other things . . . could overtake common sense, even in individuals who were normally quite sane.

No, I would stay away from the men's quarters. That would be wisest. But my trip was not wasted.

I knew, again from hearing Lucius speak, that the heavily desired champion's quarters were on this side of the ludus. If Marcus was there, I would be able to see him. To touch him, even if just for a moment.

Quietly, I made my way down the narrow corridor that led away from the baths. Torches lit my way, brilliant apricot and azure flames casting halos and giving birth to shadows that hinted of secrets. As I walked, I felt excitement begin to light a similar fire in my veins, felt my arousal grow.

I had not been able to see Marcus for far too long. Now, even just a kiss would be like ambrosia to my agitated soul.

This corridor was much shorter than the one that led in the other direction, and it had only one opening, one arch, more ornately carved than most things in the ludus. It was hung with a curtain, not as heavy or as fine as the velvet one upstairs, but still a luxury that I knew the other men were not granted.

The actual walls were another boon. From what I had been told, the generic cells contained bars, not solid divisions, so that there was no privacy, not ever—not when sleeping, not when pissing, not even when fucking.

This had to be the champion's quarters. Since the current champion was Marcus, I had enough bravery within myself to gather a fold of the curtain, which turned out to be coarsely woven and rough, in my damp fist. I pulled it aside, just enough to see in. It was not wise to startle a gladiator, even if there was no weapon at hand.

What I saw startled me, instead. Shook me to my very core.

On the narrow bed, something else this room had that I suspected the others did not, were twined two male bodies. Two hard male bodies, both of which had become as familiar to me as that of my husband's.

It was not a wonder that they did not hear me, did not see me. They were busy.

Caius and Marcus lay pressed together, arms and legs wrapped and entwined. Their mouths kissed feverishly, seeming hot with need, open wide and giving.

Marcus scrabbled his fingers over Caius' head, massaging, grabbing, looking for ruddy hair long enough to twine his fingers in, to pull the other man closer. Caius sighed into Marcus' mouth at the touch, running his hands down Marcus' back, stroking, caressing, until he reached the taut globes of the other man's ass. He dug his fingers into the man's muscle, hard enough that I winced, knowing that I would have bruised under the same pressure. But Marcus groaned at the touch, and it was a sound of pleasure.

I felt lightheaded, watching the two men who were both

my lovers make love to each other. My cunt grew slick, and my breasts felt heavy, swollen.

How I wished that I was in that room, instead of just an observer on the side. How I wished that my body was in between theirs, my skin glowing nearly white against the dark caramel that the sun had turned theirs.

But I could not, somehow, intrude on the moment. It was private, intimate, and I knew that I really should have turned away, have gone back upstairs. But not only did the sight before my eyes arouse me beyond measure—the two men who made love to me with their hands all over one another—it made me insecure, needy.

I watched because I was searching for a sign that they did not mean more to one another than I did to them. How could they want me—and I was fairly certain that they both did—when they clearly had so much more with one another?

I had thought to ask Marcus tonight what the manner of their relationship was. This was clearly not the time. No, not the time at all, as I watched the two warriors roll one way, then back again, the two men fighting for a momentary dominance.

Marcus finally pinned Caius on his back and sat up, wiping his mouth with the back of his hand. Clearly pleased with himself, he straddled Caius' hips, then leaned forward and placed his palms flat on the other man's chest.

Caius grinned up at him, and I saw that rakish nature of his in the curve of his lips. He liked being overpowered, that much was clear. And yet I knew that he also liked to have me in his control. Perhaps for him it was the best of both worlds.

I should have been jealous, but instead found myself hot and needy.

I thought that Marcus meant to kiss Caius again, on those beautiful bowed lips, but instead he pressed his mouth against skin that I knew was leather soft, right under the jaw. He worked down from that spot where the pulse of a strong heart throbbed, down to press hot, wet, open-mouthed kisses over a hard chest that was lightly dusted with whorls of hair the color of the sun. When he reached the concave dip of Caius' pelvis, where the bones of the hips jutted out on either side, he pressed his face into the skin, as if absorbing the heat and the scent.

"Marcus." Caius moaned, a sound that I knew all too well. I had heard it myself, whispered against my skin.

I was struck again, as I had been in the baths, at the degree of caring, of . . . could it be love? I did not understand. Had they known each other before coming here, to the ludus? If they cared so much for one another, why did they need me?

The answer was plain as day, and right before my eyes. They did not. And yet both professed to desire me, and I felt that it was more than my body that was wanted.

I was so confused. The only thing that I was truly clear about was the fact that I ached, so badly did I crave one of their cocks, tunneling in and out of me.

I wanted to be a part of this heated scene, rather than just an observer.

I wanted to take part in that love. I wanted to feel safe and warm and cared for. Instead I debated with myself again, telling myself to go back upstairs. I did not. I swallowed a moan, clutched at the coarse fabric of the curtain tighter and continued to watch.

"Be still." Marcus kissed small, light kisses over Caius' abdomen before pressing one final kiss to the head of the other man's cock. Opening his mouth wide, Marcus slid the length of Caius' erection against the rasp of his tongue. Caius moaned once, long and loud, and struggled against the body that held him down. Marcus ordered him back down, his tone to be obeyed. Caius fought back for a moment, a long moment in which muscles strained, before subsiding into a silence that was tense with expectation.

Spreading his knees wide in an effort to range himself low over his lover's body, Marcus let his weight be supported by his thighs, the muscles of which I could see quivering under the strain. With one hand he grasped the cock that was half in his mouth, wrapping a fist tightly. The other hand reached between the man's legs to stroke over the globes that fell softly against the coarsely woven sheet.

Caius let out a strangled cry.

"You like that?" There was amusement in Marcus' voice as he repeated the movement, a lightness laced with comfort that I had never heard in his interactions with me. Even as something that felt much like jealousy lanced through me I whimpered softly, unbearably aroused.

I could not stop myself. Though I felt so uncertain, I allowed a hand to stray to my breasts. I massaged the swollen flesh there, hoping to relieve some pressure.

I did not dare place my hand between my legs. I was too afraid of being caught.

Time slipped away from me as I watched Marcus suck

on Caius' cock, the soft, wet sounds the only noise to break the thick silence. The golden head slid up and down, and the strong hand moved in time, so that Caius was never without stimulation at any time. Caius began to tremble, his muscles standing out in sharp relief. He was about to come, I knew, and was trying to hold back.

Marcus knew it, too. "Ssh." He soothed his lover. Taking his hand away from the sack that he had been softly stroking, he slid his hand between his own legs, fisting his own erection. There he began to pump, harder and faster than I would have imagined could be pleasurable. He began to groan at the same time that Caius did, and his hips thrust forward, thick wetness spilling onto the sheet only moments before Caius grabbed the back of Marcus' head, shoving himself in roughly, as far in as he could.

The smell of sex became ripe in the air, and I very nearly whimpered. I wanted, so badly wanted, to be in that room, with those two men.

Biting my lip, wrestling with emotions that I could not quite identify, I took a step back, meaning to close the gap in the curtain, to leave. I had lost all track of time and I knew that at the very least, nosy Marina would have noticed my prolonged absence. At the very most, Lucius would be home, and I would be in a lot of trouble. I found myself strangely lethargic about the threat.

Whatever Lucius did to me, could do to me, it paled in comparison with the odd mix of feelings that were rioting through me right then, the most prominent being exclusion.

Before I could close the curtain the final crack, before I could shut the door on this particular tableau, Marcus laid down on top of the other man, spent. Caius ran his hand over Marcus' back, equally drained, and the satisfaction and contentment that seemed to seep from the very pores of both very nearly did me in.

Though I felt as though I should be crushed, I found that I was not. I could not place words to my feelings, but I did not feel despair.

As I contemplated this and quietly stepped back I thought I saw Caius raise his head, look in my direction, right at me in fact. But the curtain had already fallen shut, closing me out even more than I had already been, so I turned and walked away.

The whisper of jealousy made its presence known as I again understood that this was not my life, and would never be. Stolen moments to make things bearable were all that I could hope for. And perhaps I was being selfish, for I knew of many who would envy the position I was in.

My last thought—as I ascended the stairs that would bring me back up to my part of the house, to my world—was that damn it, it was not enough.

CHAPTER ELEVEN

By the time the sun fell the next night, marking the hour for my mating with Caius, I was feeling needier than I had ever felt in my life. And it was not just physical need. My emotions were in turmoil, and I did not know how to quiet them.

I was again beginning to suspect that it was me who was barren, not Lucius. This would be my third cycle with Caius. If this last hour had not gotten me with child, then I did not have much hope.

I hoped that the heat between us would burn the feelings away. I was ready, more than ready, when Caius entered the room. I had stripped off the thin layer of lace that covered my body, and was seated on the edge of the chaise, my legs opened in invitation.

"Domina." Caius' eyes locked onto the expanse of my naked flesh. I watched him peruse the length of my body, and the feel of his eyes seared me like a hand placed in an open flame. I saw him quiver with need and knew that he would not be able to control it.

Marcus might be able to refrain, to hold back, but not my Caius.

He crossed the room in several long strides and took me into his arms. His mouth met mine, and the kiss was feverish, like that same flame, exactly what I had wanted. I reached between us, reached into his subligaculum and rubbed a hand over the silky tip of his cock, which was already fully erect. A muffled noise escaped from his mouth into my own. Releasing his flesh, I tugged clumsily with the strings of his leathers, pulling until they loosened and fell to the floor.

His hands filled themselves with my breasts, cupping them, pinching the jutting peaks between forefinger and thumb. When I again took his cock into my hand, this time rubbing it between both palms, he bent and drew one of my nipples into his mouth. Words choked me, sticking in my throat, and all I could do was gasp. He scraped teeth gently over the tip, causing the surrounding flesh to pucker. I moaned at the heat and wet that surrounded my skin.

It was not enough. It would never be enough.

Leaning back on the chaise, I placed my weight on my hands, splayed on the softness of the cushion behind me. Sitting like this thrust forward the breasts that he was kissing, suckling. It also allowed me to open my legs wider, to twine them around Caius' hips, his hard thighs, the only part of him that I could reach from this vantage point.

"Mmm," Caius murmured against my skin. Letting my breast slip from his mouth, he slid his hands down to roam over my hips, to cup me underneath my bottom. Angling me up, he positioned himself between my thighs, right at the center of my heat, and slid inside me in one long thrust.

Reaching up, I grasped at his neck, pulled his head down toward me. I bit at the cords of muscle in his shoulder, licked my way up to his ear, and suckled the lobe into my mouth. I felt a shiver pass through him, and I nipped at that tender bit of flesh, one of the only soft parts about him.

Seeming as impatient as I, he drew back and then thrust deep, drew back and thrust again, tunneling in and out in a slow, steady rhythm. I writhed against him, wanting more, more touch, more sensation, more everything.

"More." I could barely speak. "I want more."

"Everything." He drew back until we could stare into each other's eyes. "You can have everything."

I buried my face against his neck at the sudden rush of emotion. He grasped my ass more firmly in his hands, pulling me to him and driving in deeper still. A series of shock waves set off, deep inside of me, and I let my head fall back, my mouth open in bliss. As soon as the all-encompassing sensation had passed, I found that I was not satisfied.

I wanted still more.

Pulling back, I slid my hands in between our flesh. Caius looked down at me quizzically and with lust hazing his eyes, but obliged when I pushed him away.

Rising to my feet, I pushed on his shoulders until he lay down on the floor, his back on the cool marble. Dropping to my knees at his feet, I laid a trail of quick, open-mouthed kisses from his ankles up to his inner thighs, moving up his body as my mouth moved higher.

I spared one glance at his face before returning my attention to the task at hand. His lips were pressed tightly together with tension, the skin gone nearly white and bloodless. His fists were tightly clenched as well, the skin of his knuckles matching the pale hue of his mouth. Closing my eyes, I sucked the head of his cock into my mouth without warning, felt his body jerk at the sudden onslaught of sensation.

He had had his cock in Marcus' mouth just the night before. How, I wondered, did I compare?

Deciding that I could not compete—did not even want to—I would contrast. I would be soft, I would be yielding. I would give. I pulled the fat head deep into my mouth, tasting myself on my tongue. I ran the rasp of my tongue under the ridge that divided the head from the shaft, then lightly scraped my teeth there, marveling at the slight starts that he made when I was able to sneak past his defenses and overwhelm him with pleasure.

"Domina!" He sounded like a man about to lose control. I felt the intense need to see that he did.

As I worked on his cock with my mouth, I reached a hand between my legs and worked my fingers over the hard bud of my clitoris. It was still sensitive from the release that I had been granted, but I ignored the nearly overwhelming urge to stop the pressure, concentrating on the keen edge of sensation that it was paired with, until I felt the little tremors again begin to build in my inner thighs.

It was still not enough.

When I released Caius' cock from my mouth there was a noise that sounded like a wet kiss in the still air. Placing both hands on his chest, I shimmied my way up his large frame until I was centered right on top of him, his erection pressing against the weeping wetness of my slit. I rubbed back and forth over him for a moment, enjoying the feel of his coarse hair on my inner thighs, my sensitive labia. Then I took a hand to the base of his hard shaft and positioned him so that in one quick move I could fill myself. Pistoning my hips downward, I paused for one long moment when he filled me. Then I began to move, forgoing any kind of slow, sweet loving for fast and hard. Squeezing his hips with my knees, I set a fast, nearly frantic pace, searching for pleasure that would wipe my mind of any other thoughts. I could still think, even with the jolt that passed through me every time my clitoris hit the taut skin and lean muscle of his pelvis. Still, I fisted my hands in the long coils of my hair and rode him, my hips moving as fast as bolts of lightning during a storm.

I shattered moments later, the pent-up tension in my muscles surging and then ebbing. He grunted after I had finished, pushing up into me while pulling me down with hands clasped tightly around my waist at the same time.

We remained like that for what could have been minutes or even hours, until finally I lifted myself off of him and slid down to snuggle up close beside him. Lying there after, held tight in his arms, I realized that I did not feel as I had wanted to.

Caius had made every effort to please me, had let me set the frenetic pace, and physically I was satisfied, my bones liquefied, my muscles lax. Mentally, I had many things swirling into an ever-thickening morass, and it kept me from the oblivion that I had been seeking. Even held close in Caius' impossibly large arms, I could not stop the flow of thoughts.

I could not move past the scene that I had observed the night before, in Marcus' chamber. There had been such obvious caring between the two men that I could not see where I fit into the puzzle. Though I obviously fulfilled some need for both of them, I could not see what it was.

I lay in Caius' arms, contemplating what to say, if anything, and how to say it. We had finished rather more quickly than usual, and were enjoying the sensation of lying pressed together, skin to skin.

At least, I was enjoying it. I really could not have said what the man was thinking. In the end it was Caius who broke the silence, not me.

"Why were you in the gladiators' quarters last night?"

I hesitated, the sensation of guilt causing a clutch in my gut. Lucius was away from our home again that night, and while Justinus had given his word that he would not hover outside the curtain, I was not certain what his word was worth.

"How do you know that I was?" I stroked a hand over a hard forearm that was furred with hair.

"Appius saw you." I did not respond for a long moment. Was that the only reason that Caius had known? Had he seen me in the moment before I had closed the curtain?

"Drusilla was meant to bring Christus back downstairs after . . . after." I was not certain that Christus had told the other men of the service that he had been made to perform for Hilaria. If he had not, I would not humiliate the man. It was not my information to divulge, not even to Caius or Marcus. I continued, "She was ill. Marina was busy. Justinus and Lucius were not home. Therefore I had no choice."

I had indeed had a choice, and I suspected that Caius knew it. I could easily have summoned one of our lesser slave girls to perform the task. But he did not comment, at least not on my flimsy rationale.

"Is Drusilla all right?" There was genuine concern in his voice, and though I too cared deeply about her welfare, I felt the ugly demon named jealousy clambering in my gut. I did not like what not knowing about Marcus and Caius did to me. I wanted, needed to ask what the relationship between the two men was. How I factored into it.

I could not force the words from my mouth.

"She was sleeping when I checked on her last night." I did not mention that there had been blood on her sheets that had caused me momentary concern. I had finally concluded that her monthly courses had started, but it had worried me. I did not share this with Caius. He did not need to hear about my slave girl's monthly bleeding.

He did not ask more about Drusilla, and I felt the jealousy begin to fade away. I was ashamed, and felt certain that my thoughts had been obvious. I stared at the floor, at the smoothness of the worn marble, biting my lip until I drew blood, unable to think of what next to say.

"Do you know that Marcus and I met before being purchased for the ludus?" Caius ran a hand down my arm, coming to rest on the swell of my belly. It was both comforting and a reminder that that belly was empty of child.

I knew that the touch had not been intended to bring me pain, but the emptiness never quite left.

"No." I had wondered, though. Neither man had been at the ludus for that long, only long enough for Marcus to establish himself as champion. The depth of their relationship seemed far too intense to have developed in such a short amount of time.

Caius' arm tightened around me and relaxed very slowly, as if he were willing it to do so. Not until it was again no more than firm against me did he speak again.

"Years ago, I was arrested by the Romans for refusal to join their army." My eyes narrowed; this cowardly act did not seem characteristic of the man that I knew. I could, however, see that he would have made a poor soldier—he was too impetuous, lived too much in the moment. "I lived in Thrace, and supported my two sisters and their children. Their husbands had both been killed by the Romans, and without me, they would have no means to survive."

My throat constricted; I had a suspicion that this was not going to be an easy story to hear. "Continue." I felt Caius shake his head from behind me, not as a negation, but to clear thoughts.

"In the end my actions caused more harm than good. In the army I could have sent money home, could have visited from time to time, though I could not see past the good living that I already made. I was very nearly killed on sight for refusing to join the army, and then where would they have been? But I have always been more likely to act before thinking."

His voice was self-deprecating, meant to make me smile, but I could not. After a long moment of my silence, he continued.

"So I was arrested, taken forcibly from my home in the middle of the night. Sold into slavery. I did not get to say goodbye, and did not know if the army left my family safe or not. I was taken to work in the *pits*." His voice became as hard as the rocks that lined those quarries, those rocks from which our own home was built. "You have no idea what life was like there. I have never been able to find words to describe it. It is hot, unrelentingly so, and you are not given much food or even water, for that matter, to counteract the thirst from the heat. You work all day, every day, so long as there is light."

His voice cracked, as if it had been baked for too long in the heat of which he spoke. "The people around you die, one by one, groups of them, and you wonder when your turn will come."

I could not think of anything to say that would comfort. I settled for a slight squeeze on the arm that held me, an urging to continue his story. I could not imagine the anger that this passionate warrior had felt, not being able to help those around him.

"The only comfort that I had was a man who called himself Marcus. He was from Gaul, a Celt who had been arrested for deserting the army. He had served as a soldier, but they had promised him that he would be released after two years. They changed their minds but still he left. He had a wife and a baby that he had yet to see."

Sickness began to paint itself over my skin.

"He returned home to find that both had been killed in a village raid. Then he was arrested for abandonment. He had been in the pits for two years when I arrived, an eternity given the average life expectancy there. He taught me to survive, to ration my water and food. His will was a formidable thing. He watched my back. We watched each other's backs. And we . . . found that we could provide other comforts to each other, as well."

This explained much of the affection, the closeness. Instead of satisfying me with the knowledge, however, I felt like a stone sinking in the sea. How could I ever compete with such a deep bond? They surely thought of me as vain and silly, pampered and naive.

"How did you meet him? I mean . . . the pits are huge, are they not?" I shivered as I nuzzled in closer.

"The night that I arrived in the pits I tried to escape. I was so angry at the captivity, I was nearly crazed." I could easily imagine what emotions a newly imposed slavery would bring to Caius. "I very nearly killed a guard. The guards as a whole were about to stone me to death, as an example to the others."

I anticipated the next words before Caius spoke them.

"Marcus saved my life. He had made an impression as a good worker, and he convinced them that he would be responsible for me. He convinced them that I would be a benefit, that I was strong and would be a good worker." He paused for a moment, and I could hear the ghosts of the past in his voice. "I still don't know why they listened to him, but they did. Marcus saved me."

I listened with wide eyes. The hardships that I had endured in my life, while very real to me, were nothing, absolutely nothing, compared with this.

"Often men who are owners of a ludus will visit the pits, searching for men that they think can prove themselves in the arena." Caius' voice was detached, as if he was telling a story that had happened to someone else, not to him. "It is every man's dream to be noticed on these visits. The life of a gladiator may not be easy, but it is luxury itself compared to life in the pits."

My heart ached. I could not bear that these two men, my two men, had endured such hardship when I, who had done nothing to deserve it, nothing save being born, had lived a life of comfort.

"The guards in the pits liked to rape their slaves. Men, women, children—they were not particular. The rapes were bloody, violent. On the day that your husband had come to the pit looking for new men, Marcus and I happened across one of the guards, one that we all hated, forcing himself on a young woman. She was new to the pits and terrified."

His voice lowered, and I shivered, sensing what was to come next, and not certain that I wanted to hear it. "Marcus and I tried to pull him off of her, but we were not as we are now—not as strong, you see. We were not well-fed, we did not have much water, and we were weak. So though we almost succeeded, attacking the guard by surprise, together, the brute struck the woman a blow that we could not protect her from. She fell, hit her head on a rock and died."

I was horrified. Not that they had not been able to save the poor woman, but that people died of fates like this. And I was mourning my life because my husband did not treat me well? Certainly I was permitted to feel as I felt, but this did put things into perspective.

"She looked rather like you." He reached up and threaded his hands through my long, long hair, turning my head so that he could kiss me softly on the cheek. "Dominus saw our fight with the guard and thought that we had the spirit he was looking for. He purchased us from the head of the pits, and we were taken to the ludus for training."

Another kiss, another pass of fingers through my hair.

"Once at the ludus, your fate is still not certain. You must train impossibly hard, and you must pass a strenuous and demanding test before you are permitted to take the oath, to join the brotherhood. It is nearly as grueling as being in the pits. The other men, the ones who will become your brothers, are cruel, cunning. They steal your food, they piss in your water. And you must endure it, for only through their rites of passage will you be truly accepted." His voice was quiet at this part, but held a tone that spoke well of the experience.

After the hell of the pits, perhaps it had been easy.

"Marcus and I were a comfort to each other here, as well as the pits. The bond between us is strong, stronger than any I have ever had in my life." His words were quiet, final, and caused dread to surge through me.

It sounded as if he was telling me something very specific, without saying the words. It sounded as if he was telling me that there was no room in their relationship for me.

Suddenly angry, and containing crushed hopes and dreams, I sat straight up, trying to pull his arms away from me, off of my skin. He held tight, sitting with me, and pulled me back against him, into his lap. His arms were like bands of unyielding stone. I had to go where he pulled me.

"We always felt that something was missing." He spoke softly, whispering into my ear. I reached up a hand, tucked a mussed dark lock behind my ear so that I could hear better. I did not dare to hope.

I needed him to say it before I dared to do that.

"After Marcus was first with you, he was . . . content. More content than I had been able to make him in a long time. I was jealous, but I did not understand. After I was with you the first time, I experienced that same contentment, that sense of fullness."

I could not help it. Anticipation began to blossom inside of me and twined with it was fear, fear that I was wrong.

"You contain a pureness that appeals to men who have lived the lives that we have. Your soul is kind, and you see the person, not their class."

Caius turned me so that I straddled his lap, so that my face was pressed against his and the thick curtain of my long hair sheltered us, rather as if we were in our own little world.

"But, Domina, do you not understand?" He kissed my cheeks, my forehead, my nose, and my lips before drawing back to look me in the eye. "We can never be more than this. There will never be more than stolen moments for you and me, for you and Marcus."

Ice began to form on my skin, tiny, multi-faceted crystals grown from my perspiration.

"A domina and her slaves cannot have a happy ending. You know this."

I reared back, trying to extricate myself from his arms. This time he let me go. Awkwardly I scrambled from hands and knees to my feet, crossing my hands over my breasts, though I knew that it was silly.

He had seen every part of me. Touched, tasted every part.

Regardless, I was upset, and I felt exposed. I clambered for the lacy sleep tunic that had been hastily tossed to the floor, and pulled it over my suddenly chilled skin. It did not cover much, sheer as it was, but I felt better for it. Thus armored, I turned again to face him where he still lay, on the hard floor, his eyes watching my every move with resignation. I planted my feet, angry.

"And if I become with child? Your child? His child? What then?" I knew the answer before he spoke, knew that I was being irrational.

"That child will be raised as yours, yours with your husband. You know this." Again, his words were gentle, but I felt as if each was a blow raining down on my head.

Tears welled in my eyes, though I tried to hold them back. I would not cry. I had no reason to cry. None of this was anything that I had not already known. It was my own fault that I had let myself hope, let myself dream. I thought fleetingly, frantically, of the chest of jewels that lay beneath my bed, but dismissed it just as easily. Things were not so simple as all that. Devastated, I turned on my heel and pushed through the curtain. I did not look at Caius as I left.

I found that I could not. I was not sure that I ever could again.

Many days later found me seated under the striped silk awning of the games, a munus to honor the passing of one of our so-called friends. Hilaria was thankfully not present that day, though I could not imagine what had kept her.

Baldurus had accompanied us on this outing. This was rare, a potential patron spending time publicly with his client. The class difference was simply too great for it to be a common occurrence.

Yet here he was, seated between my husband and me.

Lucius had told me in no uncertain terms before we had left the house that I was to impress the man, that I was to assure him of the immense chance that I was with child even then.

I was feeling ill, had been for days. What I wanted was to lay abed, a cool cup of water at hand, while Drusilla fanned me with a large palm leaf, to sink into a cool bath that might rinse away the sickly clamminess from my skin, and to have herbal oils rubbed into my temples with firm fingers. I had been under the weather for several days after my talk with Caius, but that had been due to nothing but my low spirits—my crushed, pulverized spirits. *This* was something else entirely, and I hoped that I had not caught a sickness.

So though I strove to keep a smile on my face, to be witty and entertaining, the truth was that the heat had made me wilt. Sweat ran down the sticky skin of my back in rivulets, and I worried that the charcoal-and-chalk powder ringing my eyes would melt and stripe my pale face. The mound of yellow hair upon my head was suffocating, even more so than usual, and my close-toed shoes seemed to have become too small.

I slipped my feet out of them and hid them under my skirts.

Baldurus had commented on my heat-flushed face and had fetched me a cup of wine, a rare act from a man who could have ordered it from any slave. The sweet liquid, when sipped into my mouth, made my tongue pucker despite the thread of melted honey that swirled through it. And the scent of roasting pig from a vendor that hovered outside our balcony made me nauseated.

"Are you feeling quite well, my dear?" Baldurus placed a hand on my shoulder, and I had to fight the urge to shrug off his touch. It was not a particularly offensive gesture—Baldurus was a kindly older man the same age that Lucius' father would be had he lived—but touch of any kind, right at that moment, did nothing but make my skin crawl.

I brightened my expression and sat up straight, wiping at my forehead surreptitiously with clenched fingers to remove the dripping sweat. "I am having a lovely time." I fanned my face with my hand and made a show of laughing gaily. "It is just so very hot."

From behind Baldurus I caught Lucius' eye, and he nodded with approval. I bit my tongue so that I did not snap at him.

The whole reason I had started to feel bad was the crushing reality that had descended after my talk with Caius. And the entire mess with both gladiators could be laid squarely at my husband's door. Well, that was not entirely true. I had seduced Marcus entirely of my own accord. But I was not feeling particularly rational at the moment. I was happy when the questioning and chatter ceased, and the games began.

I had been to too many games in my life as the domina of a ludus. I had seen many gruesome things there, injuries, death, blood. Atrocities that had given me nightmares. But none had affected me quite as they did that day. The sight of the viscous red blood, fountaining from veins that only moments earlier had been full of life, had bile rising in my throat. It coated my mouth, bitter and metallic. I fisted my hands in my tunic, fighting it back.

Lucius would never forgive me if I was to be ill in front of Baldurus.

This thought was followed by a realization that both Marcus and Caius would be taking their turns in the arena later that day. The thought of *their* blood spilling, *their* life force seeping out to soak into the dirty sand, was more than I could handle. I was upset with the pair of them, but that did not erase my feelings toward them.

A wave of incredible nausea passed through me from yellow-haired head to bare toes. I stood abruptly, pressed a clammy hand to my forehead. Despite the unrelenting heat, I was chilled, and my stomach turned, threatening to empty itself, though there was not much that could be emptied.

Lucius cast me a look of annoyance and anger, Baldurus one of concern.

"My lady?" Baldurus was the one who stood, not my husband. But when I stumbled, it was Drusilla who caught me.

Once righted, through blurred vision I looked toward the arena sands. I saw a large man with golden hair looking back at me, but I could not see who it was. That vision mixed with scarlet, and then everything faded to black.

I woke with my head cushioned in my slave girl's lap. I could hear Lucius apologizing, his voice wheedling and needy, to my ears at least. When I could focus, a cool cup with refreshing wet was pressed to my lips.

It brought me back enough to realize that I had fainted. Mortification washed over me even as my gullet tried to force the tiny sip of water back up. Looking up, I saw that Lucius looked thunderous, his hand on the shoulder of our potential patron.

Baldurus, though . . . I expected him to be angry as well,

or at least annoyed. I had ruined the day's entertainment, after all, and munera were enjoyable to all Roman citizens, not just those who could not afford any other entertainment. But the man looked overjoyed, and he knelt beside me, taking my hands in his own.

I exchanged a shocked glance with my husband. It was not common for someone of his class to kneel down to someone of mine.

"Don't you understand yet, darling girl?" The man seemed as exuberant as if he and I were very close, as if he were my pater familias and I had done something to benefit our house. "You are with child."

Chapter Twelve

That evening I still wanted nothing more than to stay in my room, alone. Lucius, however, insisted on holding yet another huge, impromptu celebration.

Marcus had sustained a painful gash to his midsection that day, but had still triumphed over his opponent. That was to be celebrated as well as my pregnancy, and, though it was not announced, I knew this was also a victory celebration of sorts for my husband.

We were now one step closer to securing Baldurus' patronage. He had asked Lucius to visit him the next week to discuss the details, which was all but a declaration of intent.

Though there was no guarantee that this child would live, this was at least confirmation that I could conceive, and that was what Baldurus had wanted. It would take years to build a family as large as his, and he was nothing if not a reasonable man.

Stretching out the stiffness in my neck, I marveled at the noise. I could not believe the din that our guests made. There did not seem to be that many of them, but the ceaseless talking, laughing, toasting had made my head throb.

I had asked to retreat to my room. Lucius had responded with scorn. He did not believe that pregnancy made a woman ill, believing instead that it was a self-fulfilling prophecy.

I resisted the urge to tell him that he should get pregnant and see if he still thought the same.

He had insisted that I join the party, and, moreover, that I be gay and as obviously happy as he.

I *was* happy, even as I cowered on a cushioned seat in a corner with Drusilla ceaselessly fanning me with a huge, waxy green leaf. My slave girl had been delighted at the news of a baby, though because of our position in society my time with the child would be limited, and the care of the infant would fall to her. She saw it as a blessing from Juno, and in my heart of hearts, I agreed.

The biggest desire I had ever carried, even more than my feelings for my gladiators, was my wish for a child. Now I would have one.

I was not barren.

My joy was double-edged, though. I was happy to be with child, yes, and even happier that that child had grown from the seed of one of two men whom I cared about, rather than from the warped seed of my husband. But that same husband would be the man to raise this child with me.

I also knew that my visits with Caius, my legitimate ones, were at an end. Though I could perhaps sneak some time with him illicitly, as I had with Marcus, things had changed.

I cringed when I saw Justinus leading the gladiators into

the room. Of course, no party at a ludus would be complete without them—they were entertainment, decoration. I would not normally have objected. Tonight, there were two men whom I very much did not want to see.

I cast my eyes to the floor. I wanted to fade away, to be invisible.

"To my wife!" Oh, it was not to be. I looked up, too sick to be startled at the words, and saw my husband toasting me, his cup of wine held high. "To my wife, and to our child!" He smiled at me then, the first kind look he had cast my way in months.

I returned the smile weakly, aware that the eyes of all of our guests were on me. I raised my cup, which contained lukewarm water, not wine, and forced a smile to my lips.

"To our child!" As Lucius spoke, I should have risen to my feet. I did not.

I could not.

Lucius appeared to be too deep in his cups to notice. He turned away with a shout of raucousness, and I raised my hands to my temples, rubbing them there.

"Let me do that, Domina." Drusilla set down the palm leaf and pressed her fingers on either side of my forehead. She had to take them away momentarily as a long, racking cough shook her slight body, and I twisted my body around to look at her with concern, though my tender abdomen protested.

"I am fine." She turned away to finish the bout, then wiped her hands on the back of her tunic and straightened her hair before turning back to me. "Close your eyes."

I meant to protest, to press and ask what was wrong. But

the pressure on my temples made me sigh, and I felt myself relax, just the slightest bit, for the first time all day. I would endure this for perhaps another hour, maybe slightly more if I had to. And then I would retire to my room.

"Pardon me, Domina, but I do believe that your attention is wanted." Drusilla's words were quiet, her voice still raspy from her coughing fit. I cracked open my eyes with reluctance, and saw that her finger pointed straight ahead.

To where the gladiators stood in a line.

I opened my eyes fully, sitting up straighter. Marcus and Caius were standing at the head of the line, in their position as champion and potential champion.

Both were looking right at me, and it sent a jolt through me. I stared back, unsure of what to do. I certainly could not go speak to them, though it looked very much like they wanted to speak to me. Tears threatened, and it was not the first time that day. What was *wrong* with me? It was just that . . . the child growing inside of me belonged to one of those two men. It was half of one of them, and half of me.

And I could not even go speak to them.

Before the tears could begin to trickle down my throat, Marcus smiled at me, just the smallest curve of his lips. Stunned that he had broken his rigidity, I blinked, and while I did, Caius, too, allowed his lips to curl briefly. His joy was more readily apparent, though I knew Marcus' would be no less deeply felt.

They returned to the stoic expression that they were ordered to keep almost immediately. But those tiny smiles told me what words could not, at least not in this situation, and I found myself warming all over, in a manner that had absolutely nothing to do with the heat in the room.

"You minx!" I groaned internally when I realized the voice belonged to Hilaria. Drusilla took her fingers away from my temples and again took up the waxy leaf, which allowed me to sit up straight.

"I'm stunned, Alba! Ogling the gladiators with a baby in your belly." Hilaria was flushed, with the consumption of too much wine and who knew what else, but she still sat much closer to me than the heat in the room should have allowed for.

I did not have a reply ready, so I said nothing. To deny too vehemently would set the patrician woman's nose for gossip-sniffing, and I would die before allowing her to know that one of those gladiators was the father of this baby.

She shoved a cup of wine into my hand. The aroma of the alcohol and spices turned my stomach, but she curled my fingers around the warm clay.

"You cannot toast your child with water!" She was giddy, and I thought she might be fully drunk. She placed an arm sloppily around my shoulders, and I cringed at the touch.

After my experience, alone in that room with her and Christus, I had no desire to have anything to do with this woman ever again. Perhaps she had reasons for why she was the way she was, but she had, ultimately, allowed herself to become the cruel, cunning woman I saw beside me.

I did not like that woman.

Perhaps this was my cue to excuse myself, even earlier than I had anticipated. Lucius looked to have consumed enough wine himself that he might not even notice.

I rose to my feet, Drusilla setting down the fan and looping a supportive arm around my waist.

"You will have to excuse me, Hilaria." I forced myself to smile, though I wanted to snarl. This woman, I thought, this woman deserved the treatment that some slaves received. "I wish I could stay and partake of your company. But I still am not feeling completely myself." Placing a hand flat on my belly, I rubbed it in a slow circle, indicating that my sickness was because of the baby.

I saw her eyes follow my hand, and saw anger flicker through them, though at first I did not understand what I had done to upset her. When she next raised her cup to her mouth, I saw the twinkle of the beads of her friendship ring, the one that matched the band she had given me.

The one that I was not wearing, that I never wanted to wear again.

Still, I did not want her upset, not when she could wreak such havoc. So I laughed weakly and made a show of flexing my hands. "They are so swollen. I cannot wear any of my rings."

The other woman considered this, then nodded slowly, though I was not convinced that she was appeased. It seemed that I was right, for even as she smiled, she reclined on the couch deliberately, as if she was mistress of our home. It was done intentionally to upset me, but I was feeling too ill to rise to the insult.

Her breast very nearly spilled out of the front of her nearly indecent tunic as she lay back on the cushions. She raised her own full cup of wine in my direction, and the red liquid slopped over the side onto her hand. With a giddy laugh, she brought the hand that had been spilled on to her lips, where a fast flickering tongue lapped at the sweetness.

"I shall see you five days hence, then, Alba." Wiping the rest of the stickiness sloppily on the side of her tunic, she narrowed her eyes and licked her lips lasciviously.

I was taken aback, both by her comment and by the sloth that she was displaying. The Hilaria I knew would never behave in such a manner in public. Confused, I cocked my head, even as Drusilla tugged at me slightly, indicating that I should leave.

"Have I been silly and forgotten an appointment?" I asked. Hilaria would be mad if I had, insulted that I would dare to not remember something as important as a meeting with her, but I truly could not recall agreeing to see her. Was she making this entire event up, to get back at me for not wearing the friendship ring?

She laughed again, showing her teeth, and fell all the way back on the couch, so that she was completely reclined. This time her breast did fall out of her tunic, hanging unfettered with its small, rosy peak out for everyone to see.

It would have been rude for me to point it out.

I forgot all about her naked flesh when she spoke.

"Did Lucius not tell you?" She made a clucking sound, her tongue slapping against her tongue and teeth. "I paid for two visits with your men. I reserved the right to take half my money back if I was not . . . satisfied . . . the first time."

She smiled then, that sly smile that made me wonder if she was as drunk as she appeared. "I was very satisfied."

My mind flashed to the image of her naked, bent over the chaise in the chamber where I met with Caius, ordering Christus to take her ass-wise. There had been something dark in her manner, in her words, something shadowed.

I really did wonder if something in the woman's mind was broken.

I then thought of the deposit of money, neatly written in Lucius' account book, and of the sum taken out immediately after. If he had needed to take it out so quickly, why had he not removed the entire sum?

Because we had not earned the entire sum.

I eyed Hilaria, unbelieving, and saw that she was watching me figure things out with glee apparent in her features. How had she discovered that I did not want her anywhere near our men? I had thought that I was discreet. But the woman had an uncanny talent for ferreting out information that others did not want her to have. Even so, I could not resist asking the question that was foremost in my mind.

It played right into her hands, but I had to know.

"Will you be meeting with Christus again, then?" I congratulated myself that my words were steady, though my voice was pitched slightly higher than usual.

I was reminded of a serpent then, a serpent from the underworld channeling itself through this woman. She spoke, and she relished every word like a delicious bite.

"Lucius really ought to confide in you more." She raised her eyebrows, and I was no longer at all certain that she was drunk, for she looked me right in the eye and, with a malicious upward curve of the lips, spoke the words I most did not want to hear.

"Christus was just a sample, just a taste. I paid well, and have proved myself discreet. I will have your champion, and your next strongest warrior. I would have them both together."

I could not respond. What was there to say? Somewhere along the line Hilaria had suspected my feelings for the men, and that, I was certain, was why she had proceeded on this path, despite Lucius' protests. She had paid a pretty sum, indeed, and now I knew why.

I would not reinforce her notions any further, no, I would not, even though I had never been so devastated.

I simply nodded, my face frozen, and turned to leave. As my feet carried me away from the party, toward my own room, my haven, I felt numb, and would look at nothing but my feet. This, this was worse than when Caius had confirmed what I had already known, that there was no future for us, no future for me and Marcus. Now, though I had a child in my belly, and though it was the child of a man whom I cared about deeply, I felt nothing but sorrow.

My belly was full, full with another life.

But I was alone.

Now that there was a babe growing in my belly, Lucius had transformed back into the husband that he had once been. Baldurus believed that a woman was indeed often ill when with child, and so Lucius changed his position on the matter. He was caring, he was attentive.

He made certain that any food, any drink that I desired was fetched immediately, no matter the cost. Any smell, sound, or touch that irritated me was eliminated promptly, and I received a gift almost every day. As my belly began to swell, just the slightest bit, and my breasts grew heavy, their tips darkening, I wanted for nothing. Regardless, my feelings for Lucius did not return, not even under his careful ministrations.

No, I wanted for nothing, nothing but the touch of the two men whom I could not, even to myself, admit I had come to... love?

I would not watch the training in the ludus, and my excuse was that the smell of the men's sweat made me ill. What I would have given to smell the sweat, the musk of either Marcus or Caius.

But I could not. It was too painful. I did not summon them, and I avoided any place where they would be. I ceased attending the games, and, to my astonishment, Lucius changed his attitude even about my public appearances by his side. He permitted my whimsies, even found them amusing.

I was again his cherished wife.

For me, it was entirely too late. I had seen the monster of greed that lurked inside, and the monster could not be erased from my memory now, could not be forced back into hiding. Truth be told, I would have found it much more pleasant to be ignored again. Then my time would have been my own.

Instead, my swollen belly and the rest of me were seated primly in my husband's office, entertaining Baldurus as he discussed yet more terms of his patronage with my husband. Though much of the nausea had passed, I was still tired, and my appetite was still off. I grew uncomfortable easily, and sitting on one of the hard-backed chairs in this dim room did not help.

At least Justinus was not present. I had noted that the better Lucius treated me, the angrier Justinus seemed to grow. I was still in awe that my husband permitted his attitude, which in my opinion was entirely inappropriate for a slave. Then again, I knew very well that I held a double standard for slaves. In my mind, all slaves save Justinus were entitled to respect, to a say in their lives. Justinus, on the other hand . . . well, I knew that my thoughts of him were not fair. Again, I reminded myself that I could not judge him.

I was freeborn.

He was a slave.

It did not make me like the man any more, and so it was refreshing that he was not present here.

"Things are well with you, my lady?" I found it a charming quirk of Baldurus' that he would address me as his lady, though I was lower in social standing than he. He was, in actuality, a delightful man, a rare find in Roman society.

I wished that I could find a tactful way to tell him that my husband, in comparison, was not.

I placed a hand on the expanse of my belly, finding it softer than it usually was. As always, touching my stomach, knowing that a life was growing beneath my very fingers, sent a thrill through me.

"I see that it is well." Baldurus smiled, then lifted his cup in toast. Lucius followed suit.

Though I was happy to be with child, I still found it difficult to share in their joy. The heart wanted what it wanted, this I knew. Unfortunately, what I wanted was not available to me.

Involved in my own thoughts as I was, I did not pay Justinus much heed when he made an abrupt, excitable appearance in the small room. Instead, I sipped at my cup of wine—slowly sipped, for I still found that the smell of the spices and honey turned my stomach. It was not until Baldurus' exclamation erupted loudly in my ear that I turned back to the conversation.

"This cannot be. Batiatus? His wife? Their children? All dead?" There was sorrow under the disbelief of our patron, a deep blue streak of it.

"I beg your pardon?" I was certain that I had missed something. Baldurus turned to me, opened his mouth to begin speaking, but Lucius interjected, setting his cup down with a decisive click.

"I am not worried. It is a lesson to others to keep a tighter rein on their slaves." His voice was disapproving, suggesting almost that these people had deserved what had happened. I looked at my husband with eyes wide in disbelief. Could he really be so dismissive of the death of another man, his wife and children? One of our colleagues, someone with whom we had shared food and drink? I knew that there was much competition between owners of the different ludi in and around Rome, but this seemed extreme to me.

There was that greed again, peering out of my husband's eyes. I understood in that moment that greed, and the pressure to live up to his father, and his father before him—to make the ludus thrive—would always take precedence over me.

It would take precedence over our children as well, and the lack of a blood bond in the relationship was not likely to help matters.

I was still having trouble believing it, certain that I had misunderstood.

"Are you saying that the slaves of the House of Batiatus have escaped? That they slaughtered their owners?" There was a lurch in my stomach as I thought of the man, whom I did not know well, and of his family.

He had young children, though; that I remembered quite clearly. Two small boys, imps really, who had a bloodthirsty fascination with their father's gladiators, and with the arena. And a small girl, barely more than a babe in arms, with a tiny tuft of black hair on the top of her small head.

I hugged my arms tightly to my stomach.

I did not care so much that the slaves had escaped. The man had not treated them well, and he was very wealthy—he could well have afforded to purchase more. But that he had been killed for their freedom—to me it spoke of a serious flaw in our so-called civilized Roman society.

"Where did they go? How many of them escaped?" This was from Baldurus, to Justinus. Lucius snorted and chugged at his wine, not seeming to think that the situation warranted as much importance as the rest of us were applying to it.

His desire for success had killed his compassion. It made me ill.

"They made their way out of the city, after stealing weapons from Roman soldiers whom they met in the street. About fifty of their two hundred, gladiators and house slaves both, escaped. They were led by Spartacus, the champion of their house. He that Marcus has not yet met. That is all I know. I knew that I should come straight here to report." I saw that Justinus stole a glance at Lucius, perhaps expecting praise, but my husband sat still with that look of disdain frozen on his face.

Batiatus and his family lived outside the city limits, in Capua. If the escaped slaves had made their way through Rome and beyond, then we were far out of harm's way by now, since our home was situated on the side of the city closest to Capua.

"I do not like this." Baldurus sat up straight in his chair—*he* was worthy of cushions, I noted, though a pregnant wife still was not—and ran shaking fingers through thinning hair the color of iron. I looked at him with concern, for he was old, and I was not sure how his constitution handled surprises.

"I am sure that your home will be fine." I reached out a hand, placed it on the man's forearm in an attempt to soothe.

Lucius again snorted air through his nose. "Yes, so long as your slaves are kept under tight control." When Baldurus looked up, looked right at him, appalled, my husband jerked as if he was a marionette on strings. "I beg apology, Bal— my lord. Of course your household is well-run. I have never thought otherwise."

Baldurus glowered at my husband, something that I noted with no small amusement. Despite the appearance of fragility wrought by his papery skin, his fine wrinkles, and his brittle bones, the man could still strike terror into one's heart when he was of a mind.

I noticed that Justinus did not look happy either, and suspected that he had not appreciated the remarks about slaves being kept under tight control.

"I should think you would be concerned about the potential danger to your wife in her condition." Baldurus mopped at a suddenly sweaty forehead with the back of his hand. "If it were my wife, I would take precautions to ensure her safety, and the safety of the babe."

Again, I found Lucius' reaction very nearly comical. Having lived with him for as many years as I had, I could read the thoughts on his face, and knew that he needed to make amends for his verbal slip. I could also see that he, too, was noting Baldurus' fragility for the first time—the man was sixty if he was a day.

It would be imperative, at least to my husband, to secure this patronage before the man died or became too sick to conduct his affairs.

"What would you suggest?" Lucius asked. Placing his cup down on his desk, he laced his fingers together and schooled his face into a mask of concern. I could see that it was not genuine, and felt disgusted.

This may not have been his child by blood or by seed, but he had had a hand in creating it all the same. And I was his wife, a part of his familia.

I would have thought that he might care, that he might be able to see past his own concerns.

Apparently that was too much to ask.

Baldurus seemed appeased by the appearance that Lucius presented, however, for he relaxed back into his chair. Gulping at his honeyed wine as if it was water, he seemed to be replenishing his strength. I turned to Justinus, intending to get him to fetch the man more, but my husband's slave was paying attention to no one but Lucius, and with him he still did not look happy.

"You have a house by the sea, do you not? A small one?" Lucius nodded slowly at Baldurus' words, not making the connection between the slaves' revolt and our other home.

We had not visited the house on the coast in years. It had once belonged to my father, and had been gifted to our household when I had made my vows to Lucius.

My spirits rose unaccountably at the thought of the tiny villa by the sea. I thought again of Drusilla and our friendship rings, of the happy hours that we had spent there as girls.

"I would dispatch Alba there, with several of your gladiators, until the upheaval in the city has died down." He nodded sharply, satisfied with the idea. "Yes, that is what I would do."

Lucius did not like this idea, or, more, did not like what it would cost. "Surely that displays an overabundance of caution?" His protests sounded thin and weedy. "This man, this Spartacus, was clearly a rebel. I do not think that this will be a recurring problem."

"Perhaps not." Baldurus inclined his head. "But perhaps it will give other slaves the idea that they had not thought of themselves. I would say to send her alone, but obviously a woman cannot travel by herself, especially not a woman who is with child. Surely there are men that you trust amongst your slaves."

The implication was that if our house was run as his was run, there would absolutely be men that one would trust with their life. I saw Lucius glance at Justinus and open his mouth to speak.

"You might trust this man, but I do not," I said. I could not keep silent, could not tolerate for even a moment the thought of being cooped up in a house alone with Justinus. Distracted from his disgruntled glares at my husband, the slave let me see the extent of his loathing for me. "He does not have the physical strength that the gladiators do. I would have a number of them accompany me, if I am to go."

Lucius sputtered, spraying droplets of tart-smelling red wine into the air. "I cannot spare several of my men from their training to stay with you at the coast for an indeterminate length of time." He very nearly laughed at the end of his words, as if the mere suggestion was ridiculous. "You will have to take Justinus, and be satisfied with that. Drusilla as well, of course." It sounded as though he was offering me a great boon by offering me the latter, and I supposed that he thought he was.

This made the affable Baldurus finally snap, his face becoming thunderous like a cloud before a storm. Standing, perhaps not that quickly or gracefully but making an impression all the same, he smacked his pottery cup onto Lucius' desk hard enough that it split into two. One of the shards sliced into the side of his thumb, and blood welled up in the cut, thick and red, but he did not seem to notice or care. With palms placed flat on the old wood, he leaned in toward Lucius, ensuring that my husband paid attention.

"We are about to enter into a very important contract, you and I." Baldurus' voice as he spoke was firm. "One of the conditions of that contract was children. The gods have blessed you with one in your wife's belly, after many years, I might add. I would protect that life before anything else."

Having gotten across that Lucius had best take his advice

if he wanted to sign this contract, he took a step back, visibly attempting to control himself.

I wanted to applaud.

"Now. Alba says that she does not trust this man, I can see for myself that he does not have the strength to physically protect her. It is a legitimate concern." With difficulty, the man sat back down in his chair. Justinus looked outraged at the comments on his physique, but at least knew enough to hold his tongue. "If the woman wants gladiators to protect her, what is the harm? You have scores, and besides, the games will not run until the fervor over this incident dies down, I assure you. Your men missing some training is a small price to pay for the safety of your wife and child."

Lucius' face looked pinched, but eventually he nodded. What other choice did he have? "Very well. I will send two gladiators. We cannot afford to send more. Theocles . . . and Animus, I think." These were not men whom I knew, and if I knew my husband, they would be two of his weakest, the two whom he would not so much miss in their absence.

For all I knew, they might be fresh purchases from the market, men who had not yet been through training or taken the vow to our house.

"Two is better than nothing." Baldurus conceded this point, having won the match.

Sensing an ally in the elderly man, I decided to press my own point. Nerves fluttered through my veins as I spoke, but I was nearly certain that I could get Baldurus to agree, that Lucius would not, could not, do anything to me.

Neither could Justinus. I eyed the man with dislike. He

might have had a tale to tell on me, but I had one on him, as well.

"No." I raised my chin and tried to settle my nerves. "No. I want two of the strongest, two of the best. I will not feel safe otherwise."

I knew, of course, exactly who I would feel safest with, though I did not try to deny, even to myself, that my safety was not the concern at the forefront of my mind.

Lucius looked as if he could spit. Baldurus, however, nodded approvingly.

I did not look at Justinus. I did not care what he thought.

"I will take Drusilla, of course. But I will also take the two gladiators that I feel are most loyal to you, and that are the strongest. Would you really send me with two whose behavior toward me cannot be anticipated?"

I took a deep breath.

Did I dare to say it?

I found that I did.

"I will have Marcus, the champion. And I will have Caius. And then this baby, this baby and I both, will certainly be safe."

Lucius looked as if he had tasted a fig that had been plucked from its branch before fully ripening.

"Alba, you know that you cannot have those two. Any other gladiators—*any* of them, and I will find a way to work around it. But Hilaria—"

He intercepted the raised eyebrow that Baldurus had sent his way, and instantly quieted.

"Surely the peace of mind of the mother of your child is not too much to ask?" Baldurus asked.

I looked to Lucius as he looked to me, words passing between us without needing to be spoken. We both knew that this was not his child, not his seed. He could hardly use that as an excuse, not when he intended to pass this child off as his own. Lucius responded slowly, as if choosing his next words carefully.

"We have a . . . meeting . . . between those two gladiators and . . . and a noble." I noticed that he did not specify that it was a noble*woman*. Money exchanged for sex was not something that Baldurus would approve it—it went against the virtues of a true Roman. It showed a measure of respect for our household that he did not question further. "It has been paid for. I cannot go back on my word."

"You do not need to go back on your word." Baldurus spoke to Lucius as he might to a child, and I saw my husband's back stiffen as he interpreted the tone. I wondered if perhaps the man was reconsidering his deal with Lucius. "You need only postpone it, until danger has passed. Any honorable Roman will understand that the safety of your wife and child comes first."

From the corner of my eye I saw Lucius cast me another look, which I did not return. We both knew what the other was thinking—Hilaria was not an honorable Roman in any sense. She was a spoiled, petty, possibly half-mad widow with enough wealth to indulge herself.

She would not be happy that her meeting with Caius and Marcus was postponed.

Of course, this could all be solved if I amended my decision, if I chose different men to accompany me to the coast.

This, I was sure, was what Lucius was trying to will me to say when he glared at me as he did, as subtly as he could.

"Well, my dear?" Baldurus turned toward me, his face kind and open. "What do you think?"

I was not accustomed to being asked what I thought. Though it was not what my husband wanted, I decided to speak the truth.

"I want Marcus and Caius."

Chapter Thirteen

Visions of a loving reunion, of a communal excitement now that we were all to have time together, were shattered like the pottery cup that Baldurus had smashed on my husband's desk.

Perhaps I had had romantic thoughts of the three of us by the sea. Certainly I had. I cared for them both, after all. But for them both to withhold any smile, any touch, any look for the past days that we had been in nearly constant company seemed cruel.

Caius and Marcus were nothing if not honorable men. Lucius had ordered them to ride in a procession, one on horseback in front of my *carpentum*—my wagon—and one with another horse behind. Neither man so much as looked my way during the entire long ride to our house by the sea... and it *was* a long, nearly interminable ride.

I supposed that I should have been grateful that they were following directions so clearly, that they truly did consider my safety their priority. But to be so close to men with whom

I had shared so much, and to not receive so much as a sweet smile, was infuriating.

But to both me and Drusilla, who rode with me, the end of the three-day journey could not come fast enough.

Normally I could have passed the time quite well with my slave girl. We had spent countless hours alone together, just like this, since our girlhoods. I feared, however, that the carpentum ride was not agreeing with her. She was nauseated and weak most of the way, regardless of whether we rode over hills or flat earth, and had a dreadful cough that would not desist, no matter how many times she tried to clear her lungs.

I had given her my palla to wrap around herself, to cover her face, in hopes of keeping the dust out of her breath, but it did not seem to help overmuch.

I noticed that she was very careful about storing away the cloths that she coughed into, and I could only assume that it was for my benefit. When I asked her why she tried so very hard to keep me from seeing, she told me that what she emptied out of her insides was not pleasant, and that she was worried that the sight might make me ill, in my condition.

I frowned at her words—I was made of sterner stuff than that, and she very well knew it. But she would not change her mind, and as such I felt guilty about the extra troubles that she went to whilst already ill.

It was with no end of relief that, by the end of the third day, I thought I detected the faintest hint of salt on the air. Sitting up straight, I wiped sweaty palms on the lap of my travel-sodden tunic and inhaled deeply.

Yes. Yes! There was salt, and the faintest hint of what I remembered being told was seaweed. I had not been to our house by the sea for many years, not since I was a girl, but I remembered asking my father once about that nearly herbal smell, tinged with brine. He had shown me a clump of the slimy green the next day. I had squealed and run away, then come back hesitantly and held it in my hand.

I was not sure why, exactly, that memory chose to surface. Yes, this house had once belonged to my family, but I had not thought of them for a very long time, not since shortly after I had married Lucius. There was no point in doing so. I was no longer part of that familia, no longer had any alliance with my mother, my father, my four brothers or two sisters. Lucius was my pater familias, and though I intended to not think of him any more than I had do on this trip away, the fact remained that I was bonded to him for life.

Or until he decided to divorce me, and now that I carried a baby in my belly, I did not think that likely.

Shaking my head, I kept it deliberately empty as we turned onto the road that I knew led to the small house. I had not thought about seeing the house again—my focus had been strictly on the two men who would accompany me, and what would happen with our relationship. I was unprepared for the surge of joy that threaded its way through my being as we rolled farther and farther down that rutted road.

The sight of grass had my lips curving into a smile. The pale green spears waved in the salty wind, and I was amazed that it had been so long since I had seen such a simple thing. And the trees were different, too—dark twisted branches that would have borne olive fruit if they were not so close to the sea.

And the house itself, when it finally came into view. It was no bigger than perhaps a quarter of my home with Lucius in Rome, but it had stood up well over time. The stones that made up the walls were perhaps a bit more worn from the stinging spray, but otherwise it looked exactly as it had, standing on the small crest of a hill that overlooked a beach with sand, sand not tainted with the blood of the arena.

I was in fine spirits when we stopped in the yard. Drusilla and I both stood in the front of the carpentum before our horse had completely stopped, anxious for both a better look, and to remove ourselves from the damnable rolling cart that we had spent entirely too much time in over the past three days.

I jumped from the carpentum before either Marcus or Caius could dismount and offer me an arm. My weariness from the trip faded considerably as soon as my feet touched the ground. I turned back to watch Drusilla also clamber down, certain that she was as excited as I to return to this place, but a fit of coughing overtook her as she stepped down.

She shook off my hand, insisting that she was all right. "I will help to unload our supplies." Since the house was located nearly a half day's journey from any town, we had several carts full of food, clothing, and the other things that we would need while we holed up by the sea. A handful of our other household slaves had journeyed with us, and they could unload before they turned around and retraced their steps. I had thought it ridiculous to have these slaves make the journey simply to help us set up house, but Baldurus had insisted. Lucius had reluctantly acquiesced.

"You will do no such thing," I said. A trickle of unease wound its way through my buoyant spirits. Drusilla had never been ill a day in her life to my recollection, not until recently. "You will go lie down. You may make up your own bed, and that is it." With arched eyebrows, I tried to sound stern; otherwise, I knew that she would disobey me and try to work.

With pinched lips, she nodded curtly. I was surprised that she did not argue the point further, and concluded that she really must not be feeling well.

"May I take linens into the slave's quarters?" Drusilla asked. I very nearly laughed. Though this house was small in comparison with the one that we inhabited in the city, it still had seven or eight sleeping chambers, and those were not counting the ones for the slaves. With only me, Drusilla, Marcus, and Caius, I thought it would be cruel to the extreme to force them all into the small, dreary area while I rattled about above, alone.

"No," I said firmly. Drusilla looked shocked that I would refuse her that, but smoothed her features over quickly, before I could continue. "No, but you may take them into any room that you like above. Then, you will make up your bed and go for a rest. I mean it."

She smiled then, and nodded before turning to walk away. I felt somewhat lost without her by my side. She had been my constant companion for the last few days, and had been a buffer, of sorts, between myself and the two men with whom I was to take up residence.

Those men were currently helping the other slaves haul supplies off the carts, and I tried not to look too intently at their muscles straining as they did so. Truth be told, I was still somewhat irritated with the pair of them, though I could not have said why, precisely. Probably it was that I was so close to them, closer than usual, and yet they did not seem as if they would welcome my touch.

This reminder put me into a bit of a snit. With pursed lips I turned and stalked down the hill, toward the sea. The closer I got, the more brisk the wind became, whipping my loose hair every which way, but instead of annoying me, I found it freeing.

Orcus take all the men, anyway. I did not need them. Stooping to remove my sandals before grains of sand could catch in them and rub the skin off my feet, I ran the last stretch to the water, inhaling a great lungful of the crisp air.

Maybe I would just stay here, me and the baby and Drusilla. I could be Lucius' wife in name, could return for public events, and otherwise just stay, raise my child by the sea.

By the sea, and away from the blood and death that was the arena. Away from gladiators, and my feelings for them.

Lucius would likely not even notice I was gone. That thought sent a thousand tiny needles into my heart, and my happy mood began to sink.

I fell to my knees with it, kneeling in the sand, not caring that I was dirtying the knees of my already filthy tunic.

I no longer had any delusions about my importance in my husband's life. He cared about my place in his life as his wife, as mother to his "children," yes, certainly. But I was no more than a placeholder, interchangeable with thousands of other Roman women.

I could perhaps have dealt with the disillusionment that this revelation had brought, had it not been for Caius and Marcus. Now, because I knew them, I knew that more existed, knew how very happy I could be if only the situation presented itself.

And yet, I knew, deep down I knew, that that happiness could not last forever. Caius' words echoed in my head, telling me that a domina and her slaves could never find happiness together.

But this seemed like a gift from the gods, this time together, unfettered by my restraints from my husband, from Caius and Marcus' duties.

And yet it seemed that they could not, would not accept that gift, though Caius had professed that they both cared for me, found something in me that they could not provide for each other.

Though being with child gave me odd rushes of emotion at inappropriate times, I found that now I felt strangely empty. It was quite odd, actually, that I should be so full, full with a burgeoning life, and feel so little.

Inhaling yet another deep breath, I lay back on the sand, stretched my legs out in front of me. I curled my toes into the mounds of tiny granules, ran my fingers through the piles and let it grind under my fingernails.

This tiny bit of peace seemed to be a gift. Or perhaps it was lethargy. Either way, I felt my body begin to relax, limb by limb.

Here, even though it seemed I would not have the special time with my two gladiators, I still would be happier than at home in the city. Here, no one would judge me, no one would watch me constantly. I would not be a pawn in my husband's political games.

Perhaps I could convince my husband, or more likely

convince Baldurus who would in turn convince Lucius, that being at the sea did wonders for both my health and the health of my baby. Perhaps I could remain here until the baby was born, postponing the arrival home.

Either way, I was grateful for the respite. I closed my eyes, lulled by the sound of the waves, cushioned by the sand that formed itself to my body. I was sad that Batiatus and his family had died, but was grateful that it had concerned Baldurus.

As I had recently learned, sometimes the only way to get through life was to take what small comforts were offered.

I was taking it, was taking this, even if it still was not exactly what my heart desired.

"Domina." I heard the title as if through water, waving and wet as it reached my ears. "Domina."

There was a touch on my shoulder, a transfer of heat.

I shifted, stretched. I felt more relaxed than I had in a very long time.

"Domina!" The voice grew more insistent. It was a male voice, one that sent shivers running down my spine.

I was too comfortable to move, let alone to speak.

"Alba!" The touch on my shoulder began to shake, jolting me out of the lovely web of relaxation that I had been floating in.

I opened my eyes, found another set of eyes directly above me, looking down into mine.

I started, not expecting a person to be right there. In a fast moment, what had happened to Batiatus and his family flashed through my mind, and I instinctively curled into a small ball, scared, with my arms wrapped tightly around my womb. It seemed that the fate of our peers had affected me more than I had realized.

"Alba. It is Marcus." A large hand rubbed over my back soothingly, and I realized that I knew that touch. Knew those eyes, those dark, nearly black eyes.

Slowly, bit by bit, I uncurled myself. As I did, I began to remember where I was. The sound of the sea lapping at the sand intruded upon my consciousness, as did the smell of brine in the air.

I was at our home by the sea, with Drusilla, Marcus, and Caius. I had fallen asleep on the sand, and given the fact that the frigid water was now threatening to lap at my toes, I had fallen asleep some hours ago.

I sat up, turning my body away from Marcus. "Where are the others?"

Undeterred by the chill I presented, Marcus sat next to me on the sand. Or perhaps he simply did not notice. Regardless, I found it disconcerting to feel the heat of his body, radiating toward me, warming my own flesh after the complete lack of attention from him the past few days.

"Drusilla is ill." He stared out to sea as he spoke. "I fear the house has not been prepared for you much in the past hours. She wanted to rise, to work, but has been unable to."

I frowned, then made to get to my feet. "I must check on her."

Fingers circled my ankle before I could move even a step. "She is sleeping." He rose as well, and stood beside me as I stared out to the open water.

Instead of feeling refreshed by my nap, I felt out of sorts, disoriented. Irritable. "And what have you been doing?" I noted that his skin was quite dry, rather than covered with the sheen of sweat that I was accustomed to seeing on it.

I felt those luminous eyes upon me, but refused to return the stare. "I have been guarding you, as per my orders from your husband. Caius has been unpacking our supplies, since Drusilla has been unable to. We have fruit and boiled beans for supper, if you are hungry."

I felt particularly nasty, given the calm tone with which he explained things to me. With an exaggerated sigh, I raked fingers through the tangles of my hair and grimaced when I found granules of sand caked in it.

"I should think that I am quite safe here. Go back inside. I wish to bathe in the sea." Crossing my arms over my soft belly, I clasped the hem of my now-damp tunic in my hands and tugged it up an inch.

Marcus did not move. Nor did he look at me.

It was infuriating, and given my current disposition, I very nearly screamed in agitation.

"I said, go inside." I glared at him and very narrowly saved myself from stomping my foot. Such an action was suited to someone with a temperament like Hilaria's. I would not stoop that low.

Finally, finally, Marcus turned to look at me. I noticed then how very large of a man he was. The top of my head barely grazed his chest.

He could do whatever he wanted with me, and I would not be able to do a thing about it.

Rather than frightening me, I found it exciting.

I stuck my chin out in stubbornness. I could not look down upon him, but I could be firm. "I am your domina. I have ordered you to go inside."

He nodded and cast his eyes to the ground. His words, however, were anything but amenable.

"Apologies, Domina. I recognize your authority. However, your husband is my pater familias, as well as yours, and his orders were that you be guarded day and night. So that is what I must do."

I laughed then, and knew very well that my laugh was tinged with hysteria. So I could not have a break from my husband's dictatorship even here, when he was miles away.

"Fine." My words were clipped, from anger and frustration. "Fine. Stay. But I will bathe in the ocean as I wish." Without bothering to wait for his reaction, I pulled my tunic up and over my head. It caught on the long ropes of my mussed hair, but one hard rip and I was free.

I dropped the cloth heedlessly on the sand, not caring how much filthier the thing got. I would burn it. I never wanted to see it again.

Naked, I was unprepared for the chill of the air off the water. It struck like a slap, causing goose pimples to hump over my skin in rapidly cresting waves. My nipples, larger and darker with pregnancy than they had ever been before, contracted so fast that it was painful. I shivered, suddenly so cold that I was unsure if my bath was a wise idea. I would be damned if I would back down before Marcus. Head held high, I walked into the water. The cold of the water now, in the early hours of night, was numbing.

It was just what I wanted.

I continued to march forward, the water reaching my ankles, my knees, my cunt. Then my hips, my belly, and finally my shoulders. Curling into a ball, I ducked my head beneath the surface, and nearly screamed with the sensation. The water intruded in my ears, my eyes, up my nose, into my mouth. It was like a thousand knives, all slicing into my flesh. But I gritted my teeth, unwilling to run back out of the water. After a long moment, a ridiculously long one, the knives stopped their stabbing, and my flesh became blissfully numb.

I was not stupid. I would not stay in the water long enough that I would get sick. But I had a point to prove, though I was not entirely sure what it was, and so I would stay until I was done.

Tilting my head back, I worked my fingers through my hair, dislodging grains of sand. Now that my body had acclimated to the water, at least a bit, it seemed warmer to be in than out, so I remained that way, head tipped back, facing the shore. I was completely submerged, but for my face, and though my lips were numb, it felt wondrous to have finally replaced the grime of travel with the salt of the sea that I so loved.

I looked toward the shore, allowing myself to float as I did. I had not forgotten how, it seemed, though it had been so many years since I had been to the coast.

Marcus was standing at the very edge of the water. Gone was his characteristic rigidity. With one hand shading his eyes, he squinted out in my direction, his face painted with uncertainty.

It seemed that I had finally managed to affect him. I had finally broken through that damned honor, that armor of his damned brotherhood.

The satisfaction that surged through me told me that that was the point I had wanted to prove. Leaning forward, waving my arms through the water, I felt my feet touch the bottom, wriggled my toes in the sand one last time. Then I began to make my way back to the shore.

I moved slowly, deliberately. I told myself that it was because I was loath to go in, but I knew that that was not the truth. I wanted to affect Marcus even more, wanted him to be affected by the sight of me. And so I moved slowly, allowing the water to swirl around my body in the reverse manner it had when I had submerged. A mirror image of my baptism in the sea, first my breasts became visible, then my belly. My hips, my legs, all were naked and open to his stare.

I held my hands out in front of me as I walked, and was struck by the contrast between their icy white sheen and the darkness of the water.

I walked straight to the edge of the water, stumbling only a bit as the suction of the liquid released me. This brought me directly in front of Marcus, who stared down at me, confused.

I kept moving, walking right into his arms.

Rising up onto the tips of my toes, I wrapped my arms around his neck, his shoulders. I pressed my body squarely against his own, and luxuriated in the juxtaposition of my icy cold temperature against the innate heat that seemed to burn inside of his skin.

I could not kiss his lips from where I stood—I was not tall

enough. But I fastened my mouth over one of his nipples and suckled it into my mouth, hard.

I felt his cock rear to life, going from semi-erect to hard and hot in the space of a breath. At the same time he recoiled from the frigidity of my skin, but for only a moment.

My assault had done as I had hoped. Though he stood stiff for that long moment, as if trying to find a way out of my embrace, out of this relationship that we both knew could never be, not for real, he gave in quickly.

Cupping his hands under the slippery globes of my bottom, he hoisted me up until our faces were level. I mashed my mouth against his, my tongue already seeking. I clasped my legs around his waist, rubbed my center, which had remained hot despite the cold, rubbed it right over the leathers that covered his erection.

I kissed him with every pent-up emotion that I possessed spilling out of my lips and into him. He swallowed them and returned the fervor, licking over my mouth, my tongue, my teeth. Finally he buried his face into my neck, kissed the corded muscle there, and groaned as if in defeat. With my arms and legs still twined about him, I pulled back, tried to search the face that he was hiding. He kept his face buried, speaking into my skin. I felt the vibrations hum over my shoulder.

"Alba." That was all that he said. "Alba."

I wanted more. I wanted an indication that this was not the last time we would touch. I wanted to know that he and Caius and I could be together, at least while we were here.

I wanted to hear him say that he wanted me, that they

both did. That they both wanted me more than the lives they had back in Rome.

That they would sacrifice for me. For me and for my child.

I wanted them to be everything that my husband was not.

Before I could express my desires, before the flood of words could start, I sensed movement. Looking up, I squinted into the distance, saw a figure at the top of the small hill on which the house sat.

It was Caius. He was watching our embrace, had possibly been watching it since it had started. His body was rigid, tense, his hands fisted, his feet planted wide.

He did not look happy.

I hummed a sound out of my throat. Marcus turned, with me still clasped in his arms. I knew when he saw what I had, for his body also tensed, the muscles contained beneath his skin pressing against me.

Now facing the other direction, I could no longer see Caius, and protested. Instead of turning back around, Marcus simply reached a big hand up, trailing over my back until it threaded into my hair. A gesture of comfort, I was not appeased, and squirmed until he put me back on my own feet.

When I turned around again, this time by myself, Caius was gone.

Chapter Fourteen

Neither Caius nor Marcus mentioned the embrace on the beach, not that evening, not in any of the days following. Neither of them tried to touch me again, either.

I was frustrated. I was angry. I did not have much time to ruminate on my feelings, however, for Drusilla continued to lie abed. She was sick, very sick, and I was thinking very seriously of sending back to Rome for a doctor.

The only thing keeping me from doing so was Drusilla herself. She insisted that it was simply the journey that had drained her, that she would be fine any day now. And as soon as I reached the end of my patience, as soon as I had decided that she needed medical attention, she would take a turn for the better, would get out of bed and bathe, even take a meal.

I vowed that I would not be convinced the next time she took a turn for the worse. I would send for a doctor, for a medic, even. I did not need to send all the way back to Rome—I would simply have Caius or Marcus ride to the town a half day's journey away. Surely they would have a medical expert of some sort.

If either of the men would go, that was. As Marcus had said, they had given their word to my husband that they would care for me, that they would not leave my side, and that was exactly what they did.

It was maddening. Wherever I went, one of them was ten paces behind me. They slept in shifts, so that one was always awake to watch over me as I slept. They even hovered outside the door while I used the chamber pot, and since I was with child, that was quite often.

I knew that they did not think me that much in danger. The revolt led by Spartacus had almost certainly been a freak occurrence. No, they did not think I was in danger . . . but they had given their word, and they would be true to it or die.

Truthfully, though I would have enjoyed just a moment's peace, knowing that I was well and truly alone, I was somewhat impressed with their unwavering attention to their vow. Not all men would have taken their duties that seriously.

I might have found the company pleasant, but for two things. The first was that, since Drusilla was sick and the four of us were alone in the house, I had to learn to do things that I had never before been expected to take on. Cooking, cleaning, washing up—I was the only other woman, and so it was my duty.

I made many mistakes. I did not appreciate an audience in the direct vicinity when I made bread that was flat and hard, or when I tried to make up a bed. I knew that I could have sent back to Rome, appealed to Lucius, and he would have sent one of our other girls to help me—Marina, most likely. But then Drusilla would have been expected to return to the ludus herself, and I knew very well that Lucius would force her back to her regular duties immediately, regardless of how sick she was.

I would much rather learn to do these things myself and let her rest, let her heal from whatever sickness this was. It did not seem to be contagious, so I was not concerned that the rest of us would fall ill. We did not need more help.

The second reason that I wanted some time alone was simply to gain some relief. Being in the company of one or both men whom I cared for so deeply, whom I *wanted* so very much, was nearly driving me insane, especially since neither of them made any move to touch me.

I found myself in a constant state of arousal. My skin would hum with nerves while I baked bread, and my nipples would contract when linens from the wash brushed against them. I was wet nearly all the time, and I dreamt of one or both men bending me over a table and taking me from behind.

Four evenings after we had arrived, the two gladiators and I sat in one of the large rooms facing the sea. Drusilla had been well enough to come downstairs, to eat a meal, but she had tired quickly and was now back in bed.

If the men found it strange that I would let my slave girl rest, that I would take the chores upon myself, they did not say it. This I appreciated. I did not feel like explaining myself. I had eaten a meal, too, but I was still hungry. I found that I was nearly always hungry now, now that I was sharing my food with the baby inside of me.

Rising, I moved across the room to where I had placed a platter of fruit earlier in the day. My fingers danced among the pile of figs, finding one that was plump and sweet with juice. Taking in hand the small knife that I had also set on the tray, I cut into the fig, intending to cut it into slices to savor on my tongue.

The metal of the blade sliced into my finger. With a shout and a curse, I raised my finger to my mouth, but the flow of blood was heavier than I thought it would be. Holding the finger out in front of me, I saw that the cut was deeper than I expected, as well.

I had never been one to feel faint at the sight of blood, but I had never had to contend with a wound myself, either. So I simply stood, the finger held out in front of me, dumbfounded.

I had no idea what to do, as the blood dripped to the floor in fat wet drops.

Both Caius and Marcus were by my side before I could again cry out.

Marcus took my hand in his, inspecting the finger, not at all taken aback by the blood. I supposed that compared with some of the wounds he had sustained in the arena, this was nothing more than a small scratch. But he treated it as if it would be fatal to me, barking at Caius to get a cloth.

Marcus squeezed the finger tightly in his palm, again not seeming to notice the blood that smeared his palm.

When Caius returned with the cloth, Marcus wrapped it carefully around my finger, then my hand. It looked rather as if my hand had been mummified, and I laughed weakly at the sight.

Marcus ran a hand over my hair then, and the gesture reminded me of the caring with which he had touched Caius after the other man's injury at the party.

"Marcus." Caius' voice was a growl, a very clear warning. I looked to him, my feelings bruised.

"It was all right for you to touch me, so long as my husband decreed it?" I felt my temper begin to rise. "But if Marcus touches me willingly, it is not permitted? No matter that it is what *I* want?"

The tears overflowed, hot and filled with the beginnings of anger. I could not see Marcus' face from where I stood beneath his chin, my hand still held in his own. But I could see Caius, and he appeared stricken. Angry, even, but with himself, not me.

I had hit the heart of the matter like a blade driving home. In a fit of emotion that I refused to attribute to my being with child, I decided that I was sick of the pair of them.

"I am going to my room. And I am going *alone*." I was furious. I was sick of being a pawn in the game of men. Yanking my hand from Marcus' grip, I shoved through the hard wall of muscle that the two men created just by being there. I would make sure that Drusilla had everything she needed, and then I would close myself in my room. At that moment, I did not care if I saw either gladiator again. I did not care if I saw my husband, either.

I simply wanted to be left alone. Life would be easier that way.

I was not pleased to hear a knock outside my door an hour later.

I ignored it.

It persisted.

I was tired, I was sore, and I was still hungry, though I would damn myself before I descended the stairs to find something to eat. My finger no longer bled, nor did it much hurt, but knowing how it would hurt when doing chores the next day made me cross. The knock only reminded me of just why I was in such low spirits, and so I gritted my teeth and yanked the curtain that separated my chamber from the hall hard enough that it tore off its hangings.

Marcus stood on the other side, his face set in the stony stillness that was habitual for him.

"I thought I told you to leave me alone." My voice was as icy as the water of the sea outside.

He nodded, but the nod seemed to have nothing to do with my words. "Come with me, if you would, Domina."

"I want to be alone. Perhaps I did not make that clear." I stepped forward, meant to brush past him and use this interruption as an excuse to head downstairs and find something to eat.

Instead I found myself lifted off of my feet. I squawked, an entirely unflattering sound, and threw my arms around his neck for fear of being dropped.

"What are you doing? Put me down *now*." I imbued my voice with every ounce of authority that I had. I was furious.

I might have been mistaken, but I thought that I detected just the ghost of a smile around Marcus' lips as he merely shifted my weight in his arms and began to walk down the hall, toward the room where he had been sleeping.

"I cannot do that, Domina. Apologies." I let loose with another sound of frustration, but I realized quite quickly that my protests were futile.

This man was a beast made of muscle. He could do as he

liked with me, and nothing I said or did could make a difference.

I subsided into bitterness. "No doubt my husband gave you more orders." It was a cheap shot and I knew it, but the man did not seem particularly disturbed by it. Rather he cocked an eyebrow, and continued the rest of the way to his room.

I turned my head away, determined to be stubborn. I did not fear him, but nor was I interested in the reason that he had hauled me here. At least, that is what I told myself. But I again found my choice taken away when Marcus adjusted me so that my weight was supported by one arm. His free hand took my chin in strong fingers and turned my face so that I had to look into the expanse of the room.

I blinked at what I saw. The bed looked to be made with fresh sheets, clumsily made, but still clean. Surrounding the bed were fat pillars of wax that burned bright at their tips, the bright orange flames dancing in the dusky air provided by the rising moon.

Marcus released my chin. I turned to look up into his face, found him looking back at me with a question that remained unspoken.

"What . . . what is this?" My voice shook.

His was solemn. "I have wanted you since the first moment that I saw you. I told myself that I could not have you unless you asked, unless you started things. I have tried to abide by this, but it seems that it has not made you happy."

I could not believe he had seen this, understood it.

"So I am taking a turn and asking you now. We cannot be

together forever, we both know this. But we can be together here and now. So I ask if you will lie with me." Uncertainty trickled over those strong, sure features, just for a moment, and it astounded me.

I could not believe that it had been caused by me, that I had been the one to break through the shields of the gladiator.

I was humbled.

"Yes." As if there was anything else I could have said. "Yes, I will lie with you."

There was a hint of a smile, which I now understood was an expression of great joy in this stoic man.

He carried me to the bed, laid me down gently on top of sheets that smelled of soap and the sea.

I was overjoyed. This, *this* was what I wanted, to be held in the arms of someone so strong who yet was soft for me. Someone to whom I did not have to tell my wishes or desires, because he already knew them.

If I was still not completely satisfied, if I still felt that something was missing, I chose to ignore it. I would be happy with what I had.

I stretched on the bed, inhaling the intoxicating scent of candle wax and the smoke that danced around the flames as the pillars burned.

Marcus stood beside the bed, looking down at me intently. Slowly, slowly, he raised his fingers to the strings of his subligaculum. I watched avidly, my skin beginning to flush, as he deftly untied them and let the soft, worn skin drop to the floor.

He stood there, proud and naked. I wanted him to come to me of his own accord, but now I understood something.

It was a show of respect for me that he would not approach me unless I asked. It was not so very hard to ask, knowing that.

I stretched an arm out to him, waited for him to take my hand in his. He came easily, sitting at the side of the bed with a grace that reminded me of who and what he was.

Bending at the waist, he kissed me softly on the lips. His hands toyed with the long strands of my hair, then traveled down over the hills of my breasts and over my belly.

There he stopped, his palms splayed over the swollen flesh. My stomach did not look quite so big against the hugeness of him.

He looked at my belly, then looked at me. I knew he wondered, as I did, if the child growing inside was his.

There was a choked noise from the direction of the doorway. I turned quickly, my head craning, and saw Caius standing just on the inside of the curtain. I had not heard him approach, so wrapped up in Marcus had I been.

I flinched, waiting for his anger, or at the very least his unhappiness, at what he saw before him. But instead he approached the bed, slowly, hesitantly.

"Apologies for my behavior earlier." He kept his gaze fastened to mine, his eyes so bright and so blue that I felt they might sear my skin. When he cast me that crooked smile, I felt something hitch in the depths of my belly.

Marcus kept his hands as they were, splayed on the mound of my stomach.

"It goes against everything that I am, to dishonor my dominus by my behavior." I knew, though he would never have said it, that the opposite did not apply, that he did not consider it dishonorable for his dominus to order him to sleep with his domina. It was not how Caius' mind worked. "But I find that . . . that I no longer care. So long as it brings you happiness."

He waited for me to reply, but I could find no words. I began to shake, I was so overwhelmed.

I knew that the joy could not last forever, but I would take it, so long as it was available.

"It brings me happiness." I smiled at him, all traces of my earlier anger and resentment gone. In their place was a playfulness, one nearly as potent as the beginnings of arousal that were creeping over me. "It would bring me more happiness still if you would remove your subligaculum."

Unlike Marcus when he was pleased, Caius allowed his entire face to break into a wide, devious smile. With what could only be termed as a playful leer, he reached for the strings of his leathers, cursing while fumbling with the knot.

Once naked, he crawled eagerly atop of me, causing Marcus to protest.

"Be careful." He snapped the words, but there was no real anger in them, just irritation. He hauled me closer to his side, his hands wrapped protectively over my stomach.

Caius merely smiled at him, then bent down to kiss me, his lips eager now that he had made up his mind.

I was so happy, so full of emotion that I let myself stop thinking, stop analyzing, stop wondering what they were thinking and feeling in turn. I let myself be swept away on the bliss.

Caius continued to kiss me, his tongue teasing my mouth

open. He tasted of figs and honeyed wine, and I drank in the sweetness.

From behind me Marcus' arms tightened. I murmured, not in protest but in enjoyment. I loved being held in his arms, loved having the bands of muscle hot against my skin.

I did not like that I could not reach him, however. When Caius paused to take in a ragged breath, I wiggled until I lay on my back, Marcus' arms still tight around me, and reached up to pull his head down for another kiss.

His lips did not taste of fruit, but rather of salt, as they had the first time I had had them against my own. I remembered what he had looked like, my first sight of that golden warrior standing so sternly by my bath, and felt myself begin to soften inside.

We continued that way for several long, drugging minutes. I would explore the mouth of one, then the other until I was breathless. I pushed both away momentarily, though they remained hovering just above me, Caius half sprawled atop me, Marcus bent at the waist.

Their heads were close, so close. One mere whisper and their skin would touch.

I wanted it. I wanted them to be together, while they were with me.

I could not ask. I did not know how.

So I bit my lower lip, drawing it between my teeth and pressing down, watching, evaluating the intensity of the intimacy that vibrated between them.

Marcus cast a sidelong glance at me, and I remembered that he would not do anything unless I asked him to. Since words were stuck in my suddenly dry throat, I simply nodded, hoping that that would be enough, that that would signal to him my acquiescence.

The moment stretched out, far too long for my liking, then the two men—*my* two men—erased the last whisper of space and pressed their lips together.

Never before had I seen something that I found so innately, completely sexual. The image of those two golden heads, one slighter darker, one the color of sunshine, made my mouth water.

I wanted not just to touch these men, not just to fuck them. I wanted to possess them, wanted to be possessed.

Their kiss was soft, hesitant. Not at all like the one that I had so illicitly watched in Marcus' quarters.

I wanted them to release all of the passion that they had for each other, that passion that I had *seen* them share. I wanted to mix it with the intensity of my feelings for them, wanted an explosion of desire. I was not sure how to ask for this, either.

I had no idea what to do with two men at once.

My uncertainty must have played out over my face. I found myself again lifted in Marcus' arms. This time I did not protest. I melted into his heat, and let him do as he would.

He sat down on the bed again, very gracefully considering that his arms were full of me. Pressing his back against the chilly stone wall, he arranged my pliant limbs so that I sat in between his legs, my back to his front. His rigid cock pressed against the small of my back, and his arms wrapped snugly around my waist.

Before those arms wrapped, though, his hands slid down

my sides, over my hips, and between my thighs. I cried out in shock, not expecting to be touched there, not yet, but all he did was to push my legs apart, far apart.

Caius quickly positioned himself between my spread legs. He lay on his front, supported on his forearms, and I could see the cords of muscle straining against the apricot-colored skin.

I could also feel the hot whisper of his breath on the sensitive skin of my inner thigh. I very nearly laughed, for it tickled, a bit, but more than that, it drew blood there, right to the very center of my cunt.

I waited, my breath held in my lungs. A moment later, the touch came, the touch of moist lips on the same skin that his breath had so recently caressed.

His lips trailed up, brushing kisses over my skin, soothing the places that the rasp of his beard scratched. He had not shaved since we had arrived, but I loved the feeling of the bristles against my skin.

Even more, I loved the feeling of his tongue on my clitoris when he parted my folds with one hand and licked me.

My back arched, pressing my hips back against Marcus. He groaned at the sudden pressure on his cock. I rocked my hips back again, just to hear his voice, before again being swept away in the sensations between my legs.

Caius swiped his tongue through my lower lips again and again, circling my clitoris, which the fingers that spread me wide helped to fully expose. When I was gasping and writhing, he thrust his tongue inside without warning, causing several small spasms to rock through my body.

After the first small quake receded and I lay boneless,

Caius replaced his tongue with a finger, thrusting in and out of my hot, tight channel. As he did, Marcus moved his hands from my waist to cup my breasts, his thumbs strumming over nipples that had grown larger in the past weeks, larger, darker and more sensitive.

The sensations were exquisite. I had never before felt the touch of so many hands, not all at once, and it was very nearly too much. I rocked back against Marcus, my head shaking violently from side to side, though I was not sure if I wanted more or if I needed the onslaught to stop.

Caius' finger found a place deep inside of me that caused my cunt to clench down on his hand. I tensed all over, not expecting the sensation. I even tried to pull back, again not sure if I loved it or if it was too much, but I had nowhere to go, not with the solid wall of Marcus at my back and Caius' mouth and hands at my front.

Caius persisted, pressing down again on the spot buried deep inside of me. My entire body clenched, but he removed his finger before I could again quake.

I shouted out loud at the loss of sensation. He merely smiled, the smile of a wicked god frolicking with a mortal. Rising to his hands and knees, he crawled up my body and straddled both my legs and Marcus'.

The sight of that tangle of limbs did funny things to my insides. It felt right, the three of us together. Tilting my head back, I kissed the only spot on Marcus that I could reach, the hollow of his neck, and in return, he squeezed my breasts once before releasing them.

He placed his hands where Caius' had been, rubbing a finger between the slick folds, rubbing over the nub of my clitoris. I felt an answering gush of moisture and was sighing with pleasure when Caius placed the head of his cock at the entrance of that wet cunt and pushed in, just the littlest bit.

I pushed back, wanting him to hilt himself in me. His face a study in concentration, he held back, moving inside of me at his own pace, which was maddeningly slow.

Marcus rubbed my clitoris with one thumb, and with his other hand made a ring of fingers through which Caius had to pass to thrust inside of me. It added pressure for both of us, and I saw sweat begin to bead on the forehead of the gladiator inside of me.

I wanted Marcus to feel what I felt, too. Reaching behind me awkwardly, I clasped the tip of his cock in my palm, and rubbed my fingers over the head of it. It was sticky, weeping, and swollen.

"Just relax." I looked up as Marcus spoke and found his eyes fogged with lust. He did not need my hand, it seemed, and I understood why when he began to thrust against my back in time with Caius' movements. Both moved in at the same time, then away in the off-beat. Marcus' cock nudged its way into the crevice of my ass, sliding up and down in the flesh there, and I could hear his breath begin to come faster.

My world became the two men whose flesh was melded so intimately with mine. The speed with which we rocked together increased, but only the slightest bit, as if we all were trying to savor this moment, this first time that we three had been together.

I felt the rolling waves begin to pull me under once again. I was helpless to do anything but let the feeling take me where it would. I felt my cunt clench around Caius' engorged cock, felt him respond. One more thrust, two, and he pushed into me as hard as he could, and I felt liquid warmth flood between my thighs.

As though our pleasure had transferred through my flesh to him, I felt Marcus move behind me, against me, the thrusts more erratic than they had been. The skin of his erection pulled at the skin of my back, a different feeling entirely from having a cock in my cunt, but still good, so good. Finally he moaned, and I felt another rush of wet, this time over the small of my back. It ran down, raining over my flesh, creating a mess, but I did not care.

We lay there, the three of us, languid and as liquid as the pools of wax from the melting candles that surrounded us. For a long moment my mind was empty of all thought; I was simply full of happiness.

I must have fallen into a light sleep, for when I woke I was snuggled in between two long, lean male bodies with no recollection of how I got there. From the snores emanating from the man on each side of me, I judged them both to be sleeping, and was pleased that, for once, they were not rigid with the idea of my safety.

Where would I have been safer, after all, than in between the two of them?

I was not tired, not anymore. Nor, however, did I want to rise. I was content, completely so, and I marveled at the blessing that the gods had bestowed upon me.

Though it would not, could not last, I knew that I would always remember this moment, this first time. I would use it to make me smile when I could not see them and my heart hurt because of it.

I would remember that Marcus was hard and unyielding, and that I did not have to make choices around him, because he already knew what I wanted. I would remember that he made me feel safe.

I would remember that Caius made me laugh, and that he was softer in manner and attentive, at least with me. I would remember that he was quick to jump to my defense, to wade in with fists flying. I would remember the wicked grin that could bring me to my knees.

I would remember that the two filled different halves of my soul, and that when we were all together, I was complete.

I did not have to remember, not just yet. For now, I could revel in the feeling of completeness.

With Caius on one side and Marcus on the other, and the promise of life in my womb, I felt full. It was the first time in my life that I had felt whole.

Chapter Fifteen

Water made rings around a stone that was thrown into its depths. Never before had I noticed this. Or perhaps I had when I was younger, on visits here, but if so the knowledge had faded from my memory long ago.

This morning I found it fascinating. That a simple object like a stone could cause such a beautiful effect caught my attention and held it. I threw rock after rock, pebble after pebble as far as I could, watching the small splashes where the stones fell, before the sea again smoothed, the stones swallowed whole.

It was nice to focus on something besides the turmoil inside of me.

I had come out to sit by the sea in the very early hours of the morning. I was rarely awake so early in Rome, for we often had social engagements that kept us out late. Rather, I had once had them. Lucius still did, he simply no longer took me with him.

Still, it had been years since I had seen the sun rise. I had forgotten how breathtaking a sight it could be, the way the colors streaked across the horizon like the gods had spilled paint mixed with light.

How could I go back to Rome after having had a taste of this? My life in Rome contained no sunrises, no stones sinking into the pale blue sea. My life in Rome contained only duty and dissatisfaction, tedium and unrelenting heat.

More, how could I go back to Lucius after having tasted the companionship, the love that I shared with my two warriors?

I did not have a choice, this I knew. But now the reality of it all seemed worse than it ever had before.

"Domina." Craning my neck, I saw Caius standing on the swell of ground above the shore. The sight of him caused excitement to rush, hot and fizzy, throughout my body.

Thinking of what we had done the night before, the two of us and Marcus, made me ache with the need for more.

"I wish you would call me by my name." My words were quiet, but I hoped that he heeded them.

I no longer felt that I was their domina. I no longer felt that they were gladiators, or slaves.

"Alba." He amended his words. "You are needed at the house. Lucius has sent a doctor to examine you."

I was alarmed. "Lucius?" I rose to my feet as quickly as I was able, which I was loath to admit was not as quickly as I had once able to move. "Is he here?" I would never be able to hide my true feelings in front of my husband. Not now, when they were so shiny and new.

Caius held his hands out and took mine in his own as I approached. He let go quickly when he realized that there was now another set of eyes present. "Calm yourself. Lucius is not here. Just the doctor. Pompeius, I believe his name is?"

Pompeius, yes, the doctor who had first suspected that it was my husband who was barren, not me. I supposed that it showed some level of caring on Lucius' part, to send the doctor all the way out here to check on the well-being of me and the baby. I rather suspected, however, that it had more to do with the well-being of our patronage. I would not have been surprised to discover that the visit had been suggested by Baldurus.

I resented the intrusion, but steeled myself. It would be beneficial to discover that all was well with the child inside of me, and while the man was here, I would have him look at Drusilla. Lucius would have balked at the expense for a slave. But Lucius was not here to say yes or no.

Pompeius was seated in the softest chair in the front room of the house, the one facing the sea. He already had a cup of honeyed wine in hand, and I assumed that he must have poured it himself, for Drusilla was still upstairs, and I could not picture Marcus pouring wine for the man.

"Alba." The doctor nodded at me. I tried to fight the anger that rose at the sight of him. He was a kindly enough man, but he had had a hand in Lucius' plan to mate me without my consent. That told me that he did not think very highly of women, or perhaps just of me. Either way, I was unimpressed.

Pompeius slurped at his wine, draining the cup before gesturing to the lounge that sat beside his chair. "Well, lie down, child. Let us have a look." I hesitated, exchanged a glance with both men.

The doctor would not have even considered that I might

be self-conscious in front of these men, for he did not see them as people. They were merely slaves, furniture. Possessions.

I knew they were so much more than that. And after my initial, knee-jerk reaction, I realized that it was silly to be self-conscious in front of either one of them.

They had both seen, touched, and tasted every part of me. They knew me better than anyone, except perhaps Drusilla.

And one of them was the father of this child. As such, their presence in the room was about so much more than just me overcoming my nerves.

It was their right.

So I lay down on the couch, bent my knees as the doctor approached. I was uncertain of what to do, having never been examined by a doctor before, let alone examined while with child. I caught first Marcus' eye, then Caius'. Both smiled at me, just enough of an expression that I would detect it, would draw comfort from it, but not so much that Pompeius would think it odd.

Amongst questions about my diet and activity, my sleep and my comfort, the doctor examined me briefly between my legs and then palpated my stomach. After running his hands over the hard ball of it, which had only recently begun to look like more than a softness around the waist, he nodded, satisfied.

"It is a girl, I think." I blinked up at him, struggled to rise to my elbows.

"How could you tell such a thing?" I thought that he must have been making up a story.

"The shape of your stomach, it is oval, rather than like a

ball." He wiped his hands on his tunic. "That suggests a girl, at least in my experience."

I was not sure what to make of this information. Part of me warmed immediately to the idea of a small daughter, one with silky curls and chubby fingers. Part of me cringed, aware that Lucius would much rather have a son.

Over Pompeius' shoulder I saw a quick rush of emotion pass over Marcus' face. It looked as though he was . . . pleased? If I could glean such a thing from such a quick glance.

A bolt of joy shot through my worries.

Done with his examination, Pompeius reached again for his cup. Finding that he had already tossed its contents down his gullet, he looked around, for a servant, I was certain. I watched with some amusement while pulling myself awkwardly into a sitting position. The man looked bewildered that the only other people to be found were the gladiators. He did not appear of a mind to ask either of the large, imposing men to fill his cup for him.

"Do you not have more help here?" He appeared amazed as I rose to take the pitcher of wine in hand and fill his cup.

"I do." This was the opening I had been looking for. "My own girl. She is upstairs. She has been ill since before we arrived here, and I do not know what to do to ease her discomfort. I would be most grateful if you would examine her before you leave."

"Examine a slave girl?" He blinked over the rim of his cup, but nodded shortly thereafter. It might have been an odd request, but I knew that he would not quibble over the extra fee that he would be paid. "Very well. Show me to her room."

The man's face again showed surprise to find that Drusilla's room was upstairs, not in the slaves' quarters. But he held his tongue, simply bending over his work. My gut clenched when I saw that Drusilla was too weak to even acknowledge that we were there.

Pompeius' mouth set in a grim line as he noted the girl's pale skin, the sheen of damp on her face, and the speckles of blood on her pillow. Alarm shot through me when I saw the blood.

"What is this from?" I gestured to Drusilla's pillow, my eyes searching the doctor's face. He shushed me and continued his inspection of the girl. I stood, worry gnawing at my insides as he worked his way over her body.

When he had concluded his work, Pompeius nodded toward the hall. I followed him out, anxious to hear what could be done to help ease Drusilla's suffering.

"It is the consumption." The words were blunt, not tempered with emotion of any kind. "The lung sickness."

I waited for him to say more. He did not.

"What does that mean?" I had not heard of this before, but then, I had been sheltered for much of my life. "What can I do?"

Puzzlement set over his face. "There is nothing to do, my dear." After a moment's thought, he reached out to pat me on the shoulder, to offer comfort. He might not understand why a slave girl meant so much to me, but he would acknowledge it. "She will die, and soon."

I cried out, feeling my blood rushing to my head in a great wave. Marcus, who had been standing at the end of the hall, moved toward me faster than I had ever seen a man move. I heard loud steps on the stairs, and assumed that Caius ran toward me, as well.

"You must stay calm, my dear. For the child." I heard the doctor's words over the sudden buzzing in my head, but shook myself, denying everything that he had said.

A gladiator stood on each side of me, ready to catch me should I fall. But I found my legs surprisingly steady. Inside I still felt as though I was screaming, but I would not fall or succumb to hysterics.

"Thank you, Pompeius." Drawing myself up, retreating into myself, I nodded as regally as I could manage. "Make certain that you charge Lucius for the extra time."

The man nodded, and the expression on his face was slightly confused.

"Escort him out, please." I pushed through the three men, not waiting to see if they would heed my words or not.

I pushed through the curtain that covered the room where Drusilla lay. I stood just inside, staring down at her, unable to identify what, exactly, it was that I felt.

Pompeius did not seem able to understand why I would be upset over the death of a slave. Perhaps I did not fully understand it, either. She had been my lover. She was the closest thing that I had to a friend. She had always been there.

And now she was dying.

For the first time I noticed the smell that hung heavy in the air of her chamber. It was a heavy musk, and it smelled of sickness, of death. I wondered that I had not noticed it before. Guilt streaked through me when I realized that I had been too wrapped up in my own life to notice much of anything. And besides that, I had not been looking for it.

I had thought that she would be fine.

Pulling a cushion over to the expanse of marble by the head of the bed, I lowered myself stiffly until I was seated there. Leaning against the wall beside the low cot, I stared down at the pale face, the snarls of brown hair.

I did not know what else to do.

I did not sleep. For the next week I sat on that same cushion by my friend's bed, brushing her hair away from her face as blood came up from her lungs, supporting her back while coughs racked her slender frame. In the quiet between her bouts, I curled into a ball on the floor, sorting through my memories of Drusilla, sharpening them desperately, lest I forget some small detail.

There was no part of my life in which she had not been a part. My very first memory, of being a small girl myself and having my hair combed out and braided, had included a tiny, wide eyed girl who watched with big eyes. The girl had been Drusilla. The slave combing my hair had been her mother.

When her mother had died several years later, Drusilla had clung to me for comfort. After the household had gone to bed, she had snuck into my own room, knowing that I had the comfort she sought, and knowing that I would never tell.

She had in turn comforted me when I took hysterics after my first kiss, that innocent slave boy who belonged to the neighboring familia. He had been beaten very nearly to death, all because of me. Drusilla had helped to alleviate my guilt.

She had calmed my nerves with copious amounts of wine on the eve of my marriage, and she had come with me to my new home. She was the sole part of my old life that had merged into my new one.

Now that last link was fading away, and with it all vestiges of my former meek self. Drusilla would no longer be here to comfort me, to protect me.

I would have to do it myself.

She drifted away a week later, her soul departing her body on one final, whispered breath. In accordance with tradition, I sealed the passage of her spirit with a kiss on lips that were already starting to cool, and closed her eyes with shaking fingers.

I was numb. I had spent the past week in a haze, growing more used to the knowledge that she was dying, but not any less grievous about it.

Marcus and Caius had done their best to comfort me, to feed us both, to make sure that I slept, but I was not in a place where I could appreciate it.

As I sat on the bed beside her body, I knew that I would not take her back to Rome. As her familia, we owed her a proper burial, but I did not care so much for the pomp and circumstance that a funeral demanded.

I did not think she would have cared for it, either. I thought I knew quite well what she would like, and a formal funeral procession led by my husband, the head of her house but whom she had never cared for, was not it. And so I resolved to amend tradition in her favor. She had been a good person. I was not afraid that her soul would not pass.

At dawn the next morning I had Caius and Marcus help me take her outside, by the water. It seemed to me that she had been happiest here, at the coast, much as I was. There I washed her in the sea, my own hands cleaning away the dredges of sickness from her body. I combed the long ribbons of hair until it was again silky smooth and I anointed her skin with the herbal oil that I used for my baths.

I dressed her in one of my own tunics, the finest one that I had with me. And while I covered her motionless, waxen form in the emerald silk, I performed the lamentations, calling her name aloud, over and over again.

I had my warriors build a *pyre* of driftwood as I prepared her. Before they lifted her atop it, I placed *Charon's obol* in her mouth—a coin ensuring special passage to the afterlife. She had been a slave without a coin of her own, but I thought she deserved that special salvation.

We watched as the pyre burned, the three of us, standing in the sand by the water. The sickly sweet smell of burning flesh should have made me sick, but I was too far into my grief to notice such things.

The two men did not have to stay with me, and I told them so, for I intended to remain until the last ember had cooled. But there they stood, one on either side of me, stern and solemn.

I knew that Drusilla would have appreciated the tribute.

Hours later, hours that seemed like mere minutes, I gathered the ashes. The fire had cooled, and so I placed them in a vase that had sat in the house. Custom said that I should seal it, but the idea did not sit well with me. Drusilla had been a slave in this lifetime. I wanted her to be free in the next. I waded out into the water, letting it lap at my knees, and tipped the vase into the wind. The salty breeze carried away the remains of my girl, and with it, the last vestiges of my old life.

Chapter Sixteen

"I am not returning to Lucius."

My two gladiators sat with me at the table, all three of us picking at the oatmeal and fruit that I had laid out in front of us. Two sets of hands stilled, and two brows furrowed.

"What is your meaning?" Caius clearly did not take my statement at face value and cocked his head in my direction inquisitively.

"I mean just as I said. I will not return to Lucius, not as his wife." I made certain to keep my face expressionless, free from emotion, so that they would understand that this was not a decision that I had come to lightly.

"How do you intend to support yourself?" This was Marcus, ever the more practical.

I ignored his question, and replied with one of my own. It was important, very important, for me to hear the answer before I told them of my jewels.

"Will you stay with me?" I looked at each in turn. Caius, with his god-like face, and Marcus with nearly black eyes. I wanted, more than anything, for them to stay with me. To be with me.

Both hesitated, and my heart sank.

"I think . . . I think that neither of us would like anything more." Marcus, when he spoke, sounded raspy and hoarse. "But we do not have enough money saved to buy our freedom, freedom for both of us. And we took an oath to the ludus, to our dominus. It would damn us both to renege."

I eyed them both warily. "Is that truly the only reason that you would return?" Doubt began to plague me. What if they really would rather return to the ludus, to the arena? To life without me?

"Yes." Caius drew the word out. "Yes. Of course."

Relief felt cool, like the ocean breeze. "I have money. Or rather, I have things to sell for money. Enough to live modestly for many years." I was still not certain what I would do when the money from the jewels ran out, but I did not pause to think of that now.

Both men shook their heads vehemently, and I started, not expecting the response at all.

"No. Our woman will not pay for our freedom." Though I warmed at being called their woman, I sighed at Marcus' stubbornness.

Caius agreed. "We will find another way."

"I am champion," Marcus said quietly. "Perhaps if I saved all that I earned, in a year . . ."

We all sat in silence, thinking of what another year would bring. I would have my child then, a child that by rights belonged to one of them, but one who would be introduced to the world as the offspring of Lucius.

I shook my head, resolute. "I will find a way. A way that does not involve my paying for you." The last was added hastily as both men opened their mouths to protest again. "I will convince Lucius."

"How?" Caius did not sound as if he did not believe that I could. No, he merely sounded curious.

"I will threaten to tell Baldurus that the child I carry does not belong to my husband." This was something that might or might not have effect. Baldurus may not care at all about parentage, so long as there was a child in the family.

I was betting everything that I held dear, however, that it would be completely against his morals.

Marcus considered, nodding. "And if Lucius will not let you go?"

I did not like to think of this, but I had. "I will run away." I would sell my jewels and travel far, far away. "With or without you." I nearly left the last words inside my mouth, as it made it sound as if I did not care whether they were with me or not.

I did care. I would be miserable without them. But if they would not come, I was leaving Lucius anyway.

Drusilla's death had taught me that life could be far too fleeting to be miserable. Now that I had had a taste of joy, I could not picture spending the rest of my days in a loveless marriage, in an existence where I was unfulfilled.

"Are you certain?" Caius asked. "Your life will not be what you are used to."

I understood that he did not think me spoiled, necessarily. He was just acknowledging something that I might not have thought of.

But I had.

"I leave tomorrow to journey back to Rome," I said, my stomach clenched with fear at the thought. "I will tell Lucius when I arrive. I will also bargain for your freedom."

I had debated telling them that I was leaving at all, knowing that they would insist on accompanying me, even though the negotiation would be easier if I was alone. I saw the two consider, communicating somehow between themselves without speaking.

"We are strong; we could find work," said Caius, summing up what they had both been thinking.

After a long moment's rumination, both men nodded, and it was Marcus who spoke.

"We will come with you."

The first day's travel on the way back to Rome had proved harder than any of the days on the way to the sea.

As evening approached, we thankfully found a room at an inn. Though the lodgings were dubious, at least there was a bath. I sank into the tub of water gratefully. Pregnancy made riding difficult, and I was sore in every single place that I could be sore.

That soreness extended to my heart, a bit. It had been difficult leaving the small house by the sea that morning. I had stood ankle deep in the water, letting the cold numb my skin, thinking of Drusilla and wondering if I would stand there again.

Though I had made up my mind, I knew that that was only the smallest part of the battle. No matter what I threatened, my husband would not be easily convinced. I still needed to somehow convince Caius and Marcus to remain outside the walls of the ludus while I told my husband of my plans, for fear that he would have them killed, something that was well within his rights as their owner.

For tonight, all that I could handle was a bath to soak away the soreness, and sleep to ease the weariness of my mind. I was grateful that we had been able to get a room with a bath. I knew that had I been traveling alone, or with any other men for that matter, it would not have happened. However, one look at my massive warriors, at the swords sheathed at their hips, and the seedy-looking innkeeper had suddenly found that his best room was free.

His best room still left much to be desired, but I could not stand the thought of riding through the night, nor would Marcus or Caius have heard of it. It had been difficult enough to convince them that I would ride on my horse's back, as taking the carpentum would slow us down. I had not thought of the pain on my already tender flesh, and so I had not argued when they had announced that we would be stopping for sleep.

Inns were not the safest of places, generally speaking. Nor were the open roads, the territory of thieves and bandits. But I knew that the men I traveled with were more than a match for anyone we should encounter.

One looked at the brand of the ludus burned into their flesh, the brand marking them as trained gladiators, would send even the most hardened criminal running.

Stretching out the tense muscles of my neck, I looked up

when I heard footsteps. Marcus stood above me, free of his subligaculum. He did not speak, but I knew that he wanted to join me in the bath.

Too weary to do anything but nod, I did so, pulling my knees to my chest to make room.

Marcus wedged his large frame into the wooden tub, facing me. Reaching out with his arms, he pulled me onto his lap, my center directly over his semi erect cock.

I wrapped my legs around his waist, my arms around his shoulders, and placed my cheek on his shoulder. I wanted to stay like this, just like this, wrapped in warmth and man.

Safe. With Marcus I was safe.

More footsteps approached. I reflected that none of us seemed to be in the mood to talk, not even Caius, who appeared sleepy as he made his way toward us.

There was no room for him to sit in the tiny tub. He settled for resting his weight on the edge, his feet in the water, one leg on either side of my hips. A very large man, he also had long arms, and did not have to bend very far to reach the water with his hands. I heard them slip through the warm water, and then felt the warmth trickle down my back as he poured it over my shoulder blades. The warmth felt like an extension of Marcus' arms around me. I sighed in pleasure and shifted position, arching my back toward the warmth.

From between my legs, I felt Marcus' cock harden fully. It nestled between the folds of my lower lips, and I gasped as it pressed against the saddle-sore flesh there.

Moving my face from his shoulder, until my nose was pressed against his own, I received a soft kiss on the lips. As he kissed me, he shifted position, just a bit, and entered me slowly, his cock coming to rest against my womb.

I moaned with the pleasure, which was mixed with a little bit of pain. Sore as I was, it felt good, so good, to be anchored against one of my warriors.

From behind me, Caius kept up the splashing of the water, his fingers trailing up and down my spine. His large, strong hands moved to my shoulders, rubbing hard, working out the tension that had manifested in knots.

When I was malleable, soft and pliant, I caught movement out of the corner of my eye, a trail of flame, and saw that my impetuous one had taken one of the dripping wax candles in his hand.

I felt heat, a searing burn, on the tender skin between the wings of my shoulder blades, and realized that he had poured the hot wax onto me.

An exclamation left my lips as my body stiffened. I half-turned to glare at the man, which caused Marcus to hiss in a breath. A tremor passed through me, as well—moving as I had tightened the hold that my cunt had on his cock.

Still, I was not over-pleased, and told Caius so. He simply grinned at me in return—the very nerve—and, bending so that his lips nearly touched the burnt skin, blew.

The cool air from his mouth felt like ice on the mild burn. A sound of enjoyment rose up from out of me before I could stop it, and my skin became prickled as the warring sensations of hot and cold entwined.

Oh, who knew that pain could feel so incredibly good? *Why* did it feel so good?

I did not care. I only knew that I wanted more.

Turning back to face Marcus, I buried my face in the nape of his neck, arching my back to expose it fully to Caius. I heard him chuckle, and I held my breath inside, waiting for the next stream of scalding wax to pour onto my skin.

When it came I hissed through my teeth. This time Caius let the wax fall for longer, crossing it over my skin in overlapping lines like a whip. Tears welled up in my eyes, but I blinked them away, jaw clenched, waiting for the pleasure.

When he leaned over, when he again blew over the inflamed skin, I felt a rush of wet to my cunt. I also felt the tears begin to trickle down my face—I was unable to hold them back any longer.

"That is enough," said Marcus, as he trailed one finger over my shoulder, where the skin was unmarred. I sat up straight, shaking my head vigorously even as the tears spilled in a salty stream down my cheeks.

"No! No." My voice was thick, a mixture of lust and upset. "More. I want more."

I caught a look of concern from Marcus before I again buried my face in his chest, but I was past caring. With his cock anchored inside of me, I felt as if I could do anything, make it through anything.

There was a moment of hesitation, during which I am certain the men exchanged a look, but finally, *finally* the burn came again. This time I let a noise of anguish escape my throat, a guttural sound, and, before Caius could breathe cool breath over my skin, I was sobbing.

It was not the pain—no, it did not hurt, at least not very much. It was more, I think, that acknowledging that pain allowed the other pain that swirled through the depths of my soul a chance to escape, to be acknowledged as well.

Rubbing my face into Marcus' large shoulder, I cried. I cried for Drusilla, and I cried for the loss of my marriage. I cried with fear for the child that grew inside of me, and I cried for things that I did not understand.

During the storm of my tears, Marcus held me close, and Caius danced firm fingers through my hair. Both were touches meant to bring comfort, but neither man tried to hurry the storm along, to deny me the tears that I obviously needed to shed.

When the last streaks of wet began to dry on my face, I found myself wrapped in arms from behind me. Caius lifted me off of Marcus' cock, which was still nestled inside of me, and took me in his arms, being careful not to touch the light welts forming on my back.

Through the damp tendrils of my hair I saw Marcus himself rising from the now-cooled tub, the water sloshing around his large frame and onto the floor. The inn did not run to such amenities as towels, and so he merely padded after us, dripping fat droplets of liquid everywhere, as we were doing.

Shifting my weight in his arms, Caius tenderly laid me down on the bed, placing me on my stomach and then, as an afterthought, rolling me to my side to accommodate for the bump of my engorged womb. I felt limp, spent.

A delicious coolness began to spread over my back. Large fingers, whose I was not sure, began to rub something slick that smelled of lemon over the angry scarlet stripes that I knew danced across my pale skin. I arched into the touch.

The salve, or balm, or whatever it was, cooled the marks that still burned.

As one set of fingers continued to paint the balm of lemon over my back, another placed a stripe of cloth over my eyes. The fabric was pulled snug, then knotted at the back of my head. I was tense for a long moment, then relaxed as the hands that had tied the cloth began to roam my torso. I did not know whose hands were whose. I could not tell from touch alone—both were large men, and both had palms calloused from training and scarred from battle.

I found that it did not matter. I cared for them equally, different as they were.

I pillowed my head on my hand, fisting my fingers in the wet strands around my face. I wanted to touch them, as well, wanted to give pleasure as well as receive. But I was so pliant, so relaxed, and so comfortable that I did no more than stretch out the length of my body, offering my two loves all the access that they wanted.

The hands at my front traced my collarbone gently, then cupped my breasts. Rough thumbs strummed over sensitive nipples, and I felt the mounds become heavier, softer under the caresses. At my back, the stripes had been fully painted with the salve, but the scent of lemon did not fade, as it would if the tin were put away.

Rather, I felt the fingers that had been tending to my burns touch the skin at the base of my neck, exposed since my hair was hanging in thick tendrils over each shoulder. I felt that lovely coolness rubbed into the top of my spine, and then that softly circling touch began to trail down.

The bright scent intensified each time more salve was

added, and then the touch would continue, making its way down my spine. At the top of my buttocks, where the crease that divided my ass into two began, the fingers hesitated for only a moment, just to get more balm, before working in between the soft mounds of flesh.

I sucked in a breath—I knew where this was going. In normal circumstances I might have felt embarrassed, maybe even inhibited. Too inhibited to allow this to happen, to actually happen.

I wanted it. With the cloth over my eyes, and with burns striping my back I felt like someone else, someone with more daring than Alba.

I said nothing, just shivered at the touch.

The hands in front of me drew attention away from the ones that were searching for my most hidden place. They danced across my belly, caressed the flesh of my hardening womb. Stroking through damp curls, they opened the petals of my lower lips, inserted a finger into flesh still wet with the wanting that Marcus' cock had ignited within me.

As the finger entered my cunt, so too did the one that pressed against my pucker from behind. I gasped out loud at the twin sensations, at being filled from both sides.

One barely eased the ache. One caused an ache of an entirely different kind.

My hand slipped out of my hair, no longer supporting my head. I lay completely on my side, rocking back and forth, wanting to roll one way or the other but not wanting to lose either sensation.

The finger at my back rotated slowly, pushing in and out, its passage eased by the balm. I felt the muscles stretch, accommodate when a second finger was added, pleasure easing me through the sting.

When those fingers were removed, I whimpered at the loss, though I still had a hand playing over my clitoris, in my channel, tunneling in and out. The man behind me urged me to my hands and knees, and I felt a sudden drop in the pit of my stomach, one borne entirely of anticipation.

The hand at my front slipped out of my channel, but before I could feel empty, a slick weight was pressed against the pucker of my ass.

Could I do this? Really, truly? With my husband I had never had a desire to, but with my gladiators . . . .

With these men, I wanted to go wherever they would take me.

I pushed back instinctively as the cock was pushed into me, just the head. I made a sound that crossed pleasure with shock—I was not at all certain that the thing would fit. But a little more entered my body, and then a little more still, and then my back entrance was as full as it could ever have been, and I found myself breathing through the startling sensations that had begun to riot through me.

The man behind me did not move, letting me adjust. I sniffed deeply, smelling lemon and candle wax, sweat and the heady musk of sex. I heard nothing but the harsh breath of three aroused people.

I could see nothing, nothing but darkness.

Slowly, testing, I rocked my hips backward. I grunted as the pleasure merged into pain and then back again, as the cock slid outwards, nearly leaving my body.

It did not leave, not entirely, beginning its journey in again in an agonizingly slow manner.

In, out. Out, in. I began to move with the man inside of me, began to ride the rush of pleasure that was entirely unlike anything I had ever experienced.

But I was greedy. I wanted more.

Shifting my weight to one arm, I groped out blindly for someone, anyone, to touch. I met with hard, slightly sticky skin gone hot, and began to pet my hands over whatever areas I could reach.

I heard the small laugh that I knew belonged to Caius, but I could not tell where the sound had come from. A moment later I sensed movement, a filling of the space around me, though nothing touched me.

Then hands cupped my cheeks, pushed my face down. I bumped my nose into hot, silky soft skin, and my eyelashes brushed over muscles that quivered. Curious, I turned my cheek and felt coarse hair.

With a sigh of contentment, I opened my mouth, licked at the skin by my lips. I felt the cock jump at the touch.

Lifting my head and opening my mouth, I tried to place my lips over the head of the erection. Not being able to see, it took me several tries. Finally I felt the swollen head against my tongue, tasted the slight bitterness of excitement, and closed my mouth around the shaft.

I sucked slowly, leisurely, lowering my head until the erection hit the back of my throat, and then moving back up to suckle just the tip again. I heard a groan, and this time thought that it came from under me, though I was not sure how.

Lowering my weight from my hands, so that I could lie flat, I found that Marcus had lain down beneath me while I balanced myself on one arm. Enjoying the feeling of his hot skin against mine, I pressed my breasts down on what I discovered were legs, while leaving my ass presented upward, so that the slow, delicious fuck might continue.

The man beneath me placed his mouth on my cunt. I might have thought that the touch came from fingers, were it not for the heated rush of breath that blew over my moisture a moment before the lick came. Fingers opened my folds, and that mouth nipped lightly at my clitoris, then suckled hard.

Losing my rhythm, I nearly collapsed. My muscles strained with the effort of supporting my body, when all that I wanted to do was go limp with pleasure. But the reward was worth the effort, and so I propped my weight again on my elbows, on top of the gladiator whom I knew could support me, and began to again bob my head over the erect cock that was in my mouth.

It should have been awkward, that tangled mass of limbs, but instead it felt as if we were all one body, flesh flowing together without pause. Though there was no rhythm, per se—I did not swallow the cock in my mouth every time the man behind me hilted—it worked, and I felt myself growing ever wetter, and felt the tightening of the muscles as my orgasm approached.

I rode the wave of bliss loudly, my cries echoing around the small room. The fingers continued to massage my clitoris after I had finished, but more firmly, and though I tried to shy away from the extra stimulation, which ran so deep that I felt as if I might drown in it, I was held in place, and a second wave crested through me, leaving me weak and boneless.

My ass was held in the air by the firm hands that clasped me at the waist. I bit lightly at the cock in my mouth, just the tiniest nip, and grunted as my mouth and throat were filled with thick liquid.

I swallowed, then swallowed again. Laying my face against my arm, I bit into the tender flesh there, hard, in defense against the quickening movements behind me. I felt the muscles that cupped my buttocks clench, and then heard a groan, long and low. I was filled, that tightest channel was filled to overflowing. As salt and stickiness dripped down my inner thighs, I laughed, a breathless sound of pure delight.

Someone laid me on my side, my head cushioned by a pillow that smelled only the slightest bit musty. A long, hard male body lay down on either side of me, limbs tangling with my own, wrapping me in warmth. Firm fingers tugged the cloth from my eyes, but I did not bother to open them, not caring who was where.

And then the only sound was that of our breath as we all three drifted to sleep, limp with satisfaction and wrapped in caring.

Chapter Seventeen

After the vast openness of the coast, the city of Rome felt closed in and grimy.

We wound our way through the streets single file, our path meandering like the curves of a snake as we avoided carpenta like the one that we had left behind at the coast, litters carried by slight, malnourished slaves, and scores of people on foot.

When we entered the market closest to our ludus, I wrinkled my nose with distaste. Once, the aroma of spices and the glitter of baubles for sale would have excited me, but today I found that I no longer wanted any of it.

I did not care if the tunics that I wore from this day forward were but rags, so long as I was happy and free.

Rounding the last corner in the market, I took a deep breath, knowing that we would be the ludus in minutes. Nerves rioted throughout my entire self, and since I was trying to calm them, I did not notice the party approaching us on the road until they were nearly upon us.

"Is that Alba?" Four slaves carried a litter, and the woman who lay upon it sat up only partway to look at me.

Though I shaded my eyes and squinted into the direct sunlight of the afternoon, I knew who it was without seeing clearly.

"Hilaria." Her litter was being carried down the path that led to the ludus. I wondered what her business had been there.

Perhaps she had grown impatient, had settled for gladiators apart from my own at last.

When the other woman saw who accompanied me, her eyes grew round with astonishment. I then caught a flash of hurt, of betrayal, which in turn gave way to a look of cunning.

"Lucius did not tell me that you were due back today." Though she referred to my return, I knew that she was speaking of the gladiators. Bending slightly at the waist, allowing her ripe breasts to press against the thin material of her tunic—for the benefit of my men, I knew—she spoke to her slaves.

"Turn around. I will accompany Alba back to the house. I will help her unpack, and then perhaps I will indulge in something . . . decadent."

Her smile was sly, and reminded me that, despite the madness I suspected her dead husband had pulled from her, she had somehow guessed that I felt more for these men than I should have.

Her return to the ludus, her accompaniment of me, was strictly to make my life difficult. This was perfectly clear. I had insulted her by taking Marcus and Caius with me to the coast. Now I would be punished.

I drew in a deep breath and reminded myself that she no longer had any hold over me. Nor would I feel sorry for a woman who had chosen to sink into the depths of depravity, rather than relish in the goodness of her freedom from an abusive man.

Yes. Any fuss that she caused was Lucius' problem, not mine.

"No." Though I had said the word so often lately, it still felt somewhat foreign on my tongue. "No. You will not accompany me."

I could not allow her to do so. I needed to speak to Lucius, and if I waited too long, I would not only lose the element of surprise that I was counting on to break through his defenses, I would also completely lose my nerve.

Hilaria reared back as if she had been slapped, and I again saw that trace of vulnerability that she had revealed to me before. Then shutters fell over her face, and the façade of arrogance that she usually shrouded herself in became apparent.

"I am afraid that you do not have a choice, Alba my dear." She sat up fully now and smoothed a hand over her shining hair. "I have a deal with your husband, if you will recall. I have not been happy, waiting for these men to come back from wherever you were. Do not think that I do not know that you chose them simply to annoy me."

I very nearly laughed at the arrogance, at the certainty that my world revolved around her, when I had not given her a thought for weeks. I maintained my stern demeanor, however, aware that I would need it to get through to her.

"Your deal is no longer valid." My words were clipped, and

shook with nerves. I drew strength from the men who stood so near to me.

"I beg your pardon?" The other woman did not look concerned, simply amused.

I inhaled deeply. "The contract allows you access to men of the ludus. As of today, these men will no longer fit that definition." I looked across to where Marcus sat on his horse, my eyes wide. He gave me the slightest smile of encouragement, then returned to his stoic self.

My warrior, ever serious.

"What is this nonsense?" Hilaria was getting angry now, her eyes glittering like hard stones. "Lucius mentioned none of this."

"Lucius does not want to return your money." I did not mention that he also did not yet know. Hilaria would seize on that detail like a bird of prey. "He would have you choose new men."

Hilaria's spine stiffened, and her eyes narrowed. "I will not." The sun shone through the thin fabric of her tunic, and the ripe curves of her body became clearly visible.

I no longer worried that Caius or Marcus would prefer her to me. They had made their decision, and she was not it.

"I was told that I could have these two, and have them I will." Rising to her knees on the litter that became unbalanced under her shifting weight, she pulled at the shoulders of her sleeveless tunic with brisk motions. "Right here, then, and now. Dismount your horses, slaves, and strip. I will have a cock in my cunt, and another in my ass, and you, Alba, will have nothing to say about it."

Pity washed over me as I watched the woman who had such noble blood strip. I remembered the thread of vulnerability that she had shown me, remembered the sad tale she had told me and tried to be kind, though I still did not care for her at all.

I looked at Caius, the impetuous man whose freedom had been stripped away. I looked at Marcus, who had lost a wife and an infant through the deceit of others. Both men could have done as Hilaria had in the aftermath of pain, could have become selfish and cunning, could have delighted in passing on the cruelty that they had received to others.

They had not. They had risen above the pain, the darkness, and were now the two most honorable Roman men I knew.

"Hilaria. You do not have to do this." Digging into the sides of my horse with my thighs, I held out my hand and touched the friendship ring that she still wore on her finger.

She looked down at the touch, the ring, as if dazed, before shrugging me off angrily. She turned to Marcus, her eyes ablaze.

"Strip, I said! Are you stupid?"

Marcus simply regarded her passively, as did Caius, though I noted that Caius tapped his heel on the side of the horse ever so slightly with agitation.

"I do not understand." Hilaria turned toward me, confused. "Why will they not do as I say?" She seemed genuinely confounded, and in her upset, reached out to me as if she had not treated me as she had a moment earlier.

"They do not want you, Hilaria." I kept my words soft, for I was beginning to understand that the problems in the other woman ran far deeper than most could ever imagine. I truly believed that she was mad. "They do not want you, and you will not have them. You will revise your deal with my husband, and you will forget that you saw us here. If you do not forget, completely forget, then I am afraid that the entire story will have to be told, not just yours."

I watched as understanding slowly dawned. She could crow far and wide about Lucius reneging on their deal, for I did not think that she would be embarrassed for others to know that she had paid to fuck a gladiator.

For others to know that the two gladiators that she wanted most had refused her, however, ignored her completely despite her beauty and her class ...

That was another thing altogether.

I watched the trembling emotions riot throughout the other woman. Slowly, she pulled her tunic back up, covering her naked flesh, and lay back down on her litter, turning her face away from me.

I felt pity as her slaves began to carry her away. That pity faded when, in a last fit of pique, she drew the twisted metal and beads of the friendship ring off of her finger and threw it into the road as hard as she could.

I watched for a long moment, observing the bright glitter fade as dust settled over it.

Then it was gone, buried in the sand.

Gone, as if it had never happened.

The walls of the ludus loomed out of the dry earth like an insurmountable barrier. I looked them over solemnly, wondering how I could ever have thought myself happy living within them.

"You need to stay here." I had told Caius and Marcus this more times than I cared to admit over the days that we had journeyed. Each time they had refused.

The sensation of victory that I had obtained during my exchange with Hilaria began to fade, all because of the stubbornness of two gladiators.

This time I made certain that my voice was as stern as I could make it, stern and serious.

"I will be safe. Lucius will not hurt me, not knowing that there is a child inside of me." I dismounted from my horse before either man could dismount theirs and help me down, simply to further prove the point—that I could take care of myself when need be. "He is many things, but in his deepest self, he is not a monster that would hurt an unborn infant."

Shielding my eyes from the sun, I squinted up at each man in turn. Caius scowled openly, as always the one whose thoughts played out over his face.

Marcus simply regarded me with his features set, but with stubbornness radiating out of his obsidian eyes.

"You two, he will want to punish. You know this." My words did not seem to be making a difference, as neither man appeared to care what my arguments were. "He sees you as possessions, things that he can do with as he will."

Two faces regarded me with looks that told me they cared not a whit about being harmed, themselves.

"It will hurt me if you are hurt," I continued. Some flickers of emotion, but still, not a large reaction. I sighed deeply and pressed my lips together.

My Wicked Gladiators   311

"Very well. If you try to enter the upstairs house with me, I will simply return down here, to the gate. I will continue to do this until you remain here, and the entire house thinks we have taken leave of our senses."

The men continued to stare at me, but I returned the hard gaze. Finally, *finally* Marcus nodded once, curtly.

"Very well," he said. "However, if you have not returned within an hour, we will come in, to make certain that you have not been harmed." I could not refrain from rolling my eyes to the heavens.

I knew, I truly knew, that I would be safe. Their protests were simply causing me no end of grief.

I also truly knew that a part of me appreciated their fierce protectiveness of me. No one in my life had ever been so concerned for my well-being, so willing to lay their life on the line, as these two warriors here.

Marcus raised an eyebrow at me as he dismounted. "I am telling you the truth." He took the rope of my horse from my hands, and I wondered for a moment at the sheer physical perfection of him.

Shading my eyes again, I looked up at Caius, who was still seated on his animal. "Where will you go while I am inside? Back to the market? We will need supplies."

Caius shifted uneasily, and I saw fiery hints of russet teased out in the gold of his hair by the sun.

"We will not buy supplies until after you have spoken to your husband. We do not want to anger the gods. We will stay here, outside the gates."

I wanted to argue. I was not concerned about angering the gods—if anything, I thought that they would be on our side.

But they were fickle creatures, and I supposed that Caius was right.

I took a step toward the gate, brushing my tangled hair from my face. I raised a hand to knock, then looked over my shoulder to make certain that the two men had disappeared. They had not.

"Stay out of sight! I mean it!" I glared at them until they moved, one to my right, one to my left. Unless someone came directly outside the gate and looked quite deliberately in each direction, they would not be seen.

The imposing gate was attached to an ancient bell inside the house, and it often took some time for someone to appear at the gate and to wrench it open. After standing there for several long minutes, finally I heard the key turning in the lock, and then the scarred wood was pulled backward, toward the house.

On the other side stood Marina, her red hair so bright in the sunlight that it hurt my eyes. Still, with that hair and her nutty skin gleaming, she looked magnificent, far tidier than many slaves did. In comparison I felt disheveled, filthy, and unattractive, and was self-conscious about it.

However, I liked that my mind-set toward slaves had evolved enough that I *could* feel threatened by one, when that one was a beautiful woman.

"Domina!" Long lids blinked over eyes as dark as olives. "What are you? Are you alone?" She stepped forward, meaning to look exactly where I did not want her to, I was sure—the girl had always had entirely too keen of an interest in gladiators, in my opinion—but I stepped forward, blocking her way.

"I am alone, Marina. I am weary. Go back inside." She had no choice but to do as I said, though I saw a flicker of resentment about her lips before she folded her hands and turned away from the gate.

"Yes, Domina." Perhaps I was imagining it, but it seemed as if the girl considered me less of her mistress than she had before I had gone. Truthfully, I reciprocated the feeling, though I did not intend to tell the girl that.

"Dominus is in his chamber," she added. "I will tell him that you have arrived home unexpectedly, but he will not be pleased." The gate swung shut behind me. Marina did not bother to lock it again, and I did not remind her.

It could only be helpful to have it unlocked.

Weeks earlier, I would have chastised Marina thoroughly for the manner in which she spoke to me. Now I found that it no longer mattered. She would be Lucius' problem entirely. I was here simply to bargain with Lucius, to collect my jewels, and to leave.

She did not ask on the whereabouts of Drusilla, and this did bother me. I did not know what I had been expecting, however—the two had never been friends. I might have been the only one to mourn Drusilla's passing, but at least she'd had me.

In the house, the girl started in the direction of my husband's room. I reached out a hand, placed it on her arm to stop her. She very nearly wrinkled her nose at my touch, and I stifled the urge to slap her. Not hard, just enough to knock the nonsense out of her. I had been traveling, yes, and I needed a bath, but I was hardly disgusting enough that my touch would contaminate her.

I swallowed all words except those I had been meaning to say before the expression crossed her face. "I will make my way there on my own, Marina. You are dismissed. Gratitude."

She cast a quick look at my tunic. "Do you not wish to bathe first? Or to change?"

Both options sounded delightful, but I had no time to waste. I had precisely one hour, and if I was not back outside before the sun had moved that fraction of space in the sky, there would be trouble, more trouble than I wanted.

"No, thank you, Marina. As I said, you may go. I wish to speak to my husband alone."

With a slight sniff, the girl spun on her heel and walked away—in the direction of the slave's quarters, I noted, and not to do more work.

Oh, well. Again, she was no longer my problem.

Lucius' room was next to my own. I debated quickly, then ducked into my own chamber first. There, I stripped my stained, torn traveling tunic off, letting it fall to the floor with haste. Around my waist was tied a leather thong, and from that braided thong dangled two skin pouches.

Naked but for those pouches, I knelt beside my bed and pulled my wooden chest from beneath the frame. I filled one pouch and then the other with all of the glittering pieces that I had accumulated over the years of my life, some from my girlhood, most from my marriage. I had a momentary pang when I realized that my own coin had bought not a single one of them.

Then I thought of that first night with my masked gladiator, and of the sickness and terror that had rolled around in my gut.

I had earned them. They were mine.

Since I was already nude, when I again stood, this time weighted down with my contraband, I slid a clean tunic over my head. It was not a fancy one, but the simple cloth would be more suited to where I intended to go.

Having accomplished all this undiscovered, I wiped damp palms over the newly clean cloth that covered my body, and willed my arms and legs to stop trembling.

It was just Lucius. I trusted that he would not harm me, not even in the worst fit of temper. I had once loved the man, after all, and I believed, deep down, that he had loved me. He might even still think that he did, though his actions told me otherwise.

Knowing this did not make telling him what I had returned here to tell him any easier.

I passed through the curtain of my chamber for the last time, letting my fingers linger on the soft fabric. At the sea house, the fabrics, the furnishings and the art were not nearly so fine.

I did not care. I would not miss the opulence, for I was gaining something far better.

I moved down the corridor, my steps deliberately soft. Outside of Lucius' room I paused, inhaling deeply, uncertain how to begin. That was when I heard the noise. It sounded like . . . crying? Like a man crying.

It could not have been Lucius. I had never seen my husband cry.

Knowing that entering unannounced would only startle him and put him on the defensive, I knocked on the wall beside the curtain, the stones scraping at the pale flesh of my knuckles.

There was no response, just the slightest pause in the odd sound.

I rapped again at the wall, this time hard enough to scrape some of the skin from my fist. Hissing, I sucked the cut into my mouth, soothing it with my tongue as I waited for a response.

Finally, my husband replied. "I said that I was to be left alone for the day." His voice could have frozen the sun, so frigid was its tone. "What will it take for you idiots to understand this?"

I raised my eyebrows, and tamped down the anger that I felt. I had never felt that slaves should be spoken to in this manner, but I knew that Lucius, and many others in Roman society, did not agree.

Aware of time ticking by, I pushed through the curtain that hung in the archway of Lucius' room, not waiting for an invitation.

"Alba?" I blinked at the sight before me, as my husband returned the stare, startled to find me there, in his room, when I was meant to be at the coast.

I could not reconcile the sight before my eyes with the picture that I held of my husband in my mind's eye.

"What has happened, Lucius?" Thinking that he had perhaps been hurt, physically hurt, I rushed across the room and perched on the edge of his bed, above where he slumped on the cold floor. Reaching down, I took his head in my hands, pulling until his face turned toward mine, searching for abrasions or blood.

He shook his head irritably, as if shooing away an insect, then in a complete change nuzzled against my hand. I realized that while there were no cuts, no abrasions, there were tears, salty tracks of them drying on his face.

Stunned and somewhat off put—more by the caress than by the tears—I jerked my hands away.

"Lucius?" My voice was wary.

I watched his face go through an array of thoughts—he had never been good at keeping what he was thinking out of his expression. I saw him try to pull himself under control, saw anger that I had caught him in such a vulnerable position, and finally—and this scared me a bit—acceptance.

"Well, now I will not have to worry about how to tell you." He laughed then, an empty laugh, and held his hands out, palm up.

Moving from the bed, I knelt on the floor in front of him. I noted that he did not ask about the baby, or about my welfare, or ask why I was home.

It hurt. I knew that he was not a bad man, he was simply the product of his upbringing, of the pressure to rise to the greatness of his ancestors, but still it hurt.

"Tell me what, Lucius?" I searched his face, saw guilt and . . . was it grief? I had never seen my husband grieve, not even when his own father had passed. I was worried. "What, Lucius? Tell me now."

He sighed, then laughed again, a maniacal sound, seeming to be on the edge of hysteria. "We have no money, Alba. None. It is all gone."

My mind flashed to the ledger that I had surreptitiously studied, thought of all of the extravagant purchases, and made the obvious conclusion.

"Have you spent it all, then?" This did not matter to me,

not with the decision that I had made. But I was not heartless. I did not like to see the man broken, not even after what he had put me through.

He looked at me sharply, insult painted over his features. I raised an eyebrow in return, wondering how he could feign innocence. True, he had no way of knowing that I had seen the account books, but still, he knew what they contained.

"No, Alba." His voice carried the irritation characteristic of it when he spoke to me, and I swallowed my own sudden anger. I was trying to console him, to find out what had happened. I was not here to be abused.

"No," he repeated, thinking of what to say or perhaps how to say it. Then his composure broke, and he looked at me, a ravaged man. "No. It was stolen. All of it, but for two hundred denarii."

A person could live off of two hundred denarii for a fair amount of time, if they lived modestly. But it could not run a household, I supposed, nor a ludus.

Two hundred denarii, I realized, was the second half of the sum that Hilaria had paid. The money meant as payment for her time with my men.

"Stolen? How was it stolen?" We kept the majority of our coins, what we did not need on a daily basis, in a large clay jar that was buried somewhere on our property, as did most Romans. I did not even know where that jar was, though I knew of its existence. No one knew where it was buried, except for Lucius.

Lucius looked up at me then, and though I was expecting to see rage on his face, all that I saw was sorrow.

"Justinus." He finally croaked out the name. "It was Justinus. He unearthed the jar, took it and every other thing of value that he could get his hands on."

I thought of my jewels, and patted the reassuring weight of one of the pouches where it brushed against my leg.

"You let Justinus see where the jar was buried?" I could not keep the judgment from my voice. Slaves were never shown where their masters buried their coin. It was simply not wise.

However, Justinus had seemed more loyal to my husband than most slaves were to their masters. I could see why my husband had trusted the man, detestable though he was.

I, however, was not overly surprised. I supposed that Justinus was not a bad man any more than Lucius was, though he was infinitely more annoying. He simply did what he needed to do to rise up in the world.

I supposed that a jar full of denarii was more than the man could pass by, no matter the loyalty to my husband. And as for that husband, I should have felt more sorrow for the loss of the money, for his ruin, in fact, but I found that I could not.

Truly, he should have known what would happen when he had shown a man such as Justinus the jar. And he would rise again, financially. He was too good a businessman to do otherwise.

Still Lucius looked up at me, clearly miserable. Though I did find some compassion for him, the man I had once loved, the thought still stirred in the depths of my mind that he looked completely pathetic.

But I did not like to see someone suffering so. I reached out a hand, patted him awkwardly on the shoulder. "You can get more money, Lucius. The authorities will be alerted. Justinus will be caught."

His eyes were rimmed with red. "The authorities cannot be told if I want to save my dignity." I squinted at him, studying his face, trying to glean his meaning. Surely it might make him look a little foolish, if it was to get out that a slave had absconded with the jar, but worse things had happened to other, more noble citizens.

"Alba, do you not see?" Again he laughed, and again I wondered at his sanity.

What was I supposed to see?

I blinked as a thought tried to worm its way through my mind, tried to make itself known. And then I did see, very clearly.

Lucius. Justinus.

Justinus. Lucius.

The unnatural closeness between a man who thought of slaves as far beneath him, and his most loyal slave. The panic on Justinus' face when I had caught him with Marina, and his insistence that I not tell my husband. The unaccounted for length of priceless blue silk in the account book, and the fine tunic that Justinus had been wearing on that same occasion. Something about that tunic had plucked at my memory, but I had not caught on to what, exactly. Then there were the other, unaccounted-for items in the accounts ledger. The ridiculously expensive ones, the ones that I had thought perhaps were future gifts for me.

How could I not have known?

I felt my lip curl in distaste. I had been made a fool of by my husband. How Justinus must have laughed behind my back! I now understood the mockery in the man's tone every time he spoke to me.

My anger fled as quickly as it had come.

Was I really any better? I was certainly of the opinion that my gladiators were worth risking it all for far more than Justinus was, but Venus did not consult us, her people, before aiming her arrow.

I could be furious with Lucius for his naiveté, for his stupidity, as well as for the way he had treated me, but I could not judge him for his choice of lover, not when I was guilty of the same.

And truly, as I turned it over in my mind, Lucius watching anxiously for my reaction, I realized that Justinus' disappearance had provided me the final thing that I needed to secure my freedom.

"You will not tell anyone, Alba?" I had never seen my husband, the man with the perpetually cruel edge to his temperament, in such a pathetic state. It did not suit him, did not look well on him. I no longer saw any vestige of the power that he wore like a fine tunic. I saw a broken man. It turned my stomach to know that I was about to break him further, but remembering his treatment of me made it easier, at least a bit.

"I will not tell." I caught my husband's eyes and stared at him, unwavering, while drawing a deep breath. The time had come. "I will not tell, but there are things that I want in return."

Lucius reared back as if I had slapped him. "You would bargain with me now, when I am so low?" The way he spoke made me feel small, as if I could be crushed beneath a well-placed sandal, but I knew that he would do exactly the same if the situation was reversed.

"I came back to Rome to tell you that I will not be returning to you, not as your wife." Emotions ran over his face like a stream of water, melting, changing, before settling on the ones so characteristic of him. Yes, here was the rage, the arrogance, filling every bit of him, inflating, as my words sunk in.

"What makes you think that you have a choice?" Slowly, forgetting his own woes in the face of the insult that I was heaping upon him, Lucius rose to his feet, leaving me kneeling on the floor. I knew that he would see this as a visual display of his power over me. "Your family gave you to me. I am your pater familias. You must do as I say. You have no choice."

"But I do." I spoke quietly, staring at my hands, which I had folded calmly in my lap. "I do have a choice."

I looked up, watched his face as he began to understand. Slowly, he sank to the bed, bracing himself on his hands.

"You would do this to me? Disgrace me so? After I have provided for you all these years?" Ah, manipulation—just another tool at my cunning husband's disposal.

I grieved for the good man that had been lost in the machinations of business.

"You need not be disgraced." My voice was still soft, quiet, but it was also firm.

I would not give in. I could not.

"You are naive as always, Alba." Again streams of tears began to fall down his face, but this time I was not as certain of their sincerity.

Still, I could not leave him suffering. It was not in my nature. Moving forward, I sat next to him on the bed, rubbing a hand over his back.

I sucked in a startled breath when he wrapped both arms

around me tightly. Thinking at first that he simply needed comfort, I did not try to extricate myself from the embrace until he cupped one of my breasts in his hand.

"Lucius! Stop it!" I tried to push him away, but he was kissing my throat, my ear, while pushing me back onto the bed. I kicked out, and as I did the skirt of my tunic rose up. Panic coated my throat when I felt the cloth give way to reveal one of the two the sacks that held my jewels.

I fought doubly hard. If Lucius found that bag, I did not know what he would do. No amount of effort from me pushed him away. When he dropped a hand to insert it between my legs, I felt his fingers brush over the lumpy cloth.

He stilled, and I panted, trying to catch my breath. I had been so certain that Lucius would never hurt me, that he truly did love me, in his own way.

I had been wrong.

"What is this?"

I lay still, quivering. He still had me pinned under his not inconsiderable weight. I could not move away, could not snatch the sacks from his hands.

He tugged until the cord of the visible sack broke away from the tie at my waist. I watched with fear painted on my face as he pried open the knot and peered inside. The range of emotions that washed over his face would have been comical had they not been so intense—astonishment, cunning, disgust, and finally rage.

"You would steal from me?" Clutching the sack tightly in fingers gone bloodless, he grabbed me by the shoulders and shook, hard. When he released me abruptly, he moved back at the same time. I felt relief to be free of him, until he slapped a hand across my cheek so hard that I saw stars. The blow had me tumbling off of the low bed and onto the marble floor.

Dazed, I pressed a cheek hot from the slap against the chilled stone. I heard Lucius laugh maniacally above my head, and the seeds of rage lodged themselves stubbornly in my belly and took root.

Slowly I pulled myself to a sitting position, my hand pressed to my injured cheek. I glared up at the man whom I no longer considered my husband.

"Everything is well! We can sell these, and we can rebuild. Why did I not think of this?" Looking as if he had completely taken leave of his senses, Lucius cradled the sack against his chest like an infant.

I rose to my knees. I felt the second sack that hung between my legs come loose.

"Those are mine," I said slowly, deliberately. I scarcely recognized my own voice.

Lucius waved a hand carelessly at me, still making incoherent sounds at the sack of jewels. "Do you not see, Alba? This fixes everything. You will stay by my side, as my wife. We will raise this child together. Baldurus will never know of Justinus. It is perfect!" Reaching a hand into the sack, he withdrew the necklace that he had given me the first night he had forced me to lie with Caius. Cackling like a bird of prey as he assessed the size of the stones, he turned to look at me, and I saw nothing of the man that I had once cared for.

Incredibly, he held his arms out for me as I rose slowly to my feet. "Come, Alba. Let us celebrate."

When I simply stared, my hand still clutched to my cheek,

he lurched forward and wrapped his fingers tightly around one of my wrists. He yanked, and I stumbled forward, but did not fall.

"Take your hands off of me." I knew that if I was to scream, Caius and Marcus would be here within moments.

I did not scream. I simply repeated my words as Lucius laughed again.

"You are mine. My wife." He tugged again, and I felt a lick of fear.

The fear gave way to pure satisfaction and relief when, with my free hand, I swung the second sack of jewels at my husband's head. It connected with his skull with a satisfying crack, and he yelped and fell backward, clutching his hands to his head. I scrambled backward, feet planted, ready to swing the sack of heavy rocks a second time if need be.

I expected to see rage when he looked at me, and it was there, but coating it was pure bewilderment.

"Why?" I saw that he truly did not understand. It seemed that Justinus' betrayal had scrambled his mind, but still I felt no pity. He was still in enough control of his faculties to manipulate.

I would not be caught in his web. I was done.

"Do not touch me again. I will kill you if I must." A hollow noise echoed from his throat, partially a sound of disbelief and partially a laugh, but it faded when he saw the intent in my eyes.

"Alba. Why?" His words this time sounded true.

I still did not drop the sack that I clutched. "I have told you why." Suddenly I was weary. I held out my hand for the other sack. "Give that to me."

Lucius narrowed his eyes and clutched it to his chest. Trepidation forced me to shake, but I did my best to conceal it.

"All I have to do is scream, and you will be dead." I was sad that it had come to this. "Give me the bag. You have no choice."

My words, and their meaning, finally sank in. Slowly, reluctantly, Lucius placed the sack at the edge of the bed, though anger again suffused his face. It was not the rage of moments earlier, however, simply anger at having been bested.

"You will go to hell." I shook my head at the petty words, for I did not believe them. Surely the gods would not punish me for finally finding joy.

Clutching the sacks tightly, one in each hand, I looked upon Lucius for one of the last times.

"You will tell whoever needs to know that I have died while at the coast for my health, a problem from the child." I had thought of nothing but this over the interminable hours of travel back to Rome. "I will leave, and I will never return to the city. No one will ever know."

"Are you forgetting that without you and that child, I have no patronage?" The bitterness now turned acidic, laying all the blame at my door—a petulant child. "And I now have no money, either. I will be out on the streets."

I looked up at him, unblinking, until he again quieted. "I suspect that if you present yourself to Baldurus, a ravaged man, wrecked from the loss of your wife and your child, he will take pity on you."

"But then I will have no wife. No one to get with child. Another problem." Clearly, Lucius cared much more about the next steps in *his* life than about losing me and the babe, now that he knew he could potentially save face.

Knowing my husband as I did, I had anticipated this question. "You will marry one of Baldurus' daughters." Never mind that the oldest was nearly fifteen years younger than Lucius. Large age differences were common in Roman marriages.

I saw a spark begin in Lucius' eye. It told me all that I needed to know.

I no longer belonged here.

"Where will you go?" I think he was simply curious, more than he actually cared.

"Back to the coast."

He narrowed his eyes as he took that in. "You are forgetting that I own that house." Jutting his chin forward, he clenched and unclenched his hands, a tick that I had often observed in him while in the middle of a business discussion.

He was mistaken. This was not a discussion at all.

"No." I raised my own chin, looking, I was sure, much more calm than I felt. "You do not."

Again Lucius reacted as if I had struck him. "And if I do not agree to any of this?" His voice was nasty, and I wondered how I had ever found it melodic or attractive.

"You do not have a choice." I firmly repeated the words I had said moments earlier, hoping that this time they would sink in. "I will tell Baldurus both that the child I carry is not yours, and that you were fooled because you opened your heart to a slave." I regarded him calmly. "Both are things that he will not want to attach his name to, I am certain."

Lucius opened his mouth, then closed it again. I realized as he worked his lips like a stunned fish that this was the longest verbal exchange that we had had in years.

Finally, understanding that he really did have no choice, he snapped, "I suppose you expect me to give you money, too, to live on after you've frittered away the money from the jewels. Too bad. I have none." He laughed harshly.

"No." I was using the word more than I ever had. "We will be fine without it."

"How do you think you will support yourself, silly woman? It costs money to live." He laughed, angrily amused with his silly young wife, until it sunk in. "We?"

"We." My gut clenched again. I was scared. This was the most important part. "You will take the money that Caius and Marcus have earned in the arena, and you will accept it as payment for their freedom."

The change in Lucius' demeanor was very nearly comical. Rage that his slaves had touched his wife, disbelief that his wife had disobeyed him and been with a gladiator. Panic at the thought of losing his champion, and the next best warrior.

"You must be mad." He ran a shaking hand through hair that was already disheveled. "They are using you to obtain their freedom. You understand that, do you not? Once they are free, they will leave you."

I did not listen. I knew the truth in my heart.

"And the money they have saved could not possibly be enough to buy their freedom." My fingers began to itch as he spoke so carelessly of my men, as if they were commodities.

"They will give you what they have, and you will consider the balance as services rendered," I said. "Stud fees, if you will." Now I rose to my own feet, aware that Lucius would see it as me putting myself on his level. In a way, I was. I would not be mistreated by this man, not ever again.

He grimaced as he ran over everything in his head, and came to the conclusion that he truly did not have a choice. I had roped him in, or rather, he had done it himself.

I had merely handed him the rope.

"And what of Hilaria?" His voice was barely more than a whisper now. "She has paid for their services."

I thought of the scene that had just occurred with the woman, and knew that Lucius would have no more trouble with her. But if I told that to Lucius, he would want to know why.

It was best to pretend that the encounter had never happened.

"Use the money from Caius and Marcus to repay her, and tell her that they escaped and ran away to join the Spartacan camp in the mountains." We had heard the newest development of the rebel slaves as we passed through the city on our way there. This would provide a story for Hilaria to latch on to, as well. "Then finalize your dealing with Baldurus. You will be fine."

There was a long moment of silence in the room, silence in which I stood, still and firm while Lucius looked around him with wild eyes. A sigh of extreme self-pity escaped his lips before he spoke, but under the theatrics, the question that he asked seemed very real.

"Do you hate me so very much?" Lucius turned away as he asked, and I felt a trickle of pity begin to work its way through me. No, I did not hate him, but I no longer loved him, cared about him, or respected him.

"I do not hate you." This was all that I could find to say. After a long, awkward moment, I stepped forward, walking around him and heading toward the entrance of his room.

With one hand caught in the curtain, I turned to say one last thing. "You will present Caius and Marcus with the palm leaves representing their freedom in the ludus below, in front of their peers. They are warriors who have bought their freedom, and they deserve an honorable release from their vow to you." I pushed through the curtain and left the room without looking back.

Lucius trailed after me like a small boy. A small, angry boy. "What of the slaves? What do I tell them?"

"I do not care."

"What of Drusilla? Will you keep her?" These words were a knife in my tender side.

No one could keep Drusilla, not any longer. I did not feel like telling him, however, he who had treated her so poorly, as he did all slaves save Justinus.

"Yes. She is mine." This, at least, was truth.

And having said it, I walked briskly away, through the large hall, toward the door that led outside. I did not stop to look at the things surrounding me, did not pause to indulge in bittersweet remembrances. I did not want to take anything more with me than I had. The rest of the things here were just that—things.

What I would leave the ludus with was so much more.

Epilogue

The gladiators assembled in the training yard of the ludus quickly, curious, I was certain, about why they had been so hastily called. They murmured amongst themselves, whispering, wondering.

Why was their domina in the yard? Why was Dominus about to make an appearance?

Where were Caius and Marcus?

Stiffly, my husband strode to the edge of the balcony where I had spent so many hours watching my gladiators. After surveying the scene below him for several long minutes, he disappeared from view, and I knew that he was making the long walk down the stairs and through the iron gate.

He reappeared after what seemed a long time, emerging from the hall where the men took their meals. He did not look over to the gate, which I stood in front of.

Perhaps he had convinced himself already that I was dead.

My lips quirked in amusement when I saw that Lucius had hung his childhood bulla around his neck. Though they put it away at the end of childhood, as did women, men were permitted to bring it out again for official occasions in which they could benefit from the protection against evil.

If he wanted to believe that I had been so possessed, then I hoped it soothed him.

Striding across the sand, his chest puffed out more than I thought necessary, he stopped directly beneath the balcony, waiting.

Moments later, Marcus and Caius appeared in the yard, from the opposite side that my husband had entered from. They had been in Marcus' quarters, I saw, and had changed clothing.

No longer wearing the subligaculum that they had all but lived in for so long, each donned a simple but clean cloth tunic. The tunic, I knew, meant more than it appeared on the surface.

Roman sumptuary laws decreed that a person's clothing tell of their status. The subligaculum had announced to the world that they were gladiators. The short tunic was the uniform of the freeman.

Both men were stiff and stoic as they walked across the yard in which they had spent so many hours, though I noticed Caius twisting his long fingers in the fabric of his tunic. They stopped directly in front of Lucius, and each offered him a small sack.

Lucius took the small, worn pouches of coins from the two men. The pouches held coin, their winnings from the arena—the payment for their freedom. I saw his fingers twitch as he accepted the bags, knew that he was dying to count the coin, but unable to do so, not at the moment. It was a sign of respect for a gladiator's integrity, accepting the contents of the sack at face value.

Tucking the coins into his waist pocket, Lucius looked to Doctore, the men's trainer. Doctore had been standing behind Lucius, but now moved forward, two large palm leaves in his scarred, rough hand. These leaves represented a slave's freedom. This was what many of the gladiators in the arena fought for, survived battles for.

Doctore turned to Marcus first, as champion, and handed him a large leaf. Though I stood on the far side of the yard, I saw a moment of wonder cross Marcus' face. He then handed the second leaf to Caius. The less reserved of the two, he allowed his face to break into a wide grin and held the leaf in the air, above his head.

I wondered what it felt like, being handed their freedom. Then I realized that I already knew, for I had achieved freedom of my own that day.

The men erupted into a huge noise, a din the likes of which I had never heard before. Though they were losing comrades, their brothers were obtaining freedom, and the other men celebrated. Surely each dreamt of the day when they, too, would earn the same.

When I heard that cheer, and saw my warriors wade into the crowd of men who hugged, slapped backs, and tousled hair, my toes curled in the dust at the base of the gate. I bounced impatiently up and down, anxious beyond words, but knowing that my men had earned this moment. It seemed hardly any time at all that they had broken free of the pack and were walking toward me.

Yes, walking toward me. Coming for *me*.

I still could scarcely believe it.

Marcus stood on one side of me, Caius on the other. After a sidelong glance exchanged among the three of us, Marcus reached forward and pulled at the wood.

The gate, still unlocked, creaked open. A small slit, it widened, getting bigger and bigger, until it framed my two warriors, framed me.

I saw that both of my men were wearing proud if slightly stunned expressions.

I imagined that mine was exactly the same.

Together we stepped out of the dust of the yard, out of the sands of the arena. I inhaled deeply, then turned back toward the ludus.

I watched the gate close, watched the figures inside fade from view, and felt not even the smallest speck of regret. With a smile, I bade it all farewell, and looked to my warriors, who were gladiators no more.

Each wore his light tunic with pride, and each had a small leather pack slung over his shoulder. Those packs contained all of the possessions that they had in this world, but none of us was overly concerned with that.

Better even than the new tunics, each man held a large, waxen palm leaf in his fist.

They were now free men. Their lives were their own.

And so was mine. So was mine.

Glossary

Balteus: a sword belt.
Bulla: a locket given to Roman children to ward off evil.
Carpentum: a common type of Roman carriage or wagon.
Charon's obol: the coin placed in or on the mouth of a dead person before burial or cremation. Possibly a bribe for safe passage to the underworld.
Cingulum: a wide leather belt, often reinforced with metal, worn about the waist by gladiators to protect from injury to the vital organs.
Dacia: a region of Central Europe during the Roman era, inhabited by the Dacian people.
Denarii/Denarius: the common silver coin of Roman currency.
Diana: Roman goddess of the hunt and the moon.
Domina: the feminine form of Dominus.
Dominus: the title meaning master or owner, particularly of slaves.
Doctore: the trainer of gladiators at a ludus.

Familia: family, a very important concept in Roman civilization.

Fortuna: Roman goddess of good fortune.

Gaul: a region of Western Europe during the Roman era, inhabited by the Gaul people, or Celts.

Juno: Roman goddess of community and fertility.

Litter: a type of human-powered transport, usually consisting of a lounge or bed attached to four posts, which are manned by people, usually slaves.

Ludus: a gladiatorial school.

Manicae: Wraps of leather and cloth worn by gladiators as arm and wrist padding.

Mars: Male god of war and virility.

Munera: provided by the wealthy, these were public works to benefit the masses. One of the most common munera was the arena games.

Orcus: a Roman god of the underworld.

Palla: a Roman woman's shawl.

Pater familias: the head of a Roman family.

Patria potestas: power that the male head of the family exercised over his family, even over his grown sons.

Patrician: refers to the elite families of ancient Rome.

Pits: The common term for the quarry from which building stones were mined. The stones, which were used for nearly all buildings in ancient Rome, were mined by slaves.

Pyre: a structure for burning a body as part of a funeral rite. Usually made of wood.

Roman Sumptuary Laws: ensured that the clothing worn by a person indicated their class and social standing.

Senator: a member of the Roman senate, a political institution and advisory/governing body in Rome. Senators were not elected, but appointed.

Spartacus: the leader of a major slave uprising against the Roman Republic.

Subligaculum: the brief garment worn by gladiators to protect their modesty.

Thrace: a historical and geographical area in Southeast Europe, inhabited by the Thracian people. The most famous historical Thracian was considered to be Spartacus.

Acknowledgments

There are always so many people who have a hand in creating a book ... and I always forget one. Let's give it a try! First, to J.L. Stermer, an awesome agent who helped give this book life, and Chelsey Emmelhainz, one of the best editors I've ever had the pleasure of working with. Along with Chelsey, thanks to the other lovely people at Avon who worked their magic on this book, especially Gail Dubov, who created the spectacular awesomeness that is this cover! For my Sirens and Scribes critique group, the most rockin' group of ladies you'll ever find—Juliana Stone, Amanda Vyne, D.L. Snow, Barbara J. Hancock, Grace Conley, Nini Angell, Elle Ricci, Cora Zane, and Suzanne Rock. These ladies are cheerleaders, editors, promoters, and lemon drop martini enablers. Love you all! To my day-job co-workers, for not shaking your heads too much when you find bits of scribbled nonsense beneath my keyboard that have nothing to do with optometry. To the Calgary chapter of the RWA ... you are all fantastic people, and so inspirational. To my parents and sister, for cheering me on. To my son, Ben, for napping so that mama can write.

To Starbucks and the Rocky Mountain Bagel Co. for the caffeine. Let's see . . . who else am I forgetting . . . oh, right. Most of all to Rob, for believing in me so much that I had to start believing in myself.

About the Author

LAUREN HAWKEYE is a writer, theater enthusiast, knitting aficionado, and animal lover who lives in the shadows of the great Rocky Mountains of Alberta, Canada. She's older than she looks—really—and younger than she feels—most of the time—and she loves to explore the journeys that take women through life in her stories. Visit her online at www.laurenhawkeye.com.